# Sweet Slow Sizzle

**Bangers Tavern Romance 4**

## Sadira Stone

# Sweet Slow Sizzle

*Loving him means risking the only family she has left.*

Bangers Tavern's hunky bouncer Jojo Williams has been flirting with server Lana Lopez for three years, but she dismisses him as a trifling joker. Determined to penetrate her prickly defenses, he plunges into the hot mess that keeps her from dating. If he screws this up, his heart and hers won't be the only ones broken.

Orphaned by a car wreck at twenty-two, Lana must keep her teen brothers on track and together in the home they grew up in. One more slip-up, and her interfering tías will separate the boys. The last thing Lana needs is a big goof like Jojo meddling with her fragile family.

But when the teens' shenanigans land them in trouble, Jojo may be the only person who can save them from the wrath of the tías. Lana's growing attraction to the gentle giant makes it harder and harder to shut him out, but loving him is a gamble that could cost her everything.

Come back to Bangers Tavern for a slow burn, sizzling hot friends to lovers workplace romance full of laughs, steam, and the glorious chaos of 21st century family—the ones we're born into, and the ones we gather to our hearts.

# Dedication

❤

To Duncan, my HEA
And to my readers
May your tots be crispy
and your love stories steamy!

# Copyright

♥

# Contents

# Chapter One

♥

"Look out. Coming through." Lana Lopez elbowed her way into the thirsty mob waiting outside Bangers Tavern. Though she'd grown up in Tacoma and should know better, she'd left the house without a jacket—and of course, the crystal September skies had given way to cold drizzle. After the day she'd had, she was in no mood to wait for this gaggle of giggling customers to finish flirting with Jojo, the hunky bouncer checking IDs. Besides, it was already ten past seven, and she hated running late, even if it wasn't her fault.

A sleek thirty-something in a leather blazer cocked her hip and blocked Lana's path. "Wait your turn, chica."

Curling her lip, she pointed to the Bangers logo on her T-shirt. "I work here."

The customer subsided with a pout as Jojo aimed his megawatt smile at Lana. After a quick head to toe inspection, he quirked his full lips to the side. "Yo, Spike. Spell me a minute?"

Tucking his thumbs into his belt loops, their second bouncer ambled to the entrance.

"No fair," Blazer Lady grumbled. "We want the cute one."

Jojo pulled Lana aside and turned so his big, bulky body sheltered her from the drizzle. Ignoring the raindrops pattering on his shaved head, he rumpled his brow. "You okay, Sunshine?"

She yanked the elastic from one of her long pigtails and tightened it to steel-cable strength as she vented her frustration. "Pedro waited until dinnertime to announce he's got a project due for biology class. Tomorrow. Needed craft supplies to make a diorama of a pond biome, biosphere, eco-whatever. So I had to run him to Artco." Satisfied with her left pigtail, she tackled the right. "He's usually Mister Overachiever, but now there's this girl, Haley, and he's losing his mind." She snapped the second elastic in place with a satisfying *thwack*. "So I'm running late and missed dinner. Tonight sucks."

"Pond, huh?" Jojo crossed his massive arms and cracked a wide grin. "Shoulda called me. I'd 'a brought you one of my brother's pond-scum protein shakes."

Kai's smoothies were legendary among the Bangers guys who trained with Jojo in his makeshift garage gym. River, the pretty-boy bartender, described them as a disgusting rite of passage. But gross smoothies were not what she needed now. Ditto Jojo's lame jokes. Was there anything he took seriously?

He closed his ginormous paw on her arm, his touch surprisingly gentle. The corners of his mouth quirked up. "You want me to talk to little bro? You know, man to man?"

Lana snorted. "That's the last thing I need."

Jojo's grin flattened. He actually kind of—winced?

*Yikes.* The big guy's juvenile humor could be annoying, but he meant well. No need to take her sour mood out on him.

She patted his muscly arm, trying hard to ignore a flutter between her thighs. Jeez, the guy was built. Ripped. Massive. Atlas in a Bangers T-shirt, keeping the bar safe from underage drinkers and rowdy drunks.

Reluctantly, she peeled her hand from his biceps. "I mean thanks, really. But Pedro's already having a manly heart-to-heart with my neighbor Kenny. Talk to you later."

She dashed through the entrance. With a Puget Sound University game this afternoon—victorious, judging by the sea of red and gold hoodies—and the Seahawks playing tomorrow, Bangers was in full football regalia, the ceiling a tangle of blue and green twinkle lights. Paper helmets and football cutouts fluttered from the old building's rafters. Bluesy rock thumped from the speakers, drowning out sports blah-blah on the TV screens. Already, every table from the back corner to the pool tables and dartboards beyond was jammed with patrons thirsty for River and Kiara's creative cocktails and hungry for Maci's Caribbean jerk wings—and, of course, Bangers' famous tater tots.

The scent of spicy, greasy goodness summoned a rumble from Lana's empty belly. Ignoring it, she fastened her apron, grabbed her tray, and headed for the servers' station at the end of the bar, collecting drink orders on the way.

Dawn O'Malley, the bar's owner, waved from the beer taps. "Hey, kiddo, can you stay after for a few minutes tonight? Time to strategize social media for the Halloween party."

"You bet," she chirped with enthusiasm she didn't quite feel. Honestly, she'd like nothing more than to crash hard as soon as possible, but she was damn lucky to have a boss who made allowances for her family crises. Like last month when her brothers Leo and Pedro were horsing around in the living room and broke a window. Handling Bangers' social media accounts was as close as Lana ever got to the marketing career she'd been training for before—

A shudder slithered down her spine. *Don't think about that now. Focus on work.*

With her electric blue curls bouncing, Rosie Chu stepped up to the servers' station and goosed Lana's butt. "Late again. Had to peel yourself out of some hottie's bed?"

"Pffsht." Lana swatted her bestie's arm. "Like I have time for that. Honestly, I don't know how single parents ever get laid."

Rosie reached past her and grabbed a stack of napkins. "Girl, you're too young to have all these worries."

She shrugged. "I've got no choice, do I? Just three more years."

"If you wait till your youngest brother graduates to have sex, your pussy will close up like an old piercing. We gotta find you a man."

If Rosie only knew how dire the situation really was.

As usual, River was busy at the far end of the bar, dazzling customers with complicated bottle flips and leaving Kiara to handle the servers.

Without breaking stride, the petite bartender handed over Lana's point of sale tablet and cash box. "Sign here, doll."

Lana scribbled her signature, then typed in her first drink order of the night. "Love the Seahawks hair clips."

No one at the bar outdid Kiara in Seahawks accessories during football season, not even Dawn, who tipped her stubby locs in blue and green glitter on game days.

"They better win Sunday," Kiara grumbled as she muddled limes and mint. "Got last night's tips riding on this game." She set a pair of Mojitos on Lana's tray. "And last night was a hot one."

While Rosie waited for a frozen blue daiquiri, she tilted her chin toward the bouncers' station at the door. "What did you say to Jojo?"

"Nothing. Why?"

"He looked like a kid who dropped his ice cream."

Lana huffed. "I just declined his offer to talk some sense into Pedro."

Rosie folded her inked-up arms. "Don't you want more healthy male role models for your brothers?"

"It's hard enough to keep those two focused on school. What's gonna happen if I bring over a musclehead who spews jokes all day? Leo's already in trouble for cutting up in class. Kenny's the kind of role model he needs, not Jojo."

"Hey, Jojo's a sweetheart. He's"—Rosie ticked off on her fingers—"educated, employed, good to his mama, and he's totally sweet on you."

Lana stabbed cherries and orange slices onto a cocktail pick. "Come on, he's sweet on anyone with boobs." She dropped the garnish into a tall rum punch. "Wait...you met his mom?"

"Last week when I dropped Eddie off for Jojo's boot-camp-slash-torture dungeon. She came by to ask for his help with something, and he was a total puppy. Adorable."

One cocktail to go, but Kiara had been waylaid by a pair of regulars halfway down the bar. A high-pitched yelp from a nearby table jerked Lana's head around. Some baby-face guy in a college hoodie was trying to snatch tater tots from a woman's platter while his knucklehead buddies laughed.

"Oh, goodie," Lana whispered to Rosie. "I love this part."

Smooth as a shadow, Jojo slid through the crowd to confront the tot raider. She couldn't hear whatever he growled at the thief, but the way he puffed out his massive chest and clenched his fists gave her shivers. Those corded forearms, those powerful shoulders! *Ungh!* She bit her lip.

Jojo jerked his chin toward the door.

Hands raised in surrender, the frat boy withdrew.

Rosie gave a low whistle. "Impressive, isn't he? If I weren't already spoken for..."

As if he could sense Lana's lustful stare, Jojo glanced their way, and his rock-hard expression melted into a goofy smile. Rosie had nailed it—he really did look like a puppy, an over-size, muscle-bound pit bull eager for a belly rub. She blew out a shaky breath and forced her attention back to her friend.

"Handling two male egos keeps me busy to the max. What would I do with a third?"

Rosie hip bumped her. "So stubborn. Always think you've gotta handle everything yourself. Jojo's been trying to catch your eye ever since you started working here. Why not let him help with your brothers? I bet they'd love him."

Kiara caught Lana's eye and held up a finger. At this rate, the ice in these drinks would melt by the time she finally delivered them.

"Look, Ro," Lana said with a huff. "I'm there for Leo and Pedro during the day, and Kenny and Carol are there at night. I've got it covered."

Truth be told, keeping house, family, and job running smoothly took every last iota of heart and brain and nerve she had. The last thing she needed was some giant jokester distracting her, no matter how her lady bits tingled when she glimpsed his luscious, tight ass.

"There's weekends," Rosie insisted with a teasing grin.

"I can't hook up with Jojo. We work together."

"So do Eddie and I. Also River and Charlie."

She was right. Diego, their former chef, found love here too with Charlie's sister. Something about Bangers Tavern seemed to bring couples together.

Rosie pointed to the carved cupid atop the antique back bar. "You can't dodge his arrows forever." Since she and Eddie hooked up at Bangers' Anti-Valentine's party, Rosie had developed a weird superstition about that chubby mahogany angel. She'd even tattooed his likeness on her own thigh.

At last, Kiara delivered the rest of their drink orders. Lana hefted her tray high overhead and shot her bestie a stern glance. "You know there's more at stake in my case. Pedro and Leo have been through enough heartache. I won't risk putting them through more."

She sailed into the mob, her embarrassing secret still locked up tight—she fantasized about Jojo all the freakin' time, a stupid, pointless habit. Until she got her brothers through high school and into college or job training, romance would have to wait.

The next three hours kept her hopping from bar to tables to kitchen to tables to bar...

But it was bound to happen eventually. It always did, at least once a shift.

While she unloaded tots, wings, and beers on a high-top near the pool tables, a customer reached behind her and yanked her braid.

Summoning her inner ninja, Lana whirled so the other pigtail smacked the perpetrator right in the face. He winced and slapped a hand over his eye.

"Oh, honey," she cooed in a saccharine tone. "Be careful. If you startle a server, she might accidentally spill her whole tray on you. We wouldn't want that to happen, would we?"

The guy's friends guffawed.

"Sorry, Miss. Just a joke. No offense intended." The grabby guy fished a ten from his pocket and dropped it on her tray.

She flashed a rictus grin. "Thanks, doll."

She couldn't win. Wearing her waist-length hair up all shift gave her a headache, and a ponytail was out of the question since that night she shed a long, black strand in someone's queso dip. Wearing it in pigtails kept it neat and out of the way, but some bozo always tried to use them for a handle.

As she collected empties from a neighboring table, a soft touch fell on her shoulder, and a wrapped burger appeared on her tray. Jojo's deep voice rumbled behind her, "You need to eat, Peanut. Gotta keep your energy up."

"Peanut?" She glared up at him through narrowed eyes.

"My bad, Ms. Lopez, ma'am." The corners of his mouth twitched, and he executed a stiff bow. "Your grace. Your excellency. Your most petite majesty."

"That's better." She gave him a tiny smile. "And thanks. Very thoughtful of you."

"Aww," a customer cooed. "That's so sweet. Wish my boyfriend took such good care of me."

Jojo barked a laugh. "Boyfriend? I should be so lucky. This little one's immune to my charms."

The customer tilted her head, the picture of puzzlement. "But why? You're so..." She waved her hand, taking in his annoying gorgeousness.

Jojo shrugged his ginormous shoulders. "Haven't figured that out yet." He gave Lana's braid a tug and returned to his post.

*Ugh.* She glared at his brawny back as he angled through the crowd. Jojo's combination of sweet and annoying left her confused, irritated, and perhaps a tiny bit tickled? Not that she was fooled by his flirty banter. He didn't mean anything by it. And even if he did, as soon as he got a clear view of all her baggage, he'd run for his life.

The customer sighed. "So cute. Just like in grade school—he pulls your braids to show he likes you."

If Lana'd had a free hand, she'd have slapped it to her forehead.

Yes, Jojo was cute. Frickin' adorable. But with her parents gone, keeping their little family together was all on her. This job was her lifeline, and she couldn't afford to think about her coworker that way. With a final glance at the delicious maleness that might have been hers, she forced her attention back to work.

Jojo eased onto his stool and lifted one aching foot, then the other, wiggling his toes inside his Vans. After pulling a double shift at the clinic to cover for a sick phlebotomist, his dogs were barking. Twelve hours of drawing blood from scared kids. Twelve hours of making funny faces and goofy jokes, of handing out temporary tattoos and glitter stickers. Crazy not to take the night off, but leaving Spike alone with this monster crowd was asking for trouble. Besides, if he stayed home, he'd just sit around wondering what Lana was up to.

How did she manage this job *and* take care of her teen brothers? A huge responsibility for someone so young. He couldn't imagine the pain of losing his parents and having to raise his younger siblings. Hell, at almost thirty, he still relied on Mama and Dad for emotional support and wisdom, not to mention Dad's amazing food.

But even that mind-blowing tragedy didn't keep Lana down for long. She returned to Bangers after a few weeks, claiming the party atmosphere helped her cope. No doubt, her Bangers family helped too—when she'd let them. Hiding her grief and stress under sass and humor, she just kept on truckin'. But tonight, her frayed edges showed in her shadowed eyes, her brittle smile. Even a powerhouse like Lana had her limits.

Seems she had help, though. Who the hell was this Kenny guy?

He huffed through his nose and forced his tense shoulders back down. Lana didn't need his jealous caveman bullshit. Checking IDs at the door, he watched her flit through the crowd like a butterfly—light, quick, unpredictable, as if she had a sixth sense for empty glasses.

"What's the Spanish word for butterfly?" he muttered under his breath as he stamped hands.

"Mariposa," his current customer chirped, batting her lash extensions.

And of course Lana caught his eye at just that moment. Was it his imagination, or did she wrinkle her nose?

He waved the flirty customer through, then pantomimed chomping into a burger.

Lana rolled her eyes, then lifted the burger and took a big bite.

*That's right. Gotta keep up your strength, Mariposa.* Grinning, he turned back to his duties.

Dawn stepped up beside him, wiping her hands on a bar towel. "Still mooning, eh, kiddo?"

"Mooning? Me?" He scoffed. "Just keeping an eye out for trouble."

"Uh huh." The boss planted her fists on her wide hips and scanned him with her X-ray vision. Then she spread her arms, demanding a hug.

No problem. Dawn gave excellent, squishy hugs. He sank into his surrogate mom's embrace. A total mother hen despite having no bio kids of her own, she kept an eye on her Bangers family, and that was fine with Jojo. After all, family equals love.

She released him. "You know I adore you, right?"

"Of course, Mama Dawn." He cocked a finger pistol. "Right back atcha."

She angled her head toward the barroom. "If I were in your shoes, I'd forget about the one who isn't interested and focus my charms on someone who appreciates me."

"Like who?"

"Take your pick." A flourish of her hand took in the whole bar.

Beside the door, a table of college cuties giggled and waved.

"See?" Dawn clapped his shoulder. "You're not exactly hurting for choices, Jojo. Quit banging your head against the wall." With a chuckle, she returned to the beer taps.

Well, shit, the boss had noticed his unrequited crush. And she spoke truth—Bangers was filled with attractive women. The trouble was, his heart was stubbornly stuck on Lana. Besides, if she saw him swapping numbers with a customer, she'd think he'd lost interest in her. Couldn't risk that.

He was a patient man, even if patience meant jerking off in the shower before work while picturing Lana's bright eyes, her sweet, snarky grin, her quick movements and husky voice, the way her long braids swung in counterpoint to the sway of her delectable, round ass. In the three years she worked at Bangers, he'd never seen her hair unbound, but in his fantasies, he loosened those tight pigtails and buried his face in soft, black silk.

With an enormous sigh, he held out his hand for the next customer's ID.

"No way, son. Come back when you're twenty-one." He slapped the obvious fake into the kid's palm.

"C'mon, man. I'm on the Lumberjacks varsity team. All my friends are in there," the baby-faced kid whined. "Can't you look the other way just this once?"

Jojo gave him a grin with lots of teeth. "And risk losing our liquor license? That's a nope."

Rosie appeared at his elbow with a cranberry and soda. Trudging past, the underage kid cast a longing glance at Rosie's tattooed cleavage.

"Thanks, gorgeous." He took a gulp of the fizzy drink. "Hey, is Lana okay?"

"Just dealing with teenage screwups." Rosie propped her tray on her hip. "Wish she didn't feel like she had to handle everything on her own."

"Right? She's got a whole family here. Any of us would be glad to help."

"Especially you, right?" She flashed a conspiratorial grin and nudged him with her elbow.

"What can I say? Kids love me."

Rosie's head shake set her blue curls bouncing. "It'll take more than a superhero Band-Aid to win over those boys—*if* Lana even lets you close to them. You've heard of Mama Bears? When it comes to her brothers, Lana's a Mama T-Rex."

Hard not to pout like one of his little patients. Of course, after losing her parents, Lana would be uber-protective of her brothers. But he worked with kids all day at the clinic, and she only had two to look after. How tough could it be?

Rosie squeezed his arm. "Look, you know I love you, but you're wasting your time. Until those boys are out of the house, Lana's not gonna let a romance distract her." The corner of her mouth quirked up. "Too bad. A tumble with a hot guy like you would loosen her up."

He rubbed the back of his neck. "Aww, you think I'm hot, Ro?"

She lifted one shoulder. "It's an objective fact. And if you tell Eddie I said so, I'll deny it with my dying breath."

Jojo raised his palms. "Don't worry. I'd never mess with Volkov's woman. Little dude would take out my kneecaps with his icepick."

"He probably would." With a saucy smile and a flip of her short skirt, Rosie strutted back into the barroom.

At a table near the bar, Lana set down a plate of wings and a pitcher of beer, then shot him a quizzical look—because of course those sharp chestnut eyes hadn't missed his conversation with her bestie.

He waggled his fingers in greeting. *That's right, beauty, we were talking about you.* He lifted his glass and gave her a smile that worked on everyone else. She held his gaze for a moment, then wrinkled her nose and turned away.

*Damn. Throw me a lifeline, Mariposa.*

# Chapter Two

♥

Lana stuffed her tip money into the pocket of her jeans shorts—as close as she and the other Bangers servers got to a uniform. Good night tonight, easily enough to cover half this week's grocery bill, despite Leo and Pedro's enormous appetites. While River distributed the bartenders' and bouncers' share, she climbed onto a barstool beside Dawn, who was scribbling something illegible on a notepad.

The boss tapped her pencil on the bar top. "Okay, kiddo. Social media for the Halloween bash. Whatcha got for me?"

Lana flipped through her phone. "We already have a Facebook event page up, and a countdown on Insta. Starting in October, we'll do daily TikTok posts with staff members. River volunteered, of course."

The handsome bartender paused his clean-up duties to execute a razzle-dazzle bottle flip and a cheesy grin. "The camera loves me."

Dawn guffawed. "He's pretty, and he knows it. Hey, I've got a bin of Halloween costumes in the back. Get footage of everyone." She waggled her eyebrows. "Especially Jojo."

*Et tu, boss?* Lana allowed herself a tiny eye roll. "The week before Halloween, we offer drink discounts to anyone who posts to social media about what they're wearing to the party and uses the Bangers hashtag. And I've still got pictures from last year's party. We'll make a montage to play on the TVs between sports games."

"Look at you, little marketing whiz. When are you opening your own PR firm?"

Lana gave a snort. "When donkeys fly."

"Hey now." Dawn squeezed her arm. "This phase of your life won't last forever. Just a few more years, then you can go back to school, right?"

"That's the plan." *So why do those three measly years feel like for-freakin'-ever?* "Okay, what events do we have on tap this year?"

"Still working on that. Costume contest for sure. October's charity is Big Brothers and Sisters of Tacoma."

"Right." She made a note on her phone. "I'll contact them for the deets and make some posts."

"Oh, before I forget." Dawn fished a business card from her breast pocket. "My buddy Alvin Wu is looking for help with social media. You know his place, Imperial Dumpling Palace?"

River paused his inventory to shoot a snarky grin over his shoulder. "Lana's your girl. She loves playing on her phone."

Passing behind the bar, Charlie smacked her boyfriend's arm. "It's called marketing, smartass."

Lana raised her chin. "If you want to run your own bar, you'll need some. You can't get by on your looks alone, blondie."

Dawn jumped into the pile-on. "Since Lana started handling our social media, attendance is up at all our events. That means more tips for everyone, River-boo."

Jojo stepped up to the bar and dropped a heavy hand onto Lana's shoulder. "Show some respect, Riv. Our Lana's an influencer. When I finally get my gym going, she's gonna make me go viral." He struck a body-builder pose, one arm flexed, the other arrowed upward, a fierce scowl on his chiseled face.

*God help me, he's so hot!* Lana ducked her head to hide the flush painting her cheeks.

Undeterred by all the teasing, River clapped back, "What'll you name your gym? Jojo's torture chamber?"

Eddie rounded the corner with a crate of bottles from the storeroom. "Home of the Bulgarian death squats. Guaranteed to make you puke or your money back."

Jojo pulled an offended face, complete with protruding lower lip. Freakin' unfair how cute he was.

Dawn patted his massive arm. "Now, now. He can't be that bad if you two keep training with him."

Eddie shrugged. "I'm just trying to impress Rosie."

"I'm impressed, baby." She called from across the room, where she helped Spike stack stools on tables.

River wiped the bar top. "To be fit, you gotta embrace the pain." He flicked his towel at Jojo. "Isn't that right, you kinky, sadistic bastard?"

An image flashed through Lana's brain: Jojo as a leather-clad dungeon master, complete with a whip and chaps. Her cheeks heated to nuclear meltdown levels. *And now he's looking at me funny. Great.*

Dawn clapped her hands. "Enough nonsense. This old broad wants to go home. You young'uns scat." With a muffled groan, she slid off her bar stool and walked off toward her office.

While Lana finalized her notes, Jojo took the seat Dawn had vacated. "Marketing, huh? Seems you're good at it."

She lifted an eyebrow. "I am. It's interesting, figuring out what makes people choose one bar over another, one beer over another, one T-shirt—" She gestured to his Bangers Security shirt, stretched tight over his bulging pecs.

Jojo shifted, and so did his mighty muscles, an endless, fascinating dance of flesh and bone and golden skin. "Will you go back to it?"

"I hope so, when my brothers leave the nest."

"How old are they again?

"Fifteen and seventeen."

Jojo nodded. "Me and my brother Kai have the same age spread. Our mama watched over us with eagle eyes and an iron fist." He covered her hand with his giant mitt and squeezed gently. "I'll bet you're the same."

For a moment, she let herself enjoy his warmth and weight, the surprising softness cocooning his strength. Then she reluctantly withdrew her hand. "My brothers are good kids. I'm proud of how well they're doing, considering what they've been through."

"Still, that's a lot to handle on your own. If you ever need a break, let me know. Nothing fixes teen attitude like a hard workout."

Lana gave a snort. Really, though, it was a tempting idea. Let Jojo work off some of the boys' adolescent hormones.

"Thanks, but between me and Kenny, I've got it covered."

Jojo's eyebrows climbed toward what would've been his hairline. How would it feel to stroke that smooth, shiny head?

She cleared her throat. "Kenny's my neighbor. The boys love him. Speaking of which, I need to go. He'll wait up until he gets my text."

Jojo wiggled on his seat. "I'm, uh, glad you got someone looking after you."

*Those eyes*— Espresso-brown, fringed with thick lashes, so intense, as if he could see right through her confident façade, straight to her aching, weary heart. For a moment, his focused attention made her forget how damn tired she was of proving, again and again, that she could handle her responsibilities.

She sucked in a steadying breath and straightened her spine. "I don't need anyone looking after me, Jojo."

If she didn't know better, she'd think the big lunk was jealous of her elderly neighbor. What a weirdo. "See ya later." She slid off her stool and onto her feet.

He did the same. Well, in Jojo's case, it was more of an upward motion. How tall was he, anyway? The top of her head barely reached his shoulder.

His powerful jaw muscles worked. "I'll walk you to your car."

She opened her mouth to protest.

He spread his hands. "Humor me, okay? It makes my caveman heart happy."

With a sigh, she headed for the door with Jojo looming behind her. In the parking lot, he stood guard, arms crossed, until she drove away.

As she navigated the nearly empty length of 6th Avenue, past bars and restaurants, vintage shops and cannabis dispensaries, she pondered what to make of Jojo. Was Rosie right? Could he really have feelings for her?

"Nah," she grumbled to her reflection in the rear-view mirror. "He's just a flirt by nature." Besides, she had no time to dwell on those soft brown eyes, those full, kissable lips, those mile-wide shoulders and arms with muscles on muscles on muscles...

With a weary sigh, she turned onto her street.

After shedding her jacket and bag, Lana peeked into Leo's room. The sour odor of gym socks drifted out, along with soft snores. Leo lay on his side, one hand dangling off the mattress, his mouth wide open. No doubt, his pillow was soaked with drool, just like when he was little. She could smile at the memory now that he'd given up the habit of sneaking into her bed and drooling all over her favorite plush unicorn. And now he was almost a grown man. Mom's voice sounded in her head, *They're always so cute when they're sleeping.* A wave of tenderness warmed Lana's chest and blurred her vision.

She tiptoed down the hallway to check on Pedro, whose room reeked of cheap body spray, a new development since he discovered girls. He'd shot up over the summer, and his voice had deepened, and lately, she'd caught him stroking his shadow of a mustache as he posed in front of the mirror. Mr. Smooth. So freakin' cute, though she'd never admit that aloud.

She closed Pedro's door softly and texted Kenny. **I'm home. Thanks much.**

He texted back. **We've got cocoa and zucchini bread. Come over?**

She found her neighbor on the couch, the coffee table laden with snacks, a crime drama on the TV. He grinned and patted the cushion beside him. "Take a load off."

Slipping off her shoes, she sat and tucked her feet beneath her. "Hey, handsome. Nice jammies." He wore a navy Henley top and flannel pajama bottoms printed with frowning teddies and "Grumpy Bear," ironic since he was the least grumpy person she knew. "Did Carol give you these?"

Laugh lines crinkled at the corners of his eyes. "Nah. Our daughter sent them from Texas."

Lana had never met their daughter and lived in fear they'd move out there, leaving her without someone to keep an eye on the boys at night while she worked at Bangers. But so far, her neighbors remained stubbornly attached to their Tacoma home.

She helped herself to a slice of zucchini bread. "You guys are up late."

Carol entered in a fuzzy robe and Tweety Bird slippers, her silver hair mussed. "Why not? We're retired. After years of getting up at the butt crack of dawn, it's a joy to finally follow our own internal clocks. Right, hon?" She smooched her husband, then set a mug of steaming cocoa in front of Lana and sank down beside her.

Lana sipped and sighed. "I can't thank you guys enough."

Kenny waved off her gratitude with a flick of his fingers. "No thanks needed. You and the boys are the closest thing we have to grandkids."

Carol leaned over and poked his shoulder. "We're far too young to have a twenty-three-year-old granddaughter."

"Twenty-four," Lana corrected her. "How were they?"

"Good as gold." Kenny reached for another slice of zucchini bread. "Leo's essay on Macbeth won't win a Pulitzer, but it'll earn him a passing grade."

"And Pedro's pond diorama?

Carol chuckled. "Oh, we had lots of fun with that. If he doesn't get at least a B, I'll march into that school and give his teacher a piece of my mind."

Lana leaned back with a sigh. "You two are angels, truly. And how lucky am I to have retired teachers as neighbors?"

Carol pursed her lips. "You work so hard, hon. Don't misunderstand me. We're glad to watch the boys while you're at the bar, but are you sure you wouldn't rather take a day job?"

"When I find one that pays what I earn at Bangers, I'll consider it."

Lana was painfully aware of the risk she was taking, leaving her brothers to fend for themselves after dinner. But Bangers was more than a flexible, well-paying job—it was family, and she prayed she wouldn't have to give it up.

When her parents died, the Bangers crew held her up through the dark days when grief and shock nearly undid her, and they stood by her through the custody battle that followed. So far, the threat of being separated to live with their strict tías in eastern Washington kept both boys in line. They knew damn well what was at stake.

"Besides," she continued, "it wasn't that different before we lost Mom and Dad. They both worked long hours, so it was on me to make sure the bros cleaned their rooms and did their homework."

Carol enfolded Lana's hands. "Oh, honey, no. The difference is enormous. Your parents had years of experience, plus that special bond parents have with their kids. I know the boys sometimes resent you for taking on that role, and I'm so full of admiration for how well you're handling it."

"Enzo and Martina were wonderful friends to us," Kenny added with a pat on her shoulder. "We could never replace them, but we're glad to help where we can."

Guilt pinched Lana hard. These two deserved to enjoy their golden years unencumbered by a couple of teens.

Better leave before she got weepy. "Thanks again, and for the bedtime snack, too." She smooched Carol's cheek, then Kenny's. "Remember, I'm at your disposal during the day. Anything you need, just ask."

Carol raised her forefinger. "Actually, Kenny has a doctor's appointment tomorrow, right when the new plumber is coming. Keep me company?"

Lana quickly checked her phone calendar. "You got it."

The phone buzzed in her hand. A text from Pedro.

**Come quick. Leo just puked.**

*Fabulous.* She dragged a hand over her mouth. Ever since he was little, Leo had a touchy tummy. Probably just overdid the greasy snacks, but she'd better check his temperature, just in case.

"Gotta go. Duty calls." Sparing Carol and Kenny the gory details, she pasted on a bright smile. "Sweet dreams, guys."

She rushed home to find the bathroom a complete disaster zone—chunky, stinky gobs everywhere. Between heaves, Leo confessed to supplementing the healthy baked chicken and veggies she'd prepared with canned chili and spray cheese.

Fighting exhaustion and the urge to spew, she tucked him into bed, pulled on rubber gloves, and got to work.

Chuckling, she recalled Jojo's sweet, concerned expression at work that night. He wanted to help with the boys? He had no freakin' idea.

# Chapter Three

♥

"Next." Perched on his barstool at Bangers' entrance, Jojo flapped his fingers in a "gimme" gesture. "C'mon, people. Sports trivia starts in fifteen minutes." He tugged his jacket zipper higher against a stiff breeze and watched the cars roll up 6th Avenue. That place across the street was set to open again, a vegan taco bar this time. Probably wouldn't last long. New restaurants came and went on The Ave, but Bangers remained, a neighborhood anchor for going on fifty years. He liked that about the squat brick building—a sense of permanence and history. Home away from home.

A whacked-out dude with wild hair staggered up the sidewalk, deep in debate with his imaginary friend. He spun and stabbed a finger at Jojo's chest. "Ain't that right?"

"Damn straight, sir."

Vindicated, the guy stumbled on, heading toward Legendary Doughnuts. Or maybe he wanted a cone from Ice Cream Social. More likely, he was looking to score some weed from that sketchy guy in the sushi place parking lot. Why anyone bothered with him on a street rich with legal dispensaries baffled Jojo, but old habits die hard.

A quartet of guys detached themselves from the competitors smoking and trash-talking outside Bangers. The first slapped his ID into Jojo's extended palm. "Gonna kick ass tonight, amirite?"

"Sure you are. Good luck, buddy." Honestly, he didn't give a crap about sports trivia. Hadn't really followed football much since he played for Stadium High School. Why grown men got so worked up about stats baffled him. *It's just math, right?*

Rosie came outside carrying a tall glass and a plate of chicken. "Virgin Mai Tai to go with your jerk wings."

Jojo seized her free hand and kissed it. "You, my inky goddess, have superb taste."

She tittered. "Don't let Eddie see you nibbling my digits. Russian guys are hot-blooded, you know."

"Not as hot as these wings." He took a bite and sucked in a breath around a mouthful of succulent, blistering bird meat. Maci, Diego's replacement since he left Bangers to run his food truck full time, had a magic hand with spices.

"Gimme one." Rosie helped herself, chomped, and did a full-body shimmy-shiver dance. "Yowza! So spicy." She wiped her mouth on her sleeve. "Thank God you're working tonight. Last week, the sports geeks got rowdy."

Jojo licked sauce off his fingers. "So? Spike can handle it."

"Spike was in a foul mood and looking to pound heads together. Gus had to step in to defuse a brawl. Fortunately, no one involved was asshole enough to punch an old guy." She patted his arm. "I like you much better than Spike."

"Aww, thanks, Rosie. I'm still waiting for my vampire tattoo." Last winter, Rosie finally found an apprenticeship at a tattoo parlor. Good to see her using her artistic talent on something besides the signs she painted on Bangers' windows.

"I've got some cute ideas. Call the studio and make an appointment."

The ship's bell rang out from behind the bar.

Jojo clapped his hands. "Last call for sports trivia. If you're playing, get your ass inside."

Patrons rushed the entrance, thrusting IDs in his face.

He checked and stamped, urging them to try the wings and River's drink special, the Tequila Touchdown.

Once the sidewalk cleared, he scanned the crowd inside for Lana. There she was, zipping from table to table, a dark scowl on her face.

His skin prickled. *Something's wrong. Must protect woman.* A stupid impulse, since she clearly didn't want his help.

When Dawn started the trivia competition, Jojo beckoned to Eddie, who came out to take his place. The skinny little squirt was surprisingly strong and quick, a good addition to Jojo's informal training group.

"I'm taking my break."

Eddie's brows contracted. "Didn't Rosie bring you an order of wings?"

"That was just an appetizer." He headed toward the kitchen for a refill and rounded the corner just as Lana sailed through the swinging doors, her tray crammed with platters.

"Maci, they changed their minds. They want the totchos, not the bacon-cheese tots."

"On it." Shelby, Maci's assistant chef, loaded the rejected tots with extra cheese goo, salsa, sliced green onions, diced chiles, avocado, olives, and sour cream. "They won't mind the bacon, right?"

Lana shrugged. "Who objects to bacon?"

"What you want, big man?" Maci asked in her sing-song Caribbean accent.

"Another plate of wings, please, extra-hot."

Maci's eyebrows climbed. "Oho. A challenge." She plunged a batch into the deep fryer.

Jojo leaned in for a closer look at the bird print of her head wrap. "Are those chickens?"

"Best I can do for now. I'm still looking for cloth printed with tater tots."

He laughed. "If you find some, let me know. I'll have a set of scrubs made."

While he waited, he turned to Lana, who glared at her phone and muttered to herself.

"Hey, bright eyes, what's got you so frowny tonight?"

Her scowl softened into a weary sigh. "My brother Leo mouthed off to his football coach."

"Coach Bauer? Ruh-roh. That's not going to end well for your brother."

"Coach wants a meeting tomorrow before school."

At last, an opening. "Bauer's a tough old fart, but he's a good coach. We won division championship my senior year."

Maci looked up. "And you played... let me guess... quarterback?"

Lana snorted. "More like offensive lineman."

*Cute, smart, and knows her football. Interesting.*

Jojo cocked a finger pistol. "Bingo. Coach straightened me out a time or two when I needed a good kick in the ass. Let him do that for your brother."

"Leo's terrified he'll get kicked off the team. He used to be such a sweet kid, but this year, he's so damn cocky. Senioritis." Her brow knitted. "If he gets cut, I'm afraid he'll blow off school entirely." She pocketed her phone and heaved a sigh. "I'll see if Kenny can come."

Again with this Kenny guy. No way could he handle Coach better than Jojo could.

He straightened his shoulders. "Let me come."

Loading her tray with the doctored tots, Lana blinked up at him. "You? Why?"

"I learned the hard way how to talk to Coach without pissing him off." He buffed his nails on his shirt. "Schmoozing is my specialty."

"I've noticed." She chewed her lip for a long moment. "Okay. Thanks. Meet me in front of the school at seven."

Once she lifted her tray and sailed through the swinging doors, Jojo permitted himself a discreet fist-pump.

Returning to his station, he clapped Eddie's shoulder. "Need you to take charge of tomorrow's workout. I'm gonna be late."

"Me?" Eddie pointed to his chest.

"Absolutely. Work 'em hard, little man. Start with walking lunges to the fire hydrant and back."

He pulled a sour face. "They won't listen to me."

"Kai will. The others will follow. Besides, no workout, no protein shakes afterward."

Eddie spluttered a laugh. "Dude, no one likes your brother's nasty shakes. They taste like pond water with a hint of dog crap."

He squeezed Eddie's shoulder, firmly muscled despite his small frame. "But look how good they work."

For the rest of his shift, Jojo alternated between guarding the entrance and watching Lana flit through the crowd. Passing with a pitcher of beer, she gifted him a shy smile that warmed him right down to his toes.

*Progress!*

After finding a parking spot near Stadium High School, Jojo drank in the view of the grand old building. The stadium bowl for which the school was named stretched out below—green sports field rimmed with red track, the far side open to a magnificent view of the Puget Sound. The school loomed above, its brown brick glowing in the September sunlight, its black-roofed turrets stretching tall. How lucky was he to have gone to school in a freakin' castle? His cousin Kapua even got to be a movie extra when they filmed that romcom here back in '98.

Visiting the site of his football glory days always brought a flood of complicated memories. This was where he transitioned from pudgy, awkward middle schooler to confident athlete, but the scars lingered just below his skin. After his growth spurt between ninth and tenth grade, he was still the same class clown, joking around to cover how hard school was and how baffling his peers were, especially girls. But people treated him differently. Teachers excused the screw-ups of the Tigers' star offensive lineman, cutting him slack they never granted before he shot up six inches and lost his baby fat.

Jojo knew better than most what was at stake for a troubled kid. Sports could be a lifesaver. He had to help Lana keep her brother on the team.

He crossed the broad courtyard, past kids in hoodies and letterman jackets who perched on the stone planters or skated outside the theater building. After patting Ballsy, the tiger statue in the lobby, for old time's sake, he signed the visitor roster and schmoozed with the receptionist, a sweet old gal who remembered him from the Class of '10. When he emerged, he spotted Lana glowering beside a lanky kid who stared at the floor, his posture slumped. She must've raided her mom's closet. Dressed in a knee-length wool skirt, plain brown pumps, and a cotton blouse, her braids wound into a knot at the base of her skull, she looked like a girl playing librarian in a school pageant. He couldn't help fantasizing about unpinning her hair, unbuttoning that prim blouse, and...

She lifted her chin in greeting and thanked him for coming, her voice tight and raspy. Hoo boy—he would not want to be in her brother's shoes.

Even though she looked peeved enough to bite through steel, her beauty sucked the air from Jojo's lungs. He hooked his thumbs into his pockets and ambled toward them, faking cool to cover the nervous vibration rattling his bones.

Lana nudged her sulking brother. "Leo, this is my work friend Jojo Williams."

The family resemblance was unmistakable. A head taller than his sister, Leo had the same sharp dark eyes, pointy chin, black-coffee hair, and olive complexion. He extended his hand and gave Jojo's a squeeze. The kid's eyes rounded when Jojo squeezed back.

*Better chill that attitude, tough guy. Coach will not be impressed.*

Lana gave Jojo an awkward half smile. God, this must be tough on her, handling parent-teacher conferences when she'd graduated, what, six years ago?

He clapped Leo's shoulder. "So, what did you say to Coach?"

Leo glared at his toes. "I just told him his stupid wind sprints don't help worth shit."

He groaned and shook his head.

"What? It's the truth. What does it accomplish to run back and forth until you puke?"

Jojo squeezed the kid's bony shoulder. "Little man, you're lucky he didn't cut you then and there. Listen up. Sometimes Coach is more hard-ass that he needs to be—and if you tell him I said that, I'll call you a liar—but the shit he teaches you makes you stronger. Not just on the field, in life."

"But—"

"Seriously, man. You're gonna face situations much harder than wind sprints. If you take the lazy route, your life will be shit. So suck it up and do your training. I'm glad I did."

Leo shot Lana an exasperated grimace.

She raised her palms. "Don't expect me to disagree, little bro. My life has been damn hard since we lost Mom and Dad. Sometimes I think back on school days and wish life was still this simple."

Leo's head jerked back like a startled turtle's.

She gentled her tone and stroked her brother's arm. "I love you and Pedro to the bottom of my soul, so I don't mind working hard. But Jojo's right. Even if you never play football again, that hard-ass coach is teaching you self-discipline. You'll need that. Now take us to your coach's classroom."

Grumbling under his breath, Leo led them up the stairs to Coach Bauer's biology lab. The kid sucked in a deep breath before knocking.

"Enter," a deep voice boomed.

When the door opened, the familiar, jungly scent brought a smile to Jojo's lips. Out on the field, Coach was a tyrant, but his classroom revealed his softer side. Well-kept aquariums burbled, gerbils ran on their exercise wheel, giant snails clung to the walls of their terrarium, and trailing plants dangled from macrame hangers. Good to see Coach still loved his little critters.

The man himself hadn't changed either. Square and stocky with a powerful jaw, he still wore his salt-and-pepper hair in a brush cut. His Stadium polo shirt stretched tight across his broad shoulders and chest.

Coach glanced up. "Killa Williams!" He flashed a mile-wide grin and stepped around his desk to pound Jojo's back. "Good to see you, son. What happened to your hair?"

"Started getting thin on top, just like Dad, so..." He swiped a hand over his scalp. "Zip."

"Suits you." Coach jerked a thumb at Leo, who stood chewing a cuticle. "You here with Numbnuts?"

Leo squeaked. Lana cleared her throat.

"Where are my manners? Miss Lopez, thanks for coming in this morning. Please have a seat." He indicated a chair facing his desk.

Jojo fetched two more from a nearby table and sat beside Leo, who whispered, "Killa?"

"Short for Mount Kilauea. You know, since I'm half Hawaiian."

"And half mad dog." Coach chuckled and sat behind his desk. His smile disappeared as he tented his fingers and pinned Leo with a stony stare. "Tell me, son, what's your definition of teamwork?"

Leo responded with a sulky shrug. Bad move.

Coach's wiry eyebrows slammed together. "You're forgetting something important, Lopez. Practice ain't about you. It's about *us*. The team." He stabbed a stubby finger toward Leo. "I don't give a flying fart how good an athlete you are. Without teamwork, your talent means nothin'. They don't pay me enough to stand out in the wind and rain with a bunch of selfish pups who just wanna screw off and make their friends laugh. If you're not here to train and win games, I don't have the time for your bull crap."

Leo shrank in his seat. Poor kid.

Coach leaned onto his fists. "So, let's clarify our intentions. Mine is to train you hard as a member of our team, no more important than any other player." His voice softened. "And no less. Now, what do you have to say for yourself?"

Leo shot Lana a pleading glance. She tilted her head toward Coach, a silent "Go on."

The kid knotted his hands in his lap. "Sorry, sir. It won't happen again."

Coach harrumphed. "Why should I believe you? This wasn't an isolated incident. You've been screwing around for weeks."

The kid was blowing it. If he didn't show convincing contrition, Coach would bounce his ass from the team.

Leo swiped at his tear-bright eyes. "It's too hard, Coach. I love to play, but the drills are kicking my ass."

"Your attitude's kicking your ass, son. The only way to get stronger is to train."

Poor kid. Jojo tasted the sour sting of humiliation on his own tongue.

Lana twisted her skirt in her lap, her voice shaky. "Coach, please give him another chance. He may not show it, but my brother cares a lot about staying on the team." She kicked his ankle. "Don't you, Leo?"

Leo nodded and sniffed hard.

Jojo weighed his approach. He was taking a chance here, but if he helped the kid, he'd be helping Lana. Even if that wasn't enough to win her heart, at least he'd get a little closer.

He straightened in his seat. "Tell you what, Coach. I run a bootcamp kinda deal with some guys from work. How about if I train Leo, build up his stamina and strength?"

Coach's jaw muscles ticked as his gaze darted from Jojo to Lana. The old bull was thinking it over. His eyes narrowed—never a good sign.

"Miss Lopez, I appreciate the difficulty of your situation, but there's no way I can let your brother off that lightly. He disrespected me in front of his teammates." He folded his hands on the desk. "Son, I'm suspending you from the team for two weeks."

Leo gulped, his eyes brimming with tears.

Coach crossed his arms and leaned back. His chair creaked under his weight. "I strongly suggest you use that time to take advantage of Williams' offer. Because when you come back to practice, if I see anything less than stellar effort and attitude, you're off the team for good. You hear me?"

Leo straightened and jutted his chin. "Yes, sir."

They filed into the hallway, where Leo grimaced and drove his fist into a locker.

Lana touched her brother's shoulder, but he shook her off.

A pang of sympathy stabbed Jojo's gut. At Leo's age, emotions hit like tsunamis. Better to let the kid swim to the surface in his own way.

His head against the metal door, Leo croaked, "What time, sir?"

"Sorry?"

"Your bootcamp thing. Where and what time?"

Jojo felt his face relax into a smile. Leo might be a snotty teen, but he had spirit. "Five o'clock." He rattled off his address.

Leo swiped his eyes on his sleeve, faced Jojo, and extended his hand. "Thanks, man." He turned to Lana. "I won't let Coach kick me off the team."

"Okay then." Lana patted Jojo's arm. "You'll be in good hands."

Her soft touch made his anatomy way too happy for a public setting. He puffed out a shaky breath and thought about multiplication tables.

She squeezed her brother's shoulder, then tilted her head toward the exit. Jojo followed her through halls now filling up with students. He hoped Leo could pull his shit together before facing his friends.

In the courtyard, surrounded by kids rushing to beat the bell, Lana clutched his arm. "Wow." She smoothed both hands over her hair. Even in her stodgy grownup clothes, she shone as bright and beautiful as the crystal September sky—and so damn young to be facing teen antics like Leo's. Most parents were in their forties by the time their kids reached this rebellious phase, but Lana was only twenty-four. And on her own too. She had no choice but to step up and protect her brothers. Who protected her?

She sucked in a breath and gifted him a heart-melting smile. "I don't know what to say except thank you."

He gave a sheepish shrug. "I'd be working out anyway. It's no big deal to add one more person."

She took his hand, and his stupid dick perked right up. Her skin was so soft, her eyes so bright, her bashful smile so sweet.

"Without your help, I think Coach would've kicked Leo off the team. If you can get through his thick head and get him back on track..." She shuffled her feet on the pavement. "Well, I'd be grateful."

*Crap. Does she think I'm only helping to win brownie points with her?*

He cleared his throat. "Listen, I was given some breaks I didn't deserve when I was your brother's age, so I'm just paying it forward. It's no big deal."

Lana touched his chest with her fingertips, and waves of tingly warmth spread across his skin like sunlit ripples in a pond. She rose on tiptoe and pecked his cheek. "It's a huge deal, Jojo. Thank you."

He watched her walk away, mesmerized by the way her quick steps shook her plush hips.

Floating inches above the ground, he made his way back to his car. Head buzzing, heart tripping over itself, he steered for the clinic, all the while replaying that sweet, soft kiss on an endless loop.

# Chapter Four

Count on Pedro to crack wise. As Lana waited for Leo to gather his workout gear, their younger brother sniped, "You got the hospital on speed dial, bro? Ya know, in case you break your delicate bones?"

Leo clenched his fist under his brother's nose. "How about I break your bones, little bro?"

"Shut it, both of you," Lana snapped and added a finger stab at Pedro's skinny chest. "And you cool it, Squirt, or I'll ask Jojo to train you too."

Pedro flexed his baby biceps. "Haley already likes my muscles."

Leo scoffed. "P gets his first kiss, and now he thinks he's grown."

Pedro smirked. "I got a lot more than a kiss, bro."

Lana threw up her hands. "Okay, Mr. Horny-pants, when we get back, you and I are having a talk about protection."

"Eew." Pedro cringed. "I don't talk about things like that with my sister."

"You do when you brag about your love life in front of me, Lothario."

Leo snort-laughed. "Ha! She called you a pasta."

"That's a famous player, Numbnuts!" Pedro shot back with a sneer.

"Enough." She shooed Leo out the door. On her way out, she pointed two fingers at her own eyes, then at Pedro.

Just what she needed, another birds and bees talk—like she was some kind of expert. Ugh.

Leo sat sullen and silent on the drive to Jojo's. Probably covering for nerves. Not much chance this scheme to keep him on the team would even work, with his snotty attitude. Worse, he'd probably get attached to Jojo. She'd caught the gleam of awe in her brother's eye when he met the gentle giant.

Her tías were right about one thing—the boys needed positive male role models, and at the moment, Kenny was all they had.

She pulled up beside a single-story stucco cottage a few blocks from Bangers. The garage door stood open, and she was surprised to see the Bangers guys inside—Eddie on a weight bench, River spotting him, Diego dangling from a chin-up bar, plus Jojo's ginormous brother Kai swinging kettle bells. Jojo stood to the side, holding a clipboard. Quite a sophisticated set-up. Band posters on the walls, an expensive-looking blender on a back counter, and heavy metal thumping from tall, old-school speakers.

Leo clutched Lana's arm. "Come with me?"

"Sure. I'll introduce you to the guys." Cute, how nervous he was. Then again, he didn't get to spend much time with young men. Maybe this would knock his teenage ego down a peg.

As they walked up the driveway, River called out, "Fresh meat."

Honestly, what did Charlie see in that smart ass—besides a model-perfect face, impossibly shiny blond hair, and a *GQ* physique? Okay, she'd just answered her own question.

Jojo approached, arms spread wide. Man, he was a sight to see in silky shorts that clung to his mighty thighs and, God help her, a sleeveless workout tank. Black-inked Polynesian tattoos swirled and danced down his right arm. Yum.

"Hey, Lana." Jojo's smile twinkled with something she'd better not think too hard about. She was here to help Leo, not encourage Jojo's flirtation. Even if that sparkle in his eyes revved her pulse and set off a tingle in her core.

"Welcome, Leo. Come meet the guys." Jojo draped his huge arm over Leo's skinny shoulders and walked him around the makeshift gym, introducing him to everyone. To Lana's relief, the guys shook Leo's hand, then got back to their workouts with a minimum of teasing. Soon, Leo was on a floor mat in the corner, his feet hooked under a low bar, cranking out sit-ups.

Jojo sauntered over. "It'll be fine, big sis. See? He's becoming one of the family, just like you." He nudged her, and the brush of his bare arm against hers dropped her IQ several points.

The slam of a car door jerked her head around. A tall, sturdy woman with golden skin a shade lighter than Jojo's strode up the driveway. "For cripes' sake, turn the music down. You're gonna get yourself evicted." Her tone was firm, but her smile glowed with warmth.

Jojo rolled his eyes. "I told you, Ma, the neighbors don't mind. Meet my work friend Lana."

Mrs. Williams enfolded Lana's hand in both of hers. "Hello, sweetheart. Clinic or bar?"

"Um—bar."

The older woman gave her son a knowing smile. "Ah, the girl with the braids." She squeezed Lana's hand before releasing it. "He's mentioned you often."

Jojo's cheeks flushed. Interesting.

"Morning, Ma. Hey, Lana." Kai trotted out to peck his mother's cheek, then Lana's—surprising, since they'd only met a few times at the bar. Probably just needling his older brother.

Jojo's clenched fists made his forearm muscles pop.

She sucked in a breath. *Quit ogling him in front of his mom!*

"Nice to meet you, Mrs. Williams. Well, I'll leave you guys to it." She backed down the driveway, prickling with embarrassment.

The older woman raised a finger. "Hang on, honey." She told her sons something about their auntie's birthday—Lana was too busy chastising herself to catch the details—then trotted back to her side.

"I'm glad to meet you, Lana. How did my son describe you?" She tapped her pursed lips. "Ah yes, he called you fierce. That's quite a compliment." Her voice took on a sign-song note. "I think he has a little crush on you."

She bit her lip. It was getting harder and harder to deny the feeling was mutual. She watched Jojo drop to the floor, demonstrating a painful-looking plank exercise to Leo. She'd never seen this much of him, and the effect was dazzling—tattoos over tawny skin and bulging muscles, a light sheen of sweat on his brow. She would have to change her sopping panties before work.

Mrs. Williams' voice jolted her out of Jojo's gym shorts and back to the driveway. "Lana. That's a Spanish name?"

"Not really. Dad wanted to name me Luna after his grandmother from Peru, but Mom vetoed that. Said kids would call me Looney Tunes."

The older woman chuckled. "Smart Mama. I'm sorry for your loss, dear. Jojo told me. And that's your brother?"

"Yes, ma'am. Jojo's helping him train for football."

"Jojo's always been good with kids." She patted Lana's arm, her touch soft and comforting. "I worried a lot about my oldest, but look at him now. He'd make a wonderful teacher, don't you think?"

Jojo looked up from his floor mat. "Don't wanna be a teacher, Ma."

Yikes! He heard all that?

Apparently, the whole Williams clan had superhero hearing, because Kai joined in. "Jojo likes to make people bleed—at the clinic, in the gym, or pounding heads at the bar."

In one smooth motion, Jojo sprang to his feet and punched Kai's arm. "Don't worry, little man," he told Leo. "No one's going to make you bleed."

Eddie snorted. "Not on your first day anyway."

Leo shot Lana a wide grin, clearly loving all this big-brother energy.

Ignoring their shenanigans, Mrs. Williams addressed her. "I'm not sure why Jojo hangs onto his job at Bangers, but I'm glad he has such nice friends."

Jojo strode toward them. "Ma, quit interrogating Lana. I won't forget Auntie's party, okay? Solemn promise."

"And you'll make sure Kai comes too?"

"Absolutely." He gave her a gentle shove. "I love you. Now go."

"Okay, okay. Don't mangle the boy."

Jojo waited until his mother drove away before swiping a hand down his glistening face and giving Lana an adorable, sheepish grin. "Sorry about that. Ma's kind of over-protective. Hey, you hungry?" Without waiting for an answer, he hollered over his shoulder, "Kai, make my friend a smoothie."

The guys chorused a groan. "I thought you liked Lana," River called out.

"I'll pass on the smoothie and leave you guys to your work-out." She took Jojo's hand and pulled him down to whisper, "I really appreciate this."

He squeezed her gently with his giant mitt. "Glad to help, sunflower."

"Gah. Still at it with the nicknames? It's La-na. Very simple. Try it with me now."

Hands raised in surrender, he backed toward the garage gym. "Fine, okay. See you at work, La-na."

Grinning like a happy fool, she drove home to deal with her amorous little brother. Hard to work up a head of righteous steam while still tingling from Jojo's touch. It was dumb to get this worked up over a coworker, but damn! For just these precious few private minutes, alone in her car, she let herself imagine his big body moving over hers, those giant hands, the humor in his warm brown eyes igniting to flame...

*Woah. Enough of that.* Now that Leo was involved, it was more crucial than ever to keep her interactions with Jojo light and friendly.

She huffed a laugh. *Easier said than done.*

Still grinning, Jojo set Leo up for decline bench presses. "That's the way. Slow and controlled. River, spot Junior, will you?" He crossed to the counter and chugged from his oversize water bottle.

Diego sidled up, wiping sweat from his brow. "You're good at this, Jojo. You've even got that kid working like he gives a shit—hard to do at that age. Why are you wasting time as a bouncer?"

Again with this question. Why all the pressure from friends and family lately?

"Habit, I guess. I started working at Bangers before I finished phlebotomy school. The bar feels like home, you know?"

Diego bent to tighten his shoelaces. "Yeah, I miss it like hell. Can't stay there forever, though. I stressed myself sick over telling Dawn I wanted to leave Bangers to open my food truck. You know what she said? She thinks of Bangers as an incubator for talented young people. She expects us to learn what we need, then leave the nest."

Jojo laughed. "What's with all the bird metaphors? Lemme guess. You making chicken empanadas this week?"

Diego grinned. "And pumpkin with chipotle and roasted corn. I'll save you a few under the counter."

"Make it three of each." Who needed the hospital cafeteria with Diego's food truck parked just outside the building? "And when are you bringing back those Hatch chili breakfast empanadas?"

Kai ambled over, one arm pulled across his chest in a stretch. "Diego's right, bro. You already finished your personal trainer cert. When you gonna open your own gym?"

"Someday, okay?" If he'd let the hairs on his neck grow, they'd be prickling. "I've already got a day job and a night job. That's enough for now."

"He wants to stick close to Lana," Diego interjected with painful accuracy. "It's been, what, three years?"

Was he really that transparent? "She'll look my way, eventually. I'm a patient man."

Diego gave his arm a playful punch. "Gotcha. A good woman is worth the wait."

"Took you a while to convince Anna you were serious, right?"

"Yup. Lots of time, lots of fixing stuff around her house and romancing her with food. Plus, I had to convince her family and mine I wasn't some creep with a pregnancy fetish. Hell, I even served divorce papers on her slimeball ex-husband." He pulled out his phone and showed them a photo of him and Anna holding baby Ellie. "It was worth it, though. We're a family now." The chef's grin could've lit the entire block.

Jostling and laughing, Diego and Kai moved off to finish their workout.

Jojo leaned against the wall and watched Leo spotting River through a set of incline bench presses. The gleam in the kid's eyes looked a lot like hero worship. Lana was right—the kid was needy. Who wouldn't be after losing both parents, then almost losing his brother and sister in a custody fight? Talk about emotional baggage—this kid came with a whole baggage carousel. As much as Jojo craved Lana's affection, now he'd involved himself in her family life, and that was sacred ground. Time to tread carefully.

# Chapter Five

♥

Only the first of October, and already Dawn had swapped football decorations for glow-in-the-dark skeletons, glittery pumpkins, and witch hats. Truly, the boss adored the spooky season.

On her way to the servers' station, Lana shook hands with a life-size skeleton propped in the corner. A pirate's tricorn hat was wired to his head. An eye patch covered one empty socket, and a skeletal parrot perched on his shoulder.

"Evening, Cap'n." She clicked her heels together.

Truth be told, she loved this season too. No heavy family obligations like Thanksgiving, no budget-killing traditions like Christmas, just lots of creepy, ghoulie fun. Plus, she got to wear her vast collection of Halloween socks and tights to work.

"Love the bats," Charlie cooed as she joined Lana at the servers' station. "How do they stay up?"

Lana peeled back the top of her thigh-high socks. "There's a sticky rubber strip—see? You got your Halloween costume yet?"

Kiara set a tall glass of Salty Dog Weizenbock on Lana's tray. "I'm coming as Medusa." She wiggled her fingers above her head like snakes. "What about you, Charlie?"

She lifted a shoulder. "I dunno, maybe a zombie?"

Rosie bopped up to the bar. "I need three Cosmos and a pitcher of Rainier." She eyed Lana and gave a wolf whistle. "Lana's hot stuff tonight. Check out the sparkly kicks."

Lana pointed her toe and admired the way her sneakers glittered under the orange and purple twinkle lights. "Found these at Vintage Treasures up the street." Since the servers usually wore jeans shorts and Bangers T-shirts to work, they made a game of accessorizing according to the season—Seahawks gear on game days, of course, plus funky holiday socks, jewelry, badges, and hair decorations. Lana loved collecting quirky things to wear at work. Not many day jobs where she could get away with goofy accessories like these.

Rosie arranged her drink order on her tray. "Wonder what Jojo will wear this year? Remember his bad-boy biker Santa at the Christmas party? That was sooo hot!"

Charlie giggled. "Don't forget his Leprechaun costume at St. Patrick's Day. That green T-shirt was tight!"

Rosie elbowed Charlie. "Lana should try his Lucky Charms. I bet they're magically delicious!"

Kiara laughed so hard she nearly spilled a pitcher of beer.

"You guys," Lana protested, "I've told you a bazillion times, Jojo's just a friend."

"Until you give him the go-ahead." Rosie hip-bumped her. "He's itching to sweep you off your feet, chica."

Charlie tapped her pursed lips. "I wonder what it'd be like. I mean, he's so huge."

Lana glanced at the bouncer station where Jojo was chatting up an older couple. As if sensing her heated gaze, he turned toward her and lifted an eyebrow.

She quickly averted her gaze. "Jesus, you're worse than the guys. Jojo's a person, not a slab of meat." She collected her drink order and escaped into the crowd. Did her friends think she'd buckle under their torment and finally jump Jojo's bones just to shut them up?

One week of Leo's two-week suspension from the football team had passed. So far, so good. His grades were holding, and he continued going to his training sessions at Jojo's without complaint. No way would she risk messing this up by cranking up the heat between her and Jojo.

By the end of her shift, the bar was so packed she expected to see the Fire Marshal. Some alumni event at PSU had drawn a crowd that adjourned to Bangers afterward, and they were in a thirsty mood. Good thing both bouncers were working. Around midnight, Dawn sent Lana out front with sodas and tots for Jojo and Spike.

Jojo accepted his snack with a wide smile and a little bow. "Why, thank you, beautiful."

Spike took his with a grunt.

Jojo smacked his arm. "Say thank you to the lady."

Spike curled his lip, barely visible under his bushy beard. "Thanks, Pippi Longstocking."

She curled her lip right back at him, slightly surprised the grumpy, fuzzy lunk had ever read a book, much less a children's classic like *Pippi*. Still, with her braids and tall socks, his zinger was pretty clever.

Jojo leaned close. "Want me to pound him?"

Spike's laugh shook his belly. "I'd like to see you try, meathead."

Lana stuck out her chin and faced the oversize grouch. "Wasn't Pippi the strongest girl in the world? And a total rule breaker? I'll take that as a compliment." She executed a sharp pivot, but Spike stepped back fast enough to avoid her flying pigtails of doom. *Drat.*

An hour before closing time, her phone sounded in her pocket—Leo's ring tone, a riff from George Thorogood's "Bad to the Bone." Her pulse sped. Leo never called during her shift. She set her tray on the bar and ducked into the break room to call him back.

Leo picked up right away and stage-whispered, "Defcon one. Read your freakin' texts." He clicked off.

Checking her screen, Lana found a string of texts. *Damn it to hell and back.* She hadn't heard the ping above the noise of the bar.

**Tía C here. WTF?**
**She's at the door!**
**What do we say?**

*Shit, shit, shit.* Her brothers were under strict orders not to answer the door to anyone but Kenny and Carol. She pictured the boys cowering in the foyer, frantically texting her while their lemon-sucking auntie leaned on the doorbell.

Pretty damn brazen of Camila to show up after midnight for a surprise inspection. In the two years since Mom and Dad's death, both of Mom's older sisters had demonstrated their total lack of confidence in Lana's parenting skills. Even after losing their bid for custody, they sent email articles about raising teens and left snarky comments on her social media posts, ragging her about her Bangers job. If Mom could see how her sisters were treating their niece and nephews, she'd be horrified.

Lana itched to invite the tías to pack sand, but her lawyer had warned her it was best to keep the peace, lest she give them ammo for another custody attempt.

A new text popped up on her phone screen.

**K and C here**

She sent back a thumbs up emoji, then whispered a prayer that Kenny and Carol could defuse this bomb, or at least delay the detonation until she got off work.

At the servers' station, waiting for her next order, Lana chewed her thumbnail and jiggled from foot to foot. She nearly jumped out of her skin when Dawn tapped her shoulder.

"What's up, kiddo?"

"My auntie paid us a surprise visit."

Dawn checked the Salty Dog Brewery clock behind the bar. "At this hour? Is it the bitchy one or the suck-up one?"

Lana's laugh tasted bitter on her tongue. "The suck-up one—who reports to the bitchy one."

"You need to go?"

*Yes!* She straightened her shoulders. "No, that wouldn't be fair to Rosie and Charlie. It's too crowded tonight. I'll stay till closing."

"Pffsht." Dawn flicked her fingers toward the door. "Go on. We can handle it."

"But—"

Dawn leveled a stern gaze. "That's what family is for. Go take care of business, kiddo. Love the socks, by the way. Reminds me of—oh, who was that redheaded kid with the braids?"

"Pippi Longstocking?"

Dawn cocked a pistol finger. "That's the one. Total badass, just like you. Go handle your business."

Flooded with relief and gratitude, Lana hugged her boss, then grabbed her things from the break room and trotted to the exit.

Jojo hooked her arm as she passed, his brow knitted. What kind of monster was she that, even in this moment of crisis, she enjoyed his hand on her bare skin?

"Everything okay?"

She hesitated, chewing her lip. But holding everything back was exhausting, and the big lunk was already involved in her family's business. "My auntie sprang another surprise inspection on us. Hell, she'll probably want to spend the night. I'd better make up the sofa bed. Ugh."

His stare bored into her. "You need anything, you call, okay?"

"It's cool." She patted his rock-hard arm. "Kenny's there to talk her down. He could charm the skin off a snake." A nervous giggle escaped her tight throat. "Actually, that saying fits my aunties to a T. Couple of snakes, both of them."

Jojo glowered.

"Something wrong?"

"I'll walk you to your car."

"Really, that's not necessary."

He dropped his huge, heavy arm over her shoulders. "Sunflower, when will you learn? I'm watching out for you whether you like it or not."

Wishing she could enjoy the delicious weight and warmth a little longer, Lana yielded. "Okay, okay. And don't call me sunflower."

The corner of his mouth quirked up. "How about mariposa?"

"Nope."

"Sunshine?"

She glared up at him. "Do I look sunshiny to you right now?"

"You look beautiful. And bright. And—" Following her, he bonked into the bouncer's stool at the entrance.

Spike grumbled, "Where the hell are you going?"

"Don't get your drawers in a knot," Jojo snarled. "I'll be right back."

"G'night, Spike," she called over her shoulder.

Spike grunted. What a charmer.

She let herself into her car. Holding the door open, Jojo squatted and gazed up at her with huge puppy dog eyes. His posture drew his jeans tight over his mighty thighs. "I'm glad you've got your neighbor to help you, but you can always call on me too. Day or night."

Heat flushed through her. "Okay. Thank you."

Danger alarms wailed in her head. This was no time for warm, fuzzy feelings and happy underpants tingles, but his earnestness was so damn touching. She drove off, fast as she dared, through the heavy Saturday night traffic on 6th Ave.

What a mess. She couldn't allow her feelings for Jojo to endanger the delicate web of support holding up her and her brothers. But this attraction was getting stickier by the day. And a web could only bear so much weight before it broke.

Lana's stomach curdled at the sight of Tía Camilla's boxy sedan in her driveway, its spotless champagne paint gleaming under the streetlight.

She hurried up the stairs and found the front door unlocked. Grasping the latch, she closed her eyes. *Breathe in calm. Breath out bullshit. I've got this.* She gently opened the door.

Kenny and Carol stood in the foyer, dressed in their PJs and robes, chatting amiably with Tía Camilla as if it were two in the afternoon. Their uptight auntie clutched her boxy purse to her chest like a shield.

At Lana's approach, Kenny's eyes crinkled with suppressed laughter. "Here's our girl. Right on time." The man deserved an Oscar for best supporting actor.

Lana forced her jaw to unclench. "Hello, Tía. So nice to see you." Good thing she wasn't in church. Did God smite people for lying in their own homes?

Kenny stepped forward. "I was just telling your aunt how much we enjoy our bedtime cocoa with you and the boys. Isn't that right, hon?"

Carol put her arm around a seasick-looking Pedro. "Every night like clockwork. We love these boys like our own grandkids."

Camilla pulled a sour face. "Isn't it a little late for someone your age to be awake?"

The nerve! Camilla was in her late fifties, only ten years younger that Kenny and Carol. Where did she get off calling them old?

Carol's eyebrows shot up, but she quickly recovered her serene smile. "Oh, we're such night owls. A privilege of retirement, right, pumpkin?" She nudged Kenny.

"Absolutely." His grin was blinding. "And we love spending time with the kids."

"Shouldn't they be in bed by now?

Leo gave Camila a sickly sweet smile. "It's Saturday, Tía."

Pedro laid it on even thicker. "If we do our homework and chores, we get to watch classic kids' movies with Kenny and Carol."

The words leapt from Lana's mouth of their own accord. "Like Pippi Longstocking."

Camila wrinkled her nose. "You're making fun of me. That's not a nice way to treat your tía who drove across the state to see you."

Lana crossed her arms. "At one in the morning?"

Camilla sniffed. "Well, there's a crafters conference in Gig Harbor, and hotel rooms are so expensive there, so I thought..."

Lana pinned her with a death stare.

Camila's beady-eyed gaze slid away and down. "Okay, I had a minor disagreement with my roommate at the hotel. Honestly, Susan is so touchy. And there were no more vacant rooms, so..."

Lana's sigh emptied her lungs. "I'll make up the sofa bed."

"Thank you. I'll get my bags." Camila stalked to the door, then turned, eyebrows raised. "Boys?"

Leo and Pedro exchanged sneers but complied without further comment. Smart kids. Lana wasn't sure she could've restrained her tongue at their age.

Camila pressed her key fob into Leo's hand. "The big suitcase and the little red one."

When the boys were gone, she glared at Lana, her posture as stiff as her lacquered hair. "They shouldn't need prompting, you know. This just goes to show they need a strong male influence, like their uncles."

*Strong male influence my ass.* Both Camila's husband and Tía Valeria's let their wives stomp all over them.

Lana raised her chin. "They have Kenny."

"He's not family. Boys need to feel connected to the older generations, and the younger ones, like their cousins."

"Their cousins are all girls." She gave a tight smile. "Carol and I have that covered."

With a "Hmph," Camila went outside, no doubt to give orders.

Kenny and Carol closed on Lana and sandwiched her in a hug.

She nestled into their comforting embrace. "Thanks for rescuing us."

Carol snickered. "That woman is puckered so tight her ass squeaks."

"You'd think," Kenny added, "after losing their custody suit, your aunts would mellow out a little."

She laughed, because it was either that or cry. "That'll happen when donkeys fly."

"And dinosaurs stroll up 6th Avenue." Carol giggled. "Speaking of dinos, did you see her car?"

Footsteps clomped up the stairs. Carol released her and flashed a smile of surprise. "Well, hello there."

*Oh God, what now?* Lana whirled to find the boys flanking Jojo, who set down three suitcases and gave her a sheepish grin. "Evening." He waved to Kenny and Carol.

She gaped. "Jojo? What are you doing here?"

He twisted his foot like a shy schoolkid. "I was just on my way home and saw your brothers out front."

*No Oscar for Jojo.*

Leo's face scrunched in confusion. "But your place is on the other side of 6th Ave., by the middle school."

Jojo rubbed the back of his neck. "There's, uh, construction. I had to detour."

Camila looked Jojo up and down, her eyes narrowed. "Aren't you going to introduce us to your... boyfriend?" She wrinkled her nose as if he smelled bad.

How dare she? Jojo smelled amazing, like sandalwood and spices. An angry flush crept up Lana's neck.

Carol, on the other hand, looked amused. "Yes, Lana, introduce us to your friend."

Lana crossed to Jojo. "Jojo Williams, meet my neighbors Kenny and Carol Dalca."

Jojo broke into a wide grin. "Pleased to meet you, ma'am." He gently gripped Carol's hand, then gave Kenny's a hearty shake. "So, you're the Kenny I've heard so much about."

Pedro cleared his throat.

"And this is my youngest brother, Pedro."

He stuck out his skinny chest. "S'up, Jojo?"

Jojo gave him a fist bump. "S'up, little man? You coming to train with your brother tomorrow?"

Tía C sniffed. "Tomorrow, the boys are going to church with me. I so rarely get to see my favorite nephews." She leveled a glare at Lana.

Pedro groaned, and Leo muttered, "We're your only nephews."

*Ugh.* There was no avoiding this part. "And this is my aunt Camila."

"A pleasure, ma'am." Jojo took her hand and turned on the high beams.

But she remained stony, immune to his charisma. How was that even possible?

Camila raised her chin. "Boys," she said, her icy eyes never leaving Jojo's face, "your sister's manners need work. One presents an older person to a younger person, not the other way around."

Kenny laughed, loud and long. "Well, I'm the oldest person in this room, and I've got no beef with Lana's manners."

Carol stepped forward, her chin equally high. "In fact, I find Lana to be a very courteous, thoughtful person. Hardworking and responsible, too. She's an excellent role model for her brothers."

"Yeah," Leo raised his nose in the air.

"My brother means yes." Pedro gave his aunt a snarky grin. Camila sniffed again.

Jojo fished a Kleenex packet from his jacket pocket. "You need a tissue for that sniffle, ma'am?" he asked with complete sincerity.

Carol and Kenny tittered. Camila looked like she'd just tasted one of Kai's smoothies.

"Well then," Jojo clapped his hands together. "See you after church, Leo. You too, Pedro?"

Biting back laughter, Lana asked her brothers to make up the sofa bed, bid Kenny and Carol good night, and wound her arm through Jojo's.

Out on the porch, she leaned against his tree trunk arm and giggled. "Touché, Jojo. But really, why did you stop by?"

His gaze slid to the side. Dude had no poker face whatsoever. Good to know.

"And don't give me that bullshit about a detour."

His chest rose and fell. "You seemed upset. I was worried about you. Sorry. Was that creepy?"

"Nah, it was sweet." She shifted so they stood toe to toe. Her feet looked half the size of his.

His wide mouth curved in a smile. "Yeah? Good. And I'm glad I got to meet Kenny."

"Why?"

"Well, from the way you talked about him—" He lifted one shoulder in a half shrug. "Let's say I was a little jealous."

Lana blinked up at him, then spluttered with laughter. Gorgeous Jojo, the guy who melted panties with one flirty glance, jealous of silver-haired Kenny? Breathless, she rested her forehead on his chest. His solid warmth felt way too good. She should step out of the danger zone. Any minute now.

His hands slid around her to cradle her lower back.

She tilted her head up and planted her chin on his breastbone. "I don't have a boyfriend, Jojo, if that's what you're worried about."

The corners of his mouth crept up. "You in the market for one?"

The million-dollar question. Part of her, the part she kept a tight lid on, jumped up and down shouting, *Yes, yes, yes!*

"The thing is, I have to put my family first right now."

He sighed and rubbed slow circles on her back. "I understand."

"My brothers have been through so much loss—"

He pressed his soft lips to her forehead. "So have you, sweet cheeks."

"Ugh." She wrinkled her nose.

"Don't like that one either, huh?"

"I'm too snarky to be a sweet cheeks."

His grin sparkled like starlight. "Give me time. I'll find a nickname you like." He toyed with the fine hairs at her nape. "Though your name is beautiful, Lana Pilar Lopez."

*How does he know my middle name? And why is that such a turn-on?*

With great reluctance, she planted her palms on his chest and pushed away. "Jojo, I'm sure you could find all kinds of things I like. But right now, keeping an eye on those two inside takes all my focus. I can't give you what you want."

His wide, rough palm cupped her jaw, his expression so tender she almost took it all back. "I understand. When you're ready, I'll be waiting."

Tears prickled her eyes. He was such a good person, so much braver than her. He didn't hide the intense emotion brimming in his gaze, but he held it in check for her sake. Hers and the boys'.

If circumstances were different, she'd give in without a second thought. Surrendering to this sweet attraction would be so delicious, so comforting and thrilling. If only she could put her desires first for once.

The air between them grew dense, electric with unspoken words and restrained desire. His lips parted. His breath fanned her skin and stirred her hair. As if drawn by his gravity, she rose on tiptoe, heart thumping, body flushed, every nerve tingling, craving—

The front door banged open. A harsh, nasal voice rang out. "Lana, dear, aren't you coming to bed?"

She thunked her head against his chest and growled, eyes scrunched shut. But no amount of wishing would make this wicked witch disappear.

Jojo chuckled into her hair. "I'd best be going. G'night, shorty."

She growled again as he backed away, hating the loss of his comforting body heat.

"That's a no on shorty then." He waved to Tía C. "Good night, Ma'am. Pleasant dreams."

Fists clenched, Lana stalked inside to tuck her brothers and their interloping auntie into bed.

# Chapter Six

♥

Powerful tremors jolted Jojo's body. Panicked, he thrashed and clutched for support but met only slippery softness, nothing solid to grasp onto and steady himself. A moment ago, he was in Lana's arms, but now she slipped away, sliding into misty darkness. Reaching for her, he screamed her name. His fingers closed on—his pillow?

He opened his bleary eyes and found his brother grinning down at him.

"What the fuck, Kai?" he grumbled, his tongue thick with sleep. He flung out a hand and knocked his alarm clock to the floor. "It's not even nine. You ruined a beautiful dream."

Kai gave the bed another kick. "I'm sick of listening to your alarms, bro. Why do you bother setting them if you're just gonna sleep through them?"

Must've set the alarms out of habit. It usually took at least two to break through his sleep-drunk brain, so he set three on weekdays, rigged to ring five minutes apart.

"It's my day off." He knew he sounded like a whiny kid, but Sunday was the one day he allowed himself to sleep in. Not this late, usually, but after last night's almost-kiss with Lana, he'd lain awake replaying the moment in his head. So damn close. She said she wanted to wait, and he would respect her wishes—but the heat in her eyes told a different tale. She felt it too, the magnetism between them, and her feelings were winning the battle over her fears. If her obnoxious auntie hadn't opened the door and screeched at them... He grinned up at the ceiling, imagining the sweet brush of her lips against his, her soft body pressed to his front, her arms around his neck. Paradise.

"Well, get your lazy ass out of bed," Kai said with a sadistic grin. "Your clients are here."

"Clients?" He rubbed his sleep-crusted eyes.

"That kid from last week. And another one."

Oh, right. He'd invited Leo's little brother, hadn't he? "Tell 'em I'll be right there." He hauled himself to his feet and stumbled to the bathroom to splash water on his face, then grinned at his dripping reflection. This was a good sign, right? If Lana sent both her brothers, she must trust him. Now to build trust with the brothers as well. Whether they knew it or not, they held the keys to his happiness.

In the garage, he found the music blasting, Kai at his blender, and both boys eyeing their smoothies as if they expected something to crawl out of them. Which was totally fair.

Pedro lifted his glass to the light. "What makes it so green?"

Kai looked up from the jumble of ingredients spread across the counter. "Spirulina and wheat grass, plus bone broth, carrot tops, and ginger kombucha." He took a big slug of his drink. "Good for ya'. Puts hair on your chest."

Pedro grimaced, took a sip, then gagged.

"Wuss." Leo downed his drink, pounded his chest, and belched.

Jojo raised his hand in greeting. "Good morning. I thought you guys were going to church with your auntie."

Pedro's grin brimmed with snark, just like his sister's. "Seven o'clock mass. You shoulda seen Tia's face when Lana started banging pots and pans at six this morning."

Leo snickered. "No one does vengeance like Lana."

Jojo filed that information away for future use. "Does she know you're here?"

The boys exchanged a look. "Kinda..." Leo scuffed the toe of his shoe on the cement floor. Kid had no lying skills whatsoever.

Pedro shrugged. "Told her I was going to study with a friend. Didn't tell her what subject." He took another sip of his smoothie and shuddered. "Thanks for tutoring me in P.E., friend."

Slippery little twerp. Lana better keep a sharp eye on him. His type always told just enough of the truth to defend his sneaky stunts.

"All righty then." He extended his hand to Kai. "Sludge me."

He gulped down his smoothie—sweet, a bit salty, with top notes of grass clippings. "Let's do this."

An hour later, they paused for a much-needed water break, with coffee for Jojo. He had to give Leo credit—the kid was putting his all into his workouts. Though sweat-soaked and trembling, Pedro was gamely trying to keep up. These kids had character, just like their big sister. Pedro resembled her even more than Leo did. He had the same bright eyes that didn't miss a trick, the same sharp edge to his smile.

Typically clueless, Kai wiped his brow and asked the kids, "So, it's just the three of you, huh? Must be tough."

Jojo shot him a harsh look. Kai didn't mean to be insensitive, he just blurted whatever was on his mind, even though Jojo had already told him the basics and warned him to keep his lip zipped around Leo.

Pedro stuck out his chin. "Yeah, just us three. And we're handling our business."

Jojo knew how much handling their business cost Lana—her freedom, her peace of mind, her career in marketing. Probably a helluva lot more, too.

Leo shot his brother a warning look, but Pedro kept on blabbing. "Tía C talks a lot of shit, but she can't touch us. I'm on the honor roll, and Leo—" He nudged him. "His grades are okay, and he's, like, a motherfuckin' sports god."

Jojo lifted his chin at Leo. "Your little bro's got a mouth on him. Does Lana know he talks like that?"

"He never does in front of her."

Pedro really perked up when Eddie, Diego, and River arrived a few minutes later. The kid's cheeks must hurt from grinning as the Bangers guys welcomed him with fist bumps and back slaps. Hero worship, much? Poor kid only had his big brother at a time when he really needed role models for what being a man looks like. That's a big responsibility to lay on a seventeen-year-old kid. Of course, they had their teachers and their neighbor Kenny, but young kids like these needed someone closer to their own age.

Eddie clasped Leo's hand. "Hey, Leo. Back for more punishment?" He grinned at Jojo. "Told you he was tough."

"Never said he wasn't. Pedro, this is Diego. Used to be our chef at Bangers. King of the tater tots."

"Did you quit?" Pedro asked.

Diego shrugged. "It was time to move on. I run a food truck now."

Just the mention of Diego's cooking brought a rumble from Jojo's belly. "His empanadas will totally blow your mind."

Diego gave a sheepish smile. "Still miss these guys, though."

Kai piped up, "Yeah, you can't work at a bar forever. Right, bro?"

First nosy questions about Lana's family, then cracks about his job. Little brother was itching for a bruising.

Leo's lips twisted in a grimace. "You sound like my tía. This morning at breakfast, she kept on hounding Lana about how she should quit working at the bar and get a respectable job." He hooked air quotes around those last words.

Of course, smart-ass Eddie had to pile on. "If Jojo quits Bangers, how will he see your sister?"

He punched Eddie's shoulder. "Shut it, squirt." He faced the boys. "You sister and I are just friends."

Leo smirked. "Uh-huh. That's why you checked up on her at midnight. And kissed her right under the streetlamp where everyone could totally see you."

Jojo flushed hot. "I didn't kiss her." Oh, he'd wanted to, more than he wanted his next breath, but until Lana's words matched the hunger in her eyes, her lips were off limits.

Pedro pressed a hand to his heart. "Love will make a man move mountains."

"Love, huh?" Leo snorted. "You mean when a girl lets you touch her tits?"

Pedro's face flushed red. Chin jutting, he stepped toe-to-toe with his brother. "You're just jealous 'cause I've got a woman and you don't."

"Jealous? Of you? Get real, twerp. I could get a woman like that." He snapped his fingers.

"Not a woman like Haley."

"Better than Haley."

Bristling, Pedro clenched his fists.

Lana wasn't going to like this, especially if her brothers returned home with bruises and split lips. "Guys, guys, let's take it down a notch. Neither of you will hang onto a woman if you don't learn to treat them with respect." He turned to Eddie and Diego. "Ain't that right?"

Eddie shook his head. "Talking about your brother's girlfriend's tits? Bad form."

Leo's lower lip protruded. "She won't find out."

River laughed. "Bro, they always find out."

Enough chit-chat. Jojo clapped his hands. "Speaking of form, everyone on the floor for plank jacks. I wanna see those backs straight as an arrow."

With a chorus of groans, the guys hit the deck. Kind of cute, the way Leo and Pedro gave it their best shot despite their trembling noodle arms. Coach Bauer would be impressed with Leo's progress. While Jojo sweated through his own more advanced workout, his mind drifted back to Lana. She had tight little arm muscles from hefting her tray at Bangers. He'd give whole worlds to see those strong, sturdy legs in Spandex.

Leo's phone pinged. "Time to go, bro." He hopped to his feet and yanked his wincing little brother upright. "Mistress Lana summons us."

Pedro executed a goofy bow. "Thank you, good sir, for the thorough trouncing." After leading Jojo through a complicated, confusing handshake that made him feel ancient, the two kids climbed into Leo's old beater and groaned as they lowered themselves into their seats.

"You'll be sore tomorrow," Jojo called. "Even worse the next day. Eat a banana and take a hot bath with Epsom salts."

River joined him in the driveway, wiping his pretty face with a towel. "Cute kids."

"Hard workers, too." Diego added.

Eddie clapped Jojo's shoulder. "Be careful, man. Those kids have been through a lot."

Jojo narrowed his eyes at the little barback. "What do you know about it?"

"Rosie told me how their aunties tried to get custody. They want a crack at straightening the boys out."

He huffed. "They don't need straightening. They're good kids."

Kai barked a laugh. "So were we, but remember all the trouble we got into?"

His brother had a point.

River steadied himself against a tree as he stretched his quads. "I'll never forget the time my friends and I got arrested by the harbor police for stealing a boat."

Diego raised a finger. "Busted for underage drinking on the pier. Someone dared me to jump into the water. Nearly drowned."

They all looked at Eddie, who gave a wry grin. "Graffiti."
Kai flapped a hand. "Man, that's just normal."
"On the assistant principal's garage door."
"Oh, shit!" Jojo doubled over with laughter.
After the guys packed up and left to enjoy their Sunday, Kai threw his sweaty arm around Jojo's shoulders. "Seriously, those kids are cute and all, but are you sure you want to get involved with a woman who's got so much baggage?"
He shook off his brother's hold. "They're not baggage, they're kids."
"Orphan kids. Probably hungry for a daddy figure. You up for the challenge?"
Ignoring that thorny question, he switched off the music and lowered the garage door. "You're making a big deal out of nothing. I'm just helping a friend."
Kai huffed through his nose. "Okay, bro. You keep telling yourself that."
Jojo waited until the house door closed behind his brother before dropping onto a weight bench and propping his elbows on his knees.
He genuinely liked Lana's brothers. Their squabbles remind him of himself and Kai at that age. But there was no denying his ulterior motives. His feelings for Lana went way beyond friendship, way deeper and stronger, angling sharply toward forever. No woman's smile ever lit him like hers did.
Lana had good reasons for being cautious and slow to trust. But her vulnerability was plain to see behind that confident, practical façade. She was hurting. Hell, she'd probably never even had time to grieve.
All he could do was try to creep a little closer every day until she finally set down her shield and opened her arms to all they could be together.

·♥·♥·♥·♥·♥·

Perched in her childhood treehouse in the front yard, Lana stared down the street in the direction Tía Camila had driven away—finally. Filled with righteous indignation after a hurried breakfast and early mass, Tía C lambasted her with criticism of everything from her housework—though the house was neat and clean, thank you very much—the boys' manners, the pancakes she served—too thin, and real maple syrup was a waste of money—Lana's appearance—"Long hair is for little girls"—and even Jojo who, according to Tía C, looked like a thug.

"It's high time you got a grownup and stopped playing house like a child, Lana. Your brothers deserve better."

*Stuck up, nosy, racist dinosaur.* Still, her aunt's criticism stung.

So here she sat in the treehouse Dad built when she was ten and the boys were tiny, her refuge when she needed time and space and peace to think. Nature had gifted her a lovely autumn morning, perfect for untangling her thoughts. The leaves on the big maple had just started to flame red and gold, and a soft breeze off the Sound carried the scent of fresh-mown grass and salt air.

Between Tía C's barrage of criticism, Pedro's slick white lie about studying with a friend, and both brothers' gushing praise for Jojo, she was finding it hard to unclench her jaw.

"He's so cool. His muscles are gi-fuckin'-normous! Did you see his tattoos? When can I get a tattoo? He stabs people with needles for a living. He stood up to Coach Bauer." On and on, the two of them heaped praise on Jojo, their eyes shining like little kids opening their Christmas loot. Even worse, they'd seen her and Jojo's almost-kiss on Friday night and assumed he'd be a regular part of their lives now. Just as she feared, they were getting attached. But when Leo's training sessions ended next week, Jojo would disappear.

God, she hated disappointing them, after all they'd been through. Despite their gangly adolescent bodies and deepening voices, she still glimpsed their sweet little-boy faces shining through, especially when they bubbled with enthusiasm over her new "boyfriend." If she could, she'd pad them in bubble wrap and keep them safe from all the disappointments of adult life.

"Ungh." She squinched her eyes shut, then opened them on a sigh. There was no other choice. She pulled out her phone and texted Jojo.

**We need to talk.**

His reply came in less than a minute.

**On my way.**

This was going to hurt.

She leaned her cheek against the wooden half-wall and gazed out at the street she'd grown up on. Though October had barely begun, most of the clapboard houses were already festooned with creepy Halloween decorations. The thirty-something couple across the way, newcomers to the neighborhood, laughed as they hung plastic ghosties from the lowest branches of their chestnut tree. Their toddler son shrieked with delight while their funny-faced bullterrier ran laps around the little family.

So many happy childhood memories—learning to ride her bike with Dad chasing her up and down this street, trick-or-treating from house to house as their parents watched from the sidewalk, after-dinner street hockey games on wobbly skates, childish shrieks as she and her friends terrified each other with ghost stories and tore up and down the block fleeing imaginary monsters.

Jojo pulled up in his lime green Dodge Challenger, its rear fenders dotted with hibiscus and flip-flop stickers. Maybe he liked the reminder of paradise during Tacoma's gloomy season.

Great, now she was imagining him in board shorts, his bare torso glistening as he emerged from the surf.

He exited the low car with surprising grace. Hidden in her elevated lookout, she seized the chance to ogle him unobserved. How could a guy look so delectable in such a casual outfit? Well-worn jeans gripped his powerful thighs, and his faded Bangers T-shirt stretched tight across his chest. Old Converse on his feet—who knew they came in aircraft carrier size? The autumn sun shone off his shaved head. How would that smooth skin feel beneath her fingers? Her tongue?

*Quit being such a weirdo. Friends don't lick friends' heads.*

He glanced at his phone, rolled his neck like a fighter warming up, squared his shoulders, and strode up the walkway toward the front door.

"I'm up here." She leaned out and waved.

Shielding his eyes, he searched for her in the treetops, his head tilted like an adorable mastiff puppy.

Should've thought this through. If they had this conversation in the house, the boys would eavesdrop. Should they go to a coffee shop? Kenny and Carol weren't home right now, and—

"Will this thing hold me?" Jojo gripped the wooden ladder.

"I don't know. How much do you weigh?"

"About two-forty."

She did some quick math—not quite double her two brothers, and the old treehouse still held the three of them. Might as well talk it out up here. Pedro and Leo might see, but they wouldn't hear. "Come on up."

Stepping carefully, he heaved his bulky body up the ladder and through the narrow door, pausing at the top to take in the wooden walls painted a faded blue, covered with childish illustrations she, Leo, and Pedro added years ago. Suddenly self-conscious, she wondered how this must look to him. Like Tía C said, she was clinging to childhood memories, playing house.

Crouching beneath the low roof, Jojo grinned. "Cute tree-house." Not the tiniest trace of snark in his expression or tone, thank God.

"Have a seat." She gestured to the cushions scattered on the floor. He chose one and folded his legs pretzel style, then patted the tree bark through an opening in the wall. "This is cool."

"My dad was a building inspector. We helped build it, if handing him nails counts, but this is mostly his work."

"It shows. Quality construction." He gave a rumbly laugh. "Kai and I made a treehouse once. Good thing my dad's a nurse." His laughter tickled deep in Lana's belly. "We were frequent fliers in the emergency room. After a while, Dad would just stitch us up at home." He pointed to the painted walls. "Which ones are yours?"

His interest in her childhood relics was so freakin' disarming. Though a grown man—magnificently grown—he wasn't too cool to be impressed with a treehouse. The scale in her heart teetered dangerously toward *yes, please* territory.

She pointed to a cloud with a rainbow. "I drew this one. And those rabbits over there." They'd faded to mere shadows from years of butts and backs pressed against the wall. "And the unicorn, of course."

Jojo traced the unicorn's horn with his fingertip. "You should repaint them. Keep the memory fresh."

Regret sliced through her. "Wow. You're making this hard."

Propping his elbows on his knees, he laced his fingers together and studied her, his gaze calm but merciless. "If this is you telling me to back off, I'm not gonna make it easy."

Her common sense told her to push him away, but everything else—mind, heart, body—urged her closer. Resisting him was as difficult and pointless as fighting gravity. "Look, I like you a lot, Jojo."

He beamed, and fairy lights twinkled inside her ribcage.

She forced herself to sit straighter. *There, project confidence.* She focused her gaze on the bridge of his broad nose, safe territory between those laser-beam brown eyes and those succulent, smiling lips. "You're a sweetheart, and you've been so generous with Leo and Pedro."

His right eyebrow inched up. "But?"

*Argh! This would be so much easier if I could be mean to you.* But hurting Jojo's feelings would be like kicking a puppy.

"I don't want them getting their hopes up. They're already getting attached to you. They'll just be heartbroken when things between us don't progress the way they hoped."

Steady and patient, he held her gaze. Was she overreacting to a mere almost-kiss? A close call, for sure, but it's not like the guy proposed. Nevertheless, she had to nip this in the bud. Or was it butt? She'd like to nip his butt.

*Focus!*

"If we keep on like this, they'll build up unrealistic expectations."

Jojo shifted his gaze to the trees beyond and sighed. The lift and fall of his sculpted chest was mesmerizing. "Are you saying I'm not a good role model for your brothers?"

*Yeah. No. I'm not sure.* She knotted her fingers in her lap.

"Ouch." He faced her, one eyebrow lifted. "Tell me why not?"

Lana flushed, embarrassed to realize she'd been stereotyping Jojo. Just because he was big and strong and funny didn't mean he wasn't smart and kind. She should be a better person. But she had to protect her brothers.

"You're, um, kind of a... joker?"

"What's wrong with that? Seems to me you've got serious covered. It takes both to make a well-balanced person."

"And you're a shameless flirt."

"So's your best friend. Flirts with all her customers. Doesn't mean she's not true to Eddie, right?"

Her cheeks flushed still hotter as her objections crumbled under the wrecking ball of Jojo's simple logic.

His probing gaze didn't help. "Have you ever heard any woman accuse me of being a player?"

She sighed and shook her head.

He scooted closer and ran his finger down her arm. "I care about you, Lana, even if you don't want to be more than a friend. To be honest, though, I want more. It's your choice."

Delicious, distracting tingles bloomed where he touched her.

"And your brothers are good kids. If you think being around me harms them, I'll stay away. But I see a lot of myself in Leo. I got through that cocky stage, and he can too, with help."

Lana shuffled her feet, feeling a deep kinship with roasted beets.

"It's all a cover for fear, you know."

Blinking in surprise, she met his gaze. "Leo afraid? Of what?"

"You'll have to ask him. But I'll venture a guess—he's scared shitless of what comes next, when he no longer has you propping him up."

"What do you mean? He'll always have me."

His broad hand closed on her wrist, a gentle pressure that demanded her focus. "He's almost an adult. Remember how scary that seemed when you started college and found your first job?"

Actually, that phase of her life wasn't all that difficult because she'd had her parents backing her up, guiding her. But she couldn't be both mom and dad to Leo. Hell, she couldn't even be his mom, just a loved but resented replacement.

His thumb traced circles on the sensitive inside of her wrist. "How do you do it, Lana?"

A wry grin twisted her lips. "With a lot of help. Kenny and Carol keep an eye on the boys while I'm at work. Their teachers answer my gazillion emails. The school's grade portal that lets me check on their classwork."

"How about a therapist?"

"Not anymore. The state paid for family counseling after Mom and Dad died. When that stipend ran out, my brothers refused to keep going. Said they just wanted to live their lives. And I get it. Talking about loss and grief every week kept us stuck in it, you know? We all needed a break." She fiddled with her shoelaces. "Besides, I couldn't afford to continue."

"Yeah, therapy's gotta be expensive."

She shrugged. "We do all right. We get a stipend from the state, and the boys receive Social Security money. Mom and Dad's insurance took care of the mortgage."

"Sounds like they thought of everything."

"Everything but appointing a guardian for their minor kids."

"And your aunties...?"

"Yeah." Her sigh emptied her lungs. "Fighting them in court was the hardest thing I've ever done except losing Mom and Dad." A dull ache spread through her, weighing her shoulders down and thickening her tongue. "I mean, you know you're going to lose your parents someday. You hope it won't happen until they're really old, but a tiny part of you knows it's coming. But when your blood relatives turn on you and try to rip your family apart? I wasn't prepared for that."

"You won, though, right?"

"Yeah, with the help of Kenny's lawyer friend. Now all I need to do is keep these two on the path of righteousness."

Jojo's fond smile was like a balm on her ragged heart. "They'll be fine. They're good kids, and they love you."

She huffed. "We're hanging onto normalcy by our fingernails."

"Sure you don't want my help?" He laced his fingers through hers, the friction of his broad, callused palm soothing.

She stared at their joined hands, astonished at how well they fit despite the vast difference in size. So much tenderness in his touch. So much kindness in his liquid brown eyes. The contrast between the crisp autumn breeze and the warmth rolling off his body was heavenly.

She wanted him. Denying desire this strong was stupid, pointless, impossible.

She licked her lips and cast a nervous glance at the house. "The boys can't know."

His grin spread as slow and sweet as spilled honey. "They won't hear it from me." His big arm settled around her waist, snugging her to his side.

He sighed her name. "I've wanted you for so long, but you never noticed." He traced her jaw, then lifted her braid and brushed the tip over his cheek. Desire simmered in his dark eyes.

Overwhelmed by his beauty, his raw honesty, she dropped her head onto his shoulder. It felt good to nestle there, safe and supported. "Oh, I noticed, but I couldn't believe you actually liked me for myself, not, you know, just another convenient female."

His chuckle rumbled beneath her cheek. "Mama taught me to never call women females. And you're not just another woman, Lana. You rule that bar floor like a little warrior, swatting away disrespect and spreading sunshine. People come to Bangers just to see you, and I get to see you every day." He cupped her cheek. "But I never got to touch you."

She nestled her cheek into his broad palm. "You're touching me now."

He closed the distance slowly. His thick, curly lashes lowered. His breath teased her skin. When his soft lips finally pressed to hers, pleasure flowed through her veins, warm and heavy, melting her last shreds of resistance. She relaxed on a sigh, and his tongue swept into her mouth in a dance of velvet heat and unbearable sweetness.

"Lana," he murmured, pulling back to gaze deep into her lust-blurred eyes. "I knew you'd be delicious." He nipped at her lower lip, then soothed the swollen flesh with languid licks.

She wound her arms around his neck and pressed her aching breasts to his chest.

The kiss went on and on, a slow, sensuous exploration that made her want to weep and sing and devour this amazing man. Her whole world contracted to their fused mouths, their shared breath—until, with a hungry growl, he pulled her onto his lap. Giddy with pleasure, she caressed his smooth, shaved head. His skin was softer and silkier than she'd expected, unlike the enormous erection prodding her hip—but he paid it no mind, patiently caressing her as if handling something rare and breakable. One broad hand moved to cup her nape. The other massaged the small of her back in slow circles.

She stroked his shoulders, chest, back, mapping the slope and curve and solid muscle of him. His heart hammered beneath her palm. He tasted of mint and fruit. His soft moan stirred a whirlwind in her belly and flooded her sex. Shooting stars zinged behind her eyelids. She kept them tightly closed, afraid to end the dream, this precious gift of living completely in the moment. No thinking, just feeling.

Downstairs, a door slammed. "Cool car." Leo's voice rang out. "Lana? You up there?"

Jojo released her, looking as breathless and dazzled as she felt. "What do you want me to do?"

She sighed as her rosy cloud of pleasure dissipated. "Looks like we've been caught." Nothing for it but to face it. Like Mom always said, "Rip off the Band-Aid, darling."

She pushed up to her knees and leaned over the half-wall. "We're up here." She beckoned to Jojo, who shot her a questioning look. She gave him a wry grin. "There's no escaping now."

He squeezed her hand, then leaned out and waved.

Leo yelled over his shoulder, "Yo, P. Jojo's in the treehouse with Lana."

"No shit." Beaming, Pedro trotted onto the porch.

She winced. *Here it comes.*

Grinning like obnoxious idiots, the boys chanted, "Lana and Jojo, sittin' in a tree. K I S S I N G."

Groaning, she shook her head. "Guess we asked for that."

Jojo laughed so hard he tipped over. Seeing him quake and roll on the floor sent her imagination to dirty, dirty places.

"We're coming up," Leo yelled.

"No!" She waved him off. "We're already at full weight capacity. We'll come down."

Kneeling, Jojo held her hand as she started down the ladder. Before releasing her, he gave it a final squeeze. "Thanks for letting me into your secret fort. I'm honored." He climbed down behind her, giving her a magnificent view of his muscular ass flexing with each step. "By the way, is there a secret password?"

"It's Pupusa," Leo hollered.

Back on solid ground, Jojo tilted his head. "Pu—what now?"

"It's a Guatemalan snack our mom used to make," Lana told him. "Kind of like Diego's empanadas, but with corn masa instead of flour dough."

She pasted on a breezy smile. If she didn't make a big deal of this, neither would her brothers, right? "Jojo and I were just discussing—"

His hand fell on her shoulder. So much for maintaining a veneer of mere friendship.

"—something private." She peered up at him with a nervous grin.

His face fell as he dropped his hand. "Right."

*Oh shit.* He thought she was going to announce their relationship, but she wasn't ready for that. And yet, he'd done so much for her and the boys. And there was no denying the strong magnetism that flowed between them. Her stubborn resolve teetered like a drunk tightrope walker.

Heart hammering, she looped her arm through his. "Look. Jojo and I, we're kind of..."

He raised an eyebrow. Tension thickened between them. Leo and Pedro watched expectantly.

Mama and Dad always said the truth was more important than pride, especially among family. Didn't she owe her brothers the truth?

She lifted her chin. "We like each other, okay? No big deal. We're just getting to know each other better."

The boys exchanged knowing grins. Leo gave a nonchalant nod. "Cool."

"Are you—" Pedro started.

Leo punched his arm. "C'mon, P. Let's give them some privacy."

And just like that, the boys retreated into the house.

"Huh." Lana rubbed the back of her neck. "I guess Leo really is growing up."

Jojo looped his arms around her, low at her hips. "You had me scared for a minute there."

A weak laugh escaped her tight throat. "You and me both. This is kinda terrifying."

"Hey now." He crooked a finger under her chin and lifted it until she met his gaze. "We can take this as slow as you want, Pupusa."

She wrinkled her nose.

"Okay, still working on a nickname. But seriously, there's no rush." He pulled her into a hug. "I'm just so happy you're finally giving me a chance."

Heart thundering, she snuggled into his embrace. This was no big deal for Jojo. He'd had lots of girlfriends. His kiss proved his skill with intimate touch. Her swagger might have fooled him, but soon he'd discover the truth. And that terrified her.

# Chapter Seven

♥

Tuesday morning, Lana ping-ponged around her empty house, fiddling with unimportant details and vibrating with nerves. It felt weird to be so jittery. After all, she'd already bared the darkest corners of her soul to Rosie—except this one embarrassing secret she'd guarded since high school. But her bestie would never judge her, right?

*God, if she laughs at me, I'll crumble into dust.*

Jaw clenched, she arranged supermarket flowers in a colorful Guatemalan vase Mom inherited from her own parents. Mom had taught her how to trim and fluff cheap flowers to make them look like an expensive bouquet. She slid the last daisy into place and sighed as a wave of longing hit her. Two years now since a distracted driver stole her parents' lives, and she still expected Mom to walk through the kitchen door, a dish towel draped over her shoulder.

When Lana had the chance to talk this painful topic over with Mom, she was too immature, too embarrassed. Now she'd never know what good advice Mama would've shared. One more regret on a miles-long list. For this thorny question, she'd have to rely on Rosie.

The doorbell jerked her from her ruminations. She trotted to the door and peered through the peephole. Grinning broadly, Rosie held up a box from Legendary Doughnuts. Charlie waved over her shoulder. Yikes! Double humiliation.

Rosie pounded on the door. "Hurry up, Lana. We're getting soaked."

For a long, tense moment, Lana gripped the latch and chewed her lip.

"Let us in or we'll eat all the doughnuts," Charlie called.

"We got your favorite, chocolate peanut butter cup," Rosie added in a sing-song voice.

Lana thunked her forehead against the cool wood.

Mama's voice rang in her memory. "Dust yourself off. Chin up. That's my brave girl."

Wincing, she opened the door. Her friends tumbled in, propelled by a rainy gust and followed by a spray of damp maple leaves. The girls hung their wet jackets on the coat tree by the door.

"Whew!" Charlie wrung out her long ponytail. "If it keeps blowing like this, the trees will be bare by Halloween." She carried the doughnuts to the dining room.

Ro halted in the foyer and narrowed her eyes. "You look queasy." She pressed the back of her hand to Lana's forehead.

She forced a smile. "I'm fine. Come sit. Coffee?"

Ignoring her, Ro called out, "Something's wrong with Lana."

Charlie opened the box and wafted the sugary scent with her hand. "Doughnuts are the best medicine."

Rosie pulled out a chair and pushed Lana into it. "Eat. Then spill."

In the kitchen, the ancient coffee machine burbled its final drops into the carafe. Mom had refused to get one of those individual-cup machines, claiming they were bad for the environment, and Lana couldn't bring herself to replace Mom's trusty machine. As Dad always said, "If it ain't broke, don't fix it."

Charlie stood. "I'll get the concentration nectar."

"Really, I'm fine," Lana protested.

Rosie sat beside her and peered, squinting, into her eyes. "Bullshit."

When they were all armed with caffeine and pastry, Lana sent up a silent prayer to the gods of humiliations avoidance, then launched.

"So, Jojo came over Sunday."

"Yeah?" Rosie and Charlie exchanged a grin, then leaned in like gossip-hungry vultures.

Lana grumbled, "This would be easier if you'd tease me like you always do."

Rosie laid a gentle hand on her arm. "Okay, Jojo liiiiikes you."

She huffed a laugh. "Yeah, he does."

Charlie smacked the table. "Finally, she admits it."

"What are you gonna do about it?" Rosie chomped her Tiger Tail, dropping cinnamon-laced crumbs down her tattooed cleavage.

"I don't knoooow." Lana curled forward and rested her forehead on the table.

Rosie drummed her fingers. "Because...?"

"He's so sweet," she muttered, face still hidden.

"Told ya."

"And he's been really kind to the boys."

"Because he's a kind person," Charlie added.

"Yeah, he is." *The kind of person whose bones I want to jump, whose mouth I want everywhere on my body, whose hands work magic.*

Ro wiped crumbs from her lips. "So, let's review. Gorgeous man, sweet as a doughnut and just as gooey, probably has a dick as big as your arm, nice to your brothers, totally smitten, and you're looking sick because..."

Lana squeezed her eyes shut. Now or never. "I've never actually, you know..."

Silence.

She gripped the table's edge. "Are you gonna make me say it?"

Still no response. The sadistic wenches were going to wait her out.

The words scraped her tight throat like barbed wire. "I'm a virgin, okay?"

She opened one eye and caught Rosie and Charlie with their mouths agape.

Finally, Charlie broke the silence. "You? Queen of sass? Mistress of dick jokes? You've never—?"

Rosie goggled. "I don't believe it. My best friend is a virgin, and I never knew?" She slumped in her chair. "I'm a shitty friend."

Lana threw her arm around Rosie's shoulders. "You're not! I've constructed this whole jaded girl persona as a protective shell. I should've told you, but the longer I waited, the harder it was to admit the truth. And it's not like I'm a total prude. I mean, I've done stuff. Lots of stuff. You know—mouths, fingers, toys. I've just never had an actual dick inside me."

"Is it a religious thing?" Charlie asked.

Lana shook her head. "I wanted my first time to mean something. My high school boyfriends were boneheads who couldn't find a clit with a map and a searchlight. And no way was I going to risk getting pregnant."

Charlie tapped her forehead. "Smart. Teen boys are terrible at sex."

"Then in college I met a few guys I liked. I'd almost talked myself into taking the plunge."

Rosie giggled and poked her finger through a doughnut hole. "Plunge?"

"Then, well, you know." A sharp ache pressed the back of her eyes. "Since Mom and Dad died, my focus has been"—a sweep of her hand took in the whole house— "keeping all this together for my brothers. I just didn't have the energy to take such a big step."

With a soft coo, Rosie rubbed Lana's shoulder while Charlie clasped her hand.

Lana sniffed hard. "Feels kind of ridiculous at my age. I mean, how old were you guys?"

Rosie narrowed her eyes and gazed into the distance. "Let's see—fifteen with a girl, sixteen with a guy."

Charlie tapped her pursed lips. "I was seventeen? No, sixteen."

"See?" She threw up her hands. "I'm way behind schedule."

Rosie scooted her chair closer. "Hon, there's no schedule. And with everything that's happened to you…"

"I had to learn to take care of myself—literally." She gave a wry laugh. "I just haven't met a guy I like enough to take that step. But the longer I wait, the bigger that step grows. Right now, it feels like a cliff."

Rosie snorted. "Jojo's tall enough to give you a boost."

At last, a laugh escaped Lana's constricted chest. Her friends joined in.

Feeling lighter, Lana grabbed another doughnut. "Seriously, though. I have to tell him. And he might not want the weight of being my first."

Charlie and Rosie exchanged sly glances. "I bet he will," Rosie said, waggling her eyebrows. "He looks at you like a lovesick puppy who wants to lick your face."

Flushing hot, Lana imagined being licked by Jojo. She already had first-hand proof of his talented tongue. "Telling him will be mortifying. And I don't want him to think I'm just using him to check a box."

Rosie leered. "Oh, he totally wants to check your box. Check it real good."

Charlie smacked Rosie's arm. "But seriously, he's a great guy. He'll recognize what an act of trust this is."

Lana leaned onto her elbow and sighed. "You know, last year I got shitfaced after the Halloween party and nearly jumped a total stranger who'd been flirting with me all night. I wish I had so Jojo and I could have a friendly fling without all this weight." She picked sprinkles off her doughnut. "But I'm just not wired that way. And I suspect he's not either."

Rosie patted her knee. "You always have a plan. Maybe it's time to loosen your grip and trust fate. After all, fate delivered a guy who cares about you *and* your brothers." Her dark gaze brimmed with wisdom. "Accept this gift. When the time is right, you'll tell him."

"How?" Lana squeaked.

"Just like you told us. Simple. Straightforward. He'll understand."

"I'm sure he will," Charlie added with a nod. "And you'll have something not many women get."

"What's that?"

"A first time that's really good."

# *Chapter Eight*

♥

Perched high in the bleachers at Stadium Bowl, the sports arena built into a natural gorge below Stadium High School, Jojo slid his arm around Lana's waist and grinned. What a freakin' glorious day. Bright sun glinted off the Sound and warmed the October breeze. Fans from both Tacoma teams filled the bleachers, sending up a merry roar with each play. And most important of all, Leo was back on the team. When she invited him to come watch Leo play, he kicked himself for not thinking of it first. Even so, here he was, his body pressed tight to Lana's as she hollered encouragement for her brother's team.

The Stadium Tigers lagged the Foss Falcons by three points. The center snapped the ball, and the Tigers' O line scrambled. Despite his hatred of wind sprints, Leo charged across the field like a beast chasing its prey. The kid had heart.

"Go, Leooooo," Lana shrieked.

He gave Lana's hip a squeeze. "Hey, was inviting me your idea or Leo's?"

Her sassy grin sparkled. "A little of both."

God, he loved her smiles. In the week since their first passionate kiss in her treehouse, her unguarded smile gradually unfurled like a gorgeous bloom. Even though his shifts at the clinic and her daytime mama bear duties kept them apart, they were creeping in a positive direction. Lana sent him playful texts throughout the day, and she was less guarded at work, stopping by his bouncer station to deliver snacks and discreet smooches. They still hadn't progressed beyond kissing, but those goodnight kisses on her porch were getting longer and hotter with each passing night. His patience was paying off, though his poor, tortured body screamed for more every time she murmured "Good night" in that sexy, husky voice of hers.

Lana nudged his ribs and proffered the popcorn bag they were sharing, then pressed tighter against his side. "You're an excellent wind shield, you know that?"

"Glad to help." He stuffed a handful of kernels in his face, smooched the top of her head, and pointed. A few rows down, Pedro huddled under a blanket with his girlfriend Haley, a cute sophomore with long brown hair whose devilish grin reminded him of Lana's.

"Should've brought a blanket for us." He reached for more popcorn.

"Uh-oh," Lana muttered. "Time for another birds and bees and condoms talk."

He laughed. "You can't get pregnant from what they're do-ing. Besides, didn't you do the same?"

Her cheeks flushed fire-engine red. Seems he'd hit the mark. Whoever had shared her blanket at football games, he was one lucky bastard.

"You want me to talk to Pedro?" he asked.

"Thanks, but I'll handle it. The boys like you, but we're not there yet."

Disappointment pinched hard. "We're getting closer, though, right?"

"Yeah, we are." She held his gaze, her smile full of promise. Man, that smile warmed him better than any blanket, or campfire, or sweet, hot cocoa, or...

"So, tell me about your week at the hospital."

He shook off his horny, lovesick fog. "Same old, same old. Making kids cry, then making them smile again with goofy faces and Sponge Bob bandages." He nudged her. "What kind of Band-Aid do you want next Wednesday?" It wasn't often his two jobs converged, but Dawn had arranged a blood drive at Bangers with drink tokens as incentives to donate—before imbibing, not after. Seemed like a weird plan, but if anyone could make it work, Dawn could. And on his birthday, no less. Good way to keep his mind off that looming milestone.

"You got any Wonder Woman Band-Aids? Or Power Puff Girls?"

"I'll make sure I do." He squeezed her knee, loving the pressure of her thigh against his.

Lana gave him an appraising glance. "Are you going to stay there? At the hospital, I mean?"

He lifted a shoulder. "It's not my forever plan, but it's meaningful work and pays well enough for now."

"Kind of like how I feel about slinging drinks and tots." She nuzzled her cheek against his shoulder. "So, what's your next step? Nursing? Medical school?"

"My parents would love that." His audiologist mom and RN dad regularly urged him to go back to school and retrain for a higher-paying job. Didn't help that half his family worked in the medical field—lots of nurses, technicians, and Gramps was a pediatrician. But healthcare, though satisfying for now, wasn't his true path.

"I've thought about starting a training business, maybe a private gym. I've got my basic personal trainer cert and want to qualify in other specialties—training people with injuries, older people, even become a health coach." He goosed her hip. "Haven't worked with many women yet. Maybe you'll let me experiment with you?"

She blushed again, as pretty as a pink rose. "Yikes, me in your gym? You're kind of intimidating, you know that?"

He traced her delicate jawline with his fingertip. "I'll be very gentle."

She sucked in a breath and shifted away. Damn.

"When?"

Flustered, he gave his head a little shake. "When what?"

"When will you open your gym?"

*Probably not until you leave Bangers.* "There's no hurry. I'm picking up clients here and there through word of mouth. I'll know when the time is right. Like my gramps used to say, slow and steady wins the race." He reached for her hand.

She took it but gave him a squinty look. "Are you talking about work or about us?"

"Yes."

She tipped her head back and laughed, a rich, mellow sound that made his belly flutter.

He joined in until a flash of movement on the field caught his eye. He tugged her to her feet and bellowed, "Go, Lopez!"

The home team crowd roared as Leo zig-zagged toward the end zone, nimbly dodging defensive players and vaulting over an attempted tackle. The booth announcer lost his ever-loving mind. "Number thirty-two is unstoppable!" he screamed into the mic, then sounded the touchdown siren. "Stadium wins!"

Hooting, Lana pumped her fist in the air, then wrapped her arms around Jojo's neck and kissed him thoroughly—in front of God and everyone, little brothers included.

Smiling into her kiss, Jojo let the feeling wash over and through him—pure, sparkling joy. With Lana in his arms, her soft lips mashed to his, her arms and—woah, one leg looped around him, life simply couldn't get any better.

When the victory cheers died down and the players headed to the locker room, Lana checked her phone. Only three o'clock. She and Jojo didn't have to report to Bangers until seven, and she hated to end their day together so soon.

Spotting Pedro and Haley at the bottom of the bleachers, she hooked her arm through Jojo's. "Want to meet Pedro's sweetie?"

His grin stretched as wide as the football field below. "I'd love that."

When they finally reached ground level, Haley's parents stood beside the kids. Her dad, a tall, tight-lipped man, frowned at Pedro, who clutched his folded blanket over his crotch, a dizzy, dreamy look on his face.

*Well, shit.* She pasted on a casual smile.

"Mr. and Mrs. Horvat, good to see you. Great game, right?" She put her arm around her horny-pants little brother and tugged him away from his ladylove. "This is my boyfriend, Jojo Williams."

Jojo's sharp inhalation switched on a mental lightbulb. Holy cats, this was the first time she'd said that out loud, wasn't it? The big guy gazed down at her, his smile as dreamy as Pedro's.

Well, why not? He'd earned the title with his generosity, patience, and unbelievable sweetness. She was damn lucky to have him. Still, she hadn't intended to jump that hurdle today. It just sort of slipped out. Huh. She liked the sound of that—my boyfriend, Jojo. A grin tugged at her lips.

After Haley left, Lana pulled Pedro aside. "Bud, you might want to rethink groping your girlfriend where her parents can see."

Pedro gaped, bug-eyed and flushed. "They couldn't see." He looked at Jojo for backup.

Jojo raised an eyebrow. "Dude."

"Aw, shit." With a wince, he pulled out his phone and moved away, thumbs flying.

Jojo chuckled. "Little man's in love."

*Are you, Jojo?* Deep in her bones, she already knew the answer, but she prayed he wouldn't say the words today. One milestone at a time was all her nervous heart could handle.

Meanwhile, Pedro needed comfort. "How about we go to Shake Shake Shake?" she called. The burger joint with ultra-crispy fries and a mile-long list of milkshake flavors was a rare delight—pricier than fast food, but so worth it.

"My treat," Jojo murmured into her ear.

"That's not—"

"My treat," he rumbled in his bouncer voice. Chills ran down her spine.

"Okay. Thank you. Gotta warn you, though, Pedro eats a lot."

Pedro rejoined them, his face tight with worry. "You think her parents will ground her?"

"Now, now." She clapped his shoulder. "Don't go spiraling into gloom."

His brow crumpled. "If they make her break up with me, I don't know what I'll do."

Jojo nudged him with his elbow. "You know what's good for worries? Fries dipped in milkshakes."

"Okay," he agreed with a shaky grin.

"Lana, Jojo!" Leo trotted over, his hair and jersey sopping with sweat, his face glowing. "Did you see?" He gave Jojo an elaborate handshake fist-bump thingy before hugging her and Pedro. The two guys heaped praise on his game-winning play, his speed, and his all-around manliness.

The sight of the three guys she loved best, celebrating together, suffused her chest with a happy glow.

She smooched Leo's cheek. "You hungry, hero?" We're going for shakes, but you probably want to hang out with your teammates." She reached for her wallet to give him some spending cash.

"Shakes sound great! Give me twenty minutes." He trotted away.

She shook her head. Leo wanted to hang with his family? Weird, but a sweet surprise. With a pang, she realized there wouldn't be many more moments like this. Her brothers were growing up fast. Was this how parents felt when their kids left the nest?

An hour later, Lana slurped up the last of her Tiger milkshake—Almond Roca bits, caramel, and chocolate—then leaned back with a contented sigh. It had been fun watching Jojo banter with the boys over deluxe burgers, crispy fries, and shakes—mud pie for Pedro, Oreo for Leo, and miso butterscotch for Jojo. She rubbed her full belly. "Well, guys, Jojo and I have to get to work."

Leo checked his phone. "Not for another two hours. Can we go to the comics store?"

"You guys like comics?" Jojo wiped fry crumbs from his lips. "I used to collect X-Men. Hung onto some in case they get valuable. You remember *X-Statix*?"

Lana zoned out, sated and relaxed, enjoying their easy boy banter. After ten more minutes of debate over DC versus Marvel, she clapped her hands. "Okay, one hour at the comics shop, then home."

They piled into Jojo's lime green Challenger.

Pedro trailed his fingers over the white leather seats. "Cool car."

Jojo patted the dashboard. "Bought it from my cousin. She's a tattoo artist, like Rosie. Did my shoulder."

"Lemme see," Pedro pleaded as they pulled into a parking space across from the comics shop.

Jojo shot her a questioning look.

"Might as well. He'll just keep bugging you until you give in."

He peeled off his jacket and shirt, and she bit her lip hard, willing her body not to respond to all that glorious, inked skin as Jojo explained the designs' symbolism. "My grandparents came to Seattle when Mama was small. We visit her family in Hawaii every year."

"Awesome," Pedro crowed. "Take us with you?"

She shot him a stern look. "Slow your roll, squirt."

Jojo grinned over his shoulder. "Maybe someday, if Lana doesn't get sick of me."

Leo jutted his jaw. "You better not."

Just as she feared, the boys pretty much super-glued themselves to Jojo whenever he came around. They tugged him toward Destiny City Comics, but Lana hooked her arm through his and tilted her head toward King's Books next door.

Like melting butter on an English muffin, Jojo's smile warmed all her nooks and crannies. "Nah, I'm gonna check out the bookstore with Lana."

Pedro opened his mouth to object, but Leo elbowed him. "Cool. See you in a few."

Herbert, the fat black and white shop cat, meowed a greeting from where he sprawled on the front display table. After petting his luxuriant fur, she led Jojo to the cookbook section behind a floor-to-ceiling bookcase. She sucked in a big breath and tried to release the tension stiffening her body.

He gently grasped her shoulders. His gaze held such tenderness, but his brows pinched together. "Am I in trouble?"

"No, but I might be. The boys are getting attached to you."

The corners of his full lips hitched upward. He hooked his fingertips into her belt loops and tugged her closer. The brush of his hips against her belly made concentration nearly impossible.

"I like your brothers. They're good kids." One hand moved to the small of her back, its warm weight delicious. "But I like their sister even better." He ducked his head and kissed her.

She pressed her palms to his broad chest. "I like you too. But I worry about them. If we don't work out—"

Jojo raised his forefinger. "We're working out fine. I've waited three years for you, Lana. I'm not backing out now."

The flutter in her stomach had nothing to do with fries and everything to do with the delectable heat of his body against hers, the sexy gleam in his eyes, his patience and persistence and kindness. She wasn't just falling for him, she was plummeting.

He continued, his voice as soft and deep as distant thunder. "And your bros are going to face all kinds of loss in their lives. They got through the biggest one I can imagine, and look at them, laughing and having fun."

And just like that, her happy cloud evaporated, dropping her back onto cold, hard earth. "You don't get it. You've never had a loss this big." Wait, she shouldn't assume. "Have you?"

"No. I'm lucky. Except for my dad's parents, my family's all still here. I can't imagine how hard this is for you. Of course you're protective of your brothers." He quirked an eyebrow. "Maybe a little too protective?"

Stung, Lana stiffened and backed out of his embrace. He was probably right. Finding the balance point between protective and permissive was incredibly difficult, especially when she was still reeling under the weight of her own grief. And no doubt she sometimes landed too far on the hard-ass side of the scale. The last thing she wanted was to drive her brothers away.

Knees wobbly, she sank into a chair and flipped through a Greek cookbook someone had left on the table.

"Mrrwaorrpp." Tail high, Herbert sauntered around the bookcase, crouched, and sprang onto the table. He stretched out on his side, half-covering the pages, and purred like a cement mixer.

Lana stroked his silky fur and just let go, let the words tumble and flow.

"My last conversation with my parents was an argument. They wanted a date night and asked me to babysit Leo and Pedro. Of course, the boys bitched. Said they were too old for a sitter. I was mad because I had to cancel a date." Her laugh rang dry and dusty. "The last date I had until today."

Jojo sat beside her and took her hand, rubbing his thumb over her knuckles.

Tears stung her eyes, but she blinked them back. If she and Jojo had any hope of a future together, she'd have to get through this.

"I tell myself they had a great time. I have to believe that." Her voice broke. "On their way home, a distracted driver hit them. The selfish bastard was gaming on his phone. And if I hadn't been there, my brothers would've been alone when they got the news." She wiped her damp cheek and gazed at him through tear-blurred eyes. "I almost wasn't there, Jojo. I almost snuck out, but something made me stay."

Ever since, she wondered if it was fate, a guardian angel, or maybe even her parents' spirits that had kept her home that night, grumbling and resentful. Whatever it was, she was grateful—and ashamed.

Jojo brought her hand to his lips. "I remember the night you came back to Bangers. You looked... hollow, I guess, like someone had scooped out your insides. I wanted to tell you how sorry I was."

She smiled through her tears. "You did. I remember." Up until that awful night, she'd never seen him drop his jokester façade. She'd endured everyone else's pity with dry eyes and a stiff spine, but Jojo's tender sweetness nearly broke her.

That same sweetness shone in his dark eyes now. "I wanted to hug you too, but I sensed you needed space. I mean, no matter how good my intentions were, it wouldn't have been fair to force my feelings on you when you were so fragile."

She cupped his cheek, skating her fingertips over soft skin and scratchy beard shadow. "You gave me two years of space. That's enough."

With a choking sound, he swept her into his arms and kissed her, deep and slow and sweet.

"Jojo, look what we—" Leo rounded the bookcase, Pedro behind him.

Pedro smirked and crossed his arms. "Oh, so you get to make out in public, but I don't."

Chuckling, Jojo pressed his lips to her forehead. "My parents won't mind." He pushed back his chair. "Come on, show me what's new at the comics shop." He squeezed her hand and left her to compose herself.

She hugged her ribs and blew out a long, quaking breath. For good or ill, she was in too deep to back out now. There was so much more to Jojo Williams than she'd given him credit for, and he'd already claimed a big chunk of her heart. This magnetism was scary, thrilling, irresistible. But could she trust her judgment, or was this powerful feeling just twenty-four years of virginity screaming for release?

She stroked the sleepy cat absently, a misty smile on her lips. When she asked Jojo to come with her to Leo's game, she'd had no idea they'd delve this deep, but baring her pain left her with an odd sense of peace. His gentle acceptance of her confession made her want to open to him further. And he'd opened his heart too, bravely laying his hopes in her hands. No artifice, no hiding, except—

She wrinkled her nose. Weird that Jojo hadn't mentioned his birthday. Rosie spilled that he was turning thirty on Wednesday and made her promise not to spoil the surprise Dawn was planning. Maybe he was one of those guys who didn't like to make a fuss. Or maybe he had a complex about that milestone year? From where she sat, Jojo had his life together—professional training, a good day job, a big circle of friends. She hoped she'd accomplish as much by that age.

Now, what to get her new boyfriend for his birthday? That word still made her giggle. She needed to find something meaningful, personal, but not too over-the-top.

An idea hit her. Perfect. Grinning, she gave the cat a final skritch, rose, and trotted out to join her guys.

·❤·❤·❤·❤·❤·

As soon as Jojo pulled into their driveway, the boys tumbled out of his car and barreled toward Kenny and Carol, out hanging Halloween decorations on their front porch. Lana lingered and laced her fingers through Jojo's.

"You were pretty awesome today. My brothers really like you."

His aw-shucks grin ignited giddy tingles behind her ribs. "I like them too. They're good kids, Lana. You've done a remarkable job with them." When he rested their joined hands on his thigh, her pulse broke into a gallop.

"Hey, would you keep next Saturday afternoon open for me?" he asked. "There's something I'd like to do with you." He waggled his eyebrows, and her heart stuttered.

He threw back his head and gave a laugh that shook his big body. "I'd like to do that with you anytime, bright eyes, but that's not what I meant. Just something fun, casual. Can you swing it?"

She checked her phone calendar. Leo had an away game, and Pedro would want to hang out with Haley and their friends. "Sure. I can swing that." Why did that phrase sound so dirty all of a sudden? And did they make those sex swing thingies big enough to hold someone like Jojo?

A rap on the window made her jump. Pedro and Leo stood there, grinning like Christmas and toting plastic storage bins. Leo set his load down and gestured for her to crank down the window.

"Carol and Kenny bought new Halloween decorations, so they're giving us their old ones. Come see!"

Their enthusiasm tickled Lana. One minute, they were posturing like adults—the next, they were squealing like sugared-up preschoolers.

Pedro poked his head through the window. "Jojo, can you help hang these lights?"

"Jojo has to get to work soon," she said as she climbed out.

"I can give you half an hour." Jojo waved to Kenny and Carol, then rubbed his palms together. "Let's see what you've got."

Lightness and warmth filled Lana's chest as she watched the three guys laugh and pelt each other with gobs of fake cobwebs. Aiming for as much normalcy as they could stomach after Mom and Dad's accident, she'd put up a few seasonal decorations, but this was the first time Leo and Pedro showed enthusiasm for this fun ritual.

Jojo might be good for them after all.

"Cider?" Carol handed her a steaming mug.

"Thanks." She inhaled the rich, cinnamon-scented steam.

"I like your young man." She patted Lana's shoulder. "It's good to see you dating again. You deserve some happiness. You're too young to be a full-time parent."

Lana's laugh sounded hollow. "I don't have much choice."

"Might be nice to have a helpmate." Carol tilted her chin toward Lana's porch, where Jojo stretched on tiptoes to hang orange and purple twinkle lights. "Someone like him, maybe?"

Lana chewed a knuckle while she ogled the tawny skin of Jojo's lower back, revealed when his shirt rode up. *Focus!*

Kenny and Carol had done so much for her and the boys, she hated to ask for more. But Carol approved of Jojo, so... "Wednesday at work we've got a surprise birthday party after closing time. I'd like to stay, but I don't want to keep you and Kenny up late. Do you think you might be able to keep the boys at your place overnight, since they've got school the next morning?"

Tilting her head, Carol gazed at Jojo, then gave her a knowing smile.

Heat crept up Lana's cheeks. Carol saw right through her story to the juicy bits she left unsaid. "Sure, hon. We'd be glad to host the boys. We'll stock up on horror movies and pizza."

Flooded with relief, Lana kissed her cheek.

Carol returned to her porch and whispered to Kenny. As Lana walked toward home, she heard Kenny laugh and say, "It's about time."

# Chapter Nine

♥

After delivering sodas and tots to Spike, Lana paused to admire the cartoon vampires Rosie and River had painted on the bar's window for tonight's blood drive. Dawn always had the best ideas for community events—one of many reasons Bangers remained the most popular bar on 6th Ave.

Of course, Dawn knew how to work a good incentive. River and Kiara had prepared fun drink specials for the occasion—Bloody Marys, of course, plus Witch's Blood martinis made with grenadine and black vodka, since it was so close to Halloween, and Bloody Vampires, a concoction of cherry vodka, gin, and grenadine, drizzled with red-dyed corn syrup. Everyone who donated blood got a free cocktail—after donating, not before, as Jojo and his phlebotomy crew had to explain again and again.

Free booze did the trick. A long line of customers snaked through the bar, awaiting their turn to donate. Tonight, the billiard and dart area was transformed to a donation station with recliners for the bleeders and a few cots for fainters. Protected by thick tarps, the pool tables held juice boxes and packaged snacks. A crew of nurses, phlebotomists, and volunteers kept the process humming smoothly.

Rosie tapped Lana's shoulder. "You donating tonight?"

"Later, when the crowd thins out. You?"

She folded her arms and gave an exaggerated shiver. "Those needles give me the heebie-jeebies."

Lana socked her arm. "Says the tattoo artist?"

"That's different. I never draw blood. Well, hardly ever. Anyway, I hid your presents in my locker."

Lana watched Jojo wrap a length of rubber tubing around a woman's biceps. His patient gave him a wan smile. He patted her arm and said something that made her laugh aloud. He had an excellent bedside manner—no surprise there.

Lana shook her head. "I can't believe he didn't tell me it's his birthday."

Charlie joined them and propped her tray on her hip. "Some people are weird about birthdays."

"Maybe he doesn't like being the center of attention," Rosie mused.

Charlie snorted. "Are you kidding? Remember the Christmas party where he played sexy Santa in that biker jacket? He was strutting like a Chippendales stripper."

"With no shirt underneath. Yum." Rosie smacked her lips.

"You two mind not drooling all over my boyfriend? Besides, you've got your own guys."

Returning from the kitchen with a net of limes, River patted Charlie's rump. "Cake's in the cooler, and Diego's coming at ten with your surprise, Lana. The whole house smelled delicious, but he wouldn't let us try one."

"There'll be plenty tonight." Lana elbowed Charlie. "Must be nice, sharing a house with a chef." She and River shared a cute Craftsman cottage with Diego and Anna, Charlie's younger sister, along with Ellie, Anna's infant daughter. Lana had spent the afternoon in their sunny kitchen cooking up a treat for Jojo's birthday celebration—and babbling gibberish to Ellie, of course.

Dawn joined them at the servers' station. "You girls let me know when it's time to start the birthday song. Like it or not, my favorite bouncer's birthday is gonna get celebrated."

Rosie clucked her tongue. "Now, now, a mom shouldn't show favoritism among her children."

Dawn rolled her eyes. "Bangers survives on its reputation as a friendly bar, and Spike's a cranky-ass curmudgeon. If he wasn't so good at tossing out knuckleheads, I'd'a canned him long ago. Glad he's here tonight, though." She tilted her chin toward the bearded ogre, perched on his stool with a box of disposable breathalyzers at his elbow. Already, he'd had to remind a few belligerent customers they couldn't donate after they drank.

A few hours later, when the line of donors thinned, Dawn hopped onto the stage in the corner and grabbed the mic. "Okay, party people. We're still twelve pints short of our goal. River's mixing up a fresh batch of Bloody Vampires, so call a friend to come donate. And staff, if you haven't donated yet, now's the time."

Passing with a bucket of ice, Eddie showed Lana his bandaged arm. "It's not so bad. Jojo's pretty good with that needle."

She got in line. After showing the nurse in charge her ID and filling out the donation forms, she asked, "Can Jojo do me?"

The woman giggled. "Everyone wants him."

Jojo looked up from his patient and waved. "This one's mine, Cassie."

He looked frickin' adorable in scrubs printed with dancing skeletons and grinning pumpkins. The short sleeves hugged his muscular arms and shoulders. Yum!

The girl in line behind Lana whined, "I wanted Jojo."

"Sorry, darlin'." He consoled her with a devilish smile. "Lana's a friend."

He gestured her into a seat. "Ready to bleed for the cause?" He fastened rubber tubing around her biceps. "I've never drawn blood from someone I'm crushing on."

"Aww, you have a crush on me?"

His grin held a glint of mischief. "What gave it away?" His thigh rubbed against her arm as he leaned in. "Make a fist for me." He swabbed the crook of her elbow with alcohol. "Just a little pinch. Let me know if you feel light-headed."

Weird to feel so turned on in this decidedly unsexy situation, but his focused concentration, the soft rumble of his voice, and his gentle touch electrified her nerve endings.

She winced as the needle slid in, then watched dark blood flowing through the tubing into the collection bag. "You're good at this."

He ran his fingertip down her arm, then pressed a spongy ball into her palm. "I like my work. It's important, and it feels good to make the process easier on people. Now give this ball a squeeze every ten seconds or so." He leaned in so close his breath tickled her cheek. "I'll be watching you."

Squeezing the ball the way she'd like to squeeze his muscular butt, she watched Jojo soothe two more patients through the process with humor, warm smiles, and gentle touches—and she fell just a little bit in love with him.

He returned to inspect her collection bag. "That's my girl. You're a good bleeder."

"Um, thanks?"

He glanced over his shoulder, then crouched beside her and cupped her hand in his. His dark eyes sparkled. "Thank you, Lana."

"For donating?"

"For all of it. This past week has been amazing. You've let me into your family circle. I'm honored." He removed the ball from her grip, lifted her hand to his lips, and pressed a soft kiss to her palm.

If she hadn't been reclining already, she would've melted onto the floor. Desire sizzled through her veins.

He looked up from removing the needle. "You okay? Feeling a little shaky?"

Shaky wasn't a strong enough word. The sweet intimacy of this moment peeled away her defenses, leaving her exposed and trembling.

"I'm okay," she croaked.

"Uh huh, Ms. I-Can-Handle-Everything-Myself." He applied a Jack-o'-lantern Band-Aid over the puncture, then helped her to her feet and, gently grasping her shoulders, led her to one of the cots. "Just rest here for a minute where I can keep an eye on you. Have you eaten tonight? Let's get you some juice."

She groaned at the filthy thoughts invading her mind. What kind of freak was she, aroused by donating blood? Licking her dry lips, she watched the shift of his back muscles as he leaned over the snack table.

He brought her a tropical punch juice box, a huge chocolate chip cookie, a blue raspberry lollipop, and an "I donated blood" sticker with a cartoon vampire. "Cute, huh? Dawn ordered these special for today."

"You're sweet, Jojo, but I'm fine, really. I should get back to work." And away from all these prying eyeballs. The registration nurse was giving the two of them funny looks.

He grasped her shoulders and pushed her onto the cot. "No, ma'am. You're going to sit right there and drink your juice. Understand?"

His commanding tone gave her shivers. The doubts and excuses she'd been hiding behind evaporated.

*Tonight's the night.*

Holding his gaze, she sucked on her straw.

His pupils darkened. "Damn, Lana," he whispered, then turned back to his work.

It was close to midnight when the blood drive finally wound up, and Jojo's back and shoulders ached from five solid hours of drawing blood—on top of his regular shift at the clinic. He'd love to prop his feet up and snarf a mountain of wings and tots, but he still had to help the blood bank team pack up and ferry the donations and equipment back to the hospital.

As he folded chairs and tables, he snuck a glance at Lana, chatting with customers at a nearby four-top. Her shapely legs in those bat-print tights pumped a jolt of energy through his exhausted body. Weird that drawing her blood affected him so strongly. Maybe because donating was an act of trust? The way she relaxed under his touch was a definite turn-on.

Kind of scary how fast he'd developed these strong, protective feelings for her and her goofy brothers. They'd had so much fun decorating Lana's porch for Halloween, clowning around with plastic skeletons and fake spider webs. If it were up to the boys, he'd be sharing that cute little clapboard house by now.

But it wasn't up to the kids, and Lana had good reasons to be so guarded. Though his body zinged with desire every time they touched, Jojo was playing the long game. The more he got to know her, the deeper he wanted to dive beneath her tightly controlled surface. Each intimate detail she revealed just made him greedy for more—of her luscious curves, sure, but also her heart and mind and trust.

Dawn climbed the four steps up to the pool tables and patted Jojo's shoulder as she passed. "Good work tonight, kiddo." She huddled with the nurse in charge, whispering and hooking a thumb in his direction. Cassie grinned and nodded, then called him over. "You're done, Jojo. Enjoy the rest of your night."

"But don't you need help with—?"

"We've got this. Your boss has other plans for you."

Plans at this hour? The crowd was already thinning. Most customers didn't stay late on a Wednesday, and Spike could easily handle bouncer duties until closing, unless... He groaned and smacked his forehead. Someone blabbed.

Kind of embarrassing how much he let this milestone birthday get to him. He'd hoped to just ignore it until the family party on Saturday—a few more days of pretending he was still in his twenties.

Even though he knew age was only a number, he'd expected to have his life's direction figured out by now. Sure, he talked a good game, telling himself and others he was in no particular hurry to choose a career, but damn, he still couldn't force himself to pick a focus. Stick with the hospital job? He enjoyed the work, and it paid well, offered benefits and a secure future, especially important as his thoughts drifted toward starting a family of his own.

But he loved his fitness training business too. Clients praised his skill at motivating them. Word was spreading, and his list of prospective clients was growing. Soon, something would have to give. The most logical choice was Bangers, but that meant no longer working beside Lana. What they had was too new and fragile to risk giving up this connection.

Dawn rang the ship's bell behind the bar. "Last call, y'all. We're closing early tonight for a private celebration."

Jojo lifted his slumped shoulders and pasted on a grin.

After he, Spike, and Dawn shooed out the last customers, the boss clapped his shoulder. "You didn't think we'd let you get away without celebrating your special day, did you? Now just park your butt right here, birthday boy. Lana, get this hard-working vampire a beer."

Lana returned with a Salty Dog Pumpkin Porter, his new favorite, and a tight-lipped expression. "Why didn't you tell me?"

He shrugged. "It's no big deal. Just another day." *Keep saying it and I might believe it.*

"Just another decade, you mean?"

Feeling suddenly a hundred pounds heavier, he took a slug from his glass. "Yeah, the big three-oh."

Lana's lips settled into a pout.

Damn, he should have told her. Huge miscalculation. Of course her feelings would be hurt, especially after all she'd shared with him about her private trauma. Compared with that, his reluctance to acknowledge this date felt weak and pathetic. Besides, she was going to find out in a few days.

He clasped her delicate hand. "So, when I asked you to save Saturday afternoon for me?"

"Yeah?"

"My family's celebrating my birthday. Kalua pig, Hawaiian rum punch, my cousins will probably dance—the whole big, rowdy deal. I hope you'll like it."

Her jaw dropped. "You want me to meet your family?"

Why was she so incredulous? Hadn't he made his feelings clear? Dancing on this line between patience and passion was exhausting.

"Yeah." He laced his fingers through hers. "I want you to meet them, even though they'll ask you nosy questions and try to get you drunk. Will you come?"

Eyes narrowed, she scrunched her lips to the side.

"I should mention Dawn's birthday gift to me—I've got Saturday night off. So do you."

When her eyes bugged out, he hurried to add, "Only if you want to. No pressure."

*Please say yes. Please, please, please.*

At last she gifted him a shy grin. "I do. I want to. Meet your family, I mean."

Her liquid gaze soothed his nerves and warmed his body right to the core.

Katy Perry's "Birthday" blasted from the speakers, and the rest of the Bangers girls pranced out from the kitchen with Dawn leading the parade, carrying a cake ablaze with candles. Diego followed with a tray of little flatbreads.

"Happy birthday to youuuuu," everyone chorused—even old Gus, who had his own unique sense of pitch, to put it kindly.

The phrase "warm fuzzies" was made for moments like this. A cozy blanket of love and friendship enveloped Jojo's body and soul. He swiped at his misty eyes. "Aww, guys, this is too much."

"Make a wish," Lana urged, mischief twinkling in her dark gaze.

"I've got a good one." He waggled his eyebrows, then blew out the candles.

Spike clapped his shoulder and flashed a rare grin. "Shut up, man, and cut the cake." The grouch eyed the table where Maci and Shelby were setting up a midnight feast. Which chef had caught his interest? Or maybe it was just the food Spike was lusting after—Maci's ultra-spicy jerk chicken wings and Shelby's loaded tots, plus whatever Diego had made.

Jojo hadn't realized how hungry he was until the heady smells hit him. He rubbed his hands together and tried not to drool. "Holy cats, you guys are the best."

Maci gave him a teasing grin as she dished up his plate. "A big boy like you needs fuel, and I know you like a little spice." She nudged Lana with her elbow. "And tots to soak up all the birthday shots."

Diego dropped a steaming, flat pastry on his plate. "And this is from Lana and me."

"Smells amazing. What are they?"

"Pupusas with cheese and pork belly. Lana taught me how to make them."

Lana scoffed. "More like Diego taught me." Her smile grew misty. "Mom would be proud. These are almost as good as hers."

Jojo chomped into savory corn dough surrounding crispy pork and gooey cheese. He rolled his eyes heavenward and moaned. "Wow. Even better than Diego's empanadas. I'm honored, Lana."

"A toast!" Kiara brought out a tray of dark red cocktails, their rims drizzled with syrupy fake blood. "To Jojo, our favorite vampire. Long may he—um, suck?"

"To Jojo!"

He sampled the sweet-tart concoction. Better go slow—he was tired, and these babies were jet-fuel strong.

Next came presents. From his workout crew, an "Over the Hill" T-shirt and an assortment of protein bars. From Rosie, a certificate for a tattoo. Kiara gave him an oversize water bottle, and Spike gifted him a plush rat wearing gym shorts. "It's a gym rat. Get it?"

Lana handed him a shiny gift bag. "From Leo and Pedro"

He unwrapped a long-sleeved T-shirt with the Stadium High School tiger on the front and "Coach Jojo" on the back.

His heart squeezed.

"And this is from me." Lana bit her lip, her cheeks flushed as he unwrapped a fleece blanket, also imprinted with a Stadium Tiger. "In case we go to another game."

Understanding dawned. Jojo's face heated, and his grin spread so wide his cheeks cramped.

"I love it." He gripped her waist and gently kneaded that soft curve.

She rose on tiptoe and whispered, "The boys are staying with Kenny and Carol tonight."

His pulse stuttered, then sprinted. "You sure?"

She trailed a fingertip down his chest. "Yeah. I'm sure."

He went hard in an instant, barely able to breathe, much less speak. Clutching the blanket to cover his arousal, he thanked everyone. "It's been a long day, y'all. Thanks for a birthday I'll never forget."

If Lana delivered on her smile's steamy promise, it truly would be his best birthday ever.

Gus grumbled, "We went to all this trouble and now you're leaving?"

Dawn gave Jojo a knowing smile. "Let him go, Gus. He's got another celebration to go to."

Lana wound her arm through Jojo's. "You ready?"

The gesture slammed him right in the feels. She was declaring her intentions for the entire crew to see. She was claiming him. This was huge.

One arm around the woman of his dreams, the other loaded with birthday loot, he kicked the door open and strode out into the magical night.

# Chapter Ten

Lana pulled into her driveway and sat in silence, listening to the tick, tick, tick of her car's cooling engine. A traffic delayed Jojo, but he'd be along any minute now. Countdown to the most awkward moment of her life.

She had to tell him. He was an experienced lover—how could he not be, looking like he did? As tempting as it was to bluff her way through this, he'd know. And he'd been so sweet and open with her. Lying would be unfair to both of them.

She gripped her steering wheel with damp, trembling hands. *What if this isn't good for him? What if I get stuck in my head and can't enjoy the experience?* There was no denying her body's enthusiastic response to his touch. The other night, when he slid his big, warm hand beneath her sweater to cup her breast, she'd nearly come, right there on her porch.

"Stop overthinking," she snapped aloud. She was determined to jump this hurdle. Tonight. She needed to put this anxiety behind her so she could finally relax and enjoy their growing closeness.

She texted Carol and got an immediate reply.

**Boys asleep. Have fun.** She added a wink emoji.

Lana winced, then sucked in a deep breath as Jojo's headlights flared behind her. She bolted to her feet and slammed her car door much too hard, then leaned against it to keep herself upright.

An easy smile lit his face, but every step he took toward her pounded her heart like kettle drum. With a white-knuckled grip, she clutched her jacket over her chest. He bracketed her legs with his and gently gripped her shoulders. "You sure about this, Lana?"

She gave a sharp nod, seized the back of his neck, and mashed her lips to his in a bruising kiss.

"Mmmf." Chuckling, he pulled back and rubbed his mouth. "Fierce, aren't you?"

Embarrassed, she jutted her chin, faking the courage she wished she felt. "Let's go inside."

The house felt eerily dark and quiet as she kicked off her shoes. Jojo did the same and set them neatly beside hers.

Rubbing her hands on her thighs, she stared down at his enormous sneakers, nearly twice the size of hers. *God, he's huge. Will he even fit inside me?*

She flicked on the living room lights, dialed down the dimmer, then connected her phone to the Bluetooth speaker and pulled up music to cover the awkward silence before fleeing to the kitchen. "Something to drink? I've got, um—" Damn, should've stocked up on beer, but she didn't keep alcohol in the house. Too much temptation for a couple of teen boys left alone. She surveyed the fridge. "Sorry, just seltzers and sodas."

"A seltzer would be great." Moving behind her, he rested his hands on her waist and his chin atop her head. "Orange, please."

She handed him a can and fetched glasses, then poured her own drink to quench her parched, tight throat. Her hands shook so hard she sloshed seltzer onto the counter.

Gripping her shoulders, he gently turned her to face him. "Hey, this doesn't have to be a big step." He brushed a soft kiss across her lips. "You set the pace, little warrior. When you say stop, we stop." Another kiss, sweet and lingering. "That's a solemn promise."

Gazing into his sparkling, coffee-brown eyes helped her summon the courage to continue. "Thank you, Jojo." She gulped her drink, took his hand, and led him into the living room.

*Oh shit, what now?*

A new song floated from the speaker, a smoky ballad about love lost and found again. She drew his hand to her waist. "Dance with me?"

Cradled in Jojo's brawny arms, she relaxed into the rhythm and hid her face against his shoulder. Swaying to the beat, she sank into the sensation of his body against hers—graceful despite his bulk, gentle despite his strength. He massaged her lower back in slow circles, bringing her other hand to his lips before draping it across his shoulder. Anticipation thrummed along her nerves and pulsed in her core. When he hummed along to the music, the rumble of his voice against her cheek weakened her knees.

"You okay, angel?"

"Kinda tired." *And so turned on I can barely breathe.* "It's been a long day."

"Well then, let's get you off your feet." He danced her backward to the couch, tugged her down so they sat hip to hip, and scooped her legs across his lap. Heat smoldered in his heavy-lidded eyes as he stroked her jawline with a fingertip. "I need to confess something."

Her heart boomed. Her sex throbbed in counterpoint.

"I have this secret fantasy." He toyed with one of her pigtails. "Can I share it?"

"Please do."

"I really want to unbraid your hair. I've never seen it loose."

*Whew!* She peeled off the elastics and dropped them on the coffee table.

His gaze rapt, he slowly teased her hair free of the tight braids, then lifted a lock and stroked it against his cheek.

Her hands ached to touch him, but she clenched them in her lap, spellbound by the pleasure he took in caressing her hair.

Closing his eyes, he inhaled its scent. With a sexy grunt, he raked his fingers into the strands and fisted a handful, the tug sharply arousing.

Heat curled down her spine. *He's making love to my hair.*

"So beautiful," he murmured. "Like moonlight on dark water." His eyes glittered. "Lana, I can't explain the effect you have on me. When I touch you, everything gets brighter, sharper, sweeter." His lips grazed the sensitive skin below her ear. "You're magical."

She felt herself melting, flesh and bones liquified by his tender touch. She had to force the words out now, before she lost the power of speech.

"I have a confession too. It's a big one." She nuzzled his neck, relishing the contrast of soft skin over corded muscle and coarse beard shadow.

He chuckled. "Hope it doesn't involve hair, 'cause that's not a strong point for me."

She skated her palm over his smooth scalp, so silky and sensual. His eyes drifted closed as he purred like a tiger. Good. This gave her something to focus on during this excruciating part.

"The thing is, I'm not very experienced. With, you know, sex." She screwed her eyes shut. *Please don't be squicked out.*

He feathered kisses beneath her jaw. "Really? You seem so confident."

Her belly tightened. "I mean, I've fooled around with guys, but I never quite... made it across the finish line."

Jojo straightened, eyes solemn, but his hands continued to massage her nape and thigh.

Fighting the urge to hide from his penetrating gaze, she plunged ahead. "After Mom and Dad died, I had no chance to get comfortable with anyone. And the more time passed, the harder it was to cross that barrier." She caressed the muscular curve of his shoulder. "Until I met you."

Lips parting on a swift inhalation, he cupped her jaw in both hands. "Lana, are you telling me I'm your first?"

She forced herself to breathe. "Yeah."

"And you want to take that step tonight? With me?" His thumbs stroked her cheekbones.

The thundering of her heart echoed in every nerve. Tight with tension and arousal, she whispered, "Yes. I want that very much."

With a low groan, he pulled her into his arms and captured her mouth, the tip of his tongue parting her lips in a light, teasing touch. He broke the kiss and pressed his forehead to hers. "What an incredible gift. I promise I'll make it good for you."

"I know you will." Urgent need drove her to her knees. She straddled him, pressing her aching breasts to his broad, firm chest. His powerful thighs were warm stone beneath her. Cradling her head, he devoured her mouth, his tongue dancing over and around hers while his free hand skimmed her side, her hip, her thigh.

Dizzy with pleasure, she laced her hands behind his neck and held on. Jojo stroked her ribs, his thumb brushing the edge of her breast. She felt drunk, floating on waves of sparkling sensation.

"So beautiful," he murmured into the crook of her neck. "Do you know how long I've wanted you? How scared I was to approach you?"

She slid greedy hands beneath his scrubs to stroke his satiny skin. "You? Scared of me?"

"Scared of losing you. What if I asked you out and you turned me down? What if moving too fast made things awkward between us?" He trailed kisses along her collarbones. "What if I never got a second chance?"

She palmed the broad planes of his pecs. "You are a patient man."

"Not right now, I'm not." With a swift tug, he pulled her shirt over her head and tossed it away. His low, hungry growls echoed between her thighs as his hands closed over the cups of her bra. "Can I open this?"

Biting her lip, Lana popped the center clasp. Her breasts spilled free. Jojo's lips parted on a moan as he kneaded her sensitive flesh. One rock of his hips brought his rigid cock into perfect alignment with her core. Pleasure cascaded through her, need overtaking fear.

When he lifted her to lick and suckle her aching nipples, her clit lit up like neon.

"I want to feel your skin against mine," she moaned.

Some asshole with a souped-up motor roared up the street, his headlights illuminating the living room through the closed curtains.

With a sexy grunt, he hefted her in his arms and vaulted from the couch. "Bedroom in the back?"

"Second door on the right." Giggling, she clung to him as he strode down the hallway.

Shifting his grip, he claimed another deep, probing kiss and kicked the door open. He crossed the floor in three long strides and deposited her gently on the bed. The room lay dark except for the streetlight's faint glow. She switched on the bedside lamp. "I want to see you."

"Likewise, beauty." Jojo flashed a devilish smile as he peeled off his shirt.

The sight of his glorious bare chest stole her breath. Tawny skin over sculpted muscles, black-inked Hawaiian tattoos covering his right shoulder and arm—sharp points, swirling lines, a stylized sea turtle. She skimmed her fingertips over his stunning curves and planes. Splaying her hands over his pecs, she leaned in and licked the column of his throat. He smelled of sandalwood and spice. She wanted to feast on him.

"You're so beautiful, Jojo. A walking, breathing masterpiece. Do these tattoos have a story?"

"I'll tell you each one—after." He pressed soft lips to her collarbone, neck, breasts, then hooked his thumbs into the waistband of her shorts. "Can we take these off?"

His rapt attention pumped up her confidence. "Yours first."

"Yes, ma'am." With a dazzling smile, he unfastened his belt and grasped his zipper pull.

"Let me." Giddy with arousal, she unzipped his fly and tugged his jeans down, enraptured by his sturdy thighs and powerful calves dusted with tiny curls. Even his feet were sexy—broad but graceful. He stood before her, a marble statue come to life. And at the juncture of those thick thighs, beneath snug black boxer-briefs, his hefty erection angled toward his hipbone, its fat head and vein-roped shaft clearly visible through the thin cloth.

With a happy sigh, she crouched to nuzzle the line of dark hairs descending from his navel, then traced it with her tongue.

Jojo hissed through clenched teeth.

Giggling, she hooked a finger in his waistband and glanced up at his face, as hungry for his reaction as for his touch. His pupils shone inky with desire, and his chest rose and fell in rapid, shallow breaths. Holding his gaze, she trailed her fingertip up the hard ridge of his shaft. His breath caught. His abs jerked.

Pride swelled in her chest. This beautiful, powerful man was at her mercy. Such a heady, delicious feeling. She tugged his waistband down until his cock sprang free, heavy and ruddy, pointing at her chin. When she pressed a kiss to its plush crown, a crystal tear of pleasure appeared. Grasping him gently, she slid her hand up and down his hot, heavy erection, then swirled her tongue over the velvety head. His hips jerked forward.

"Mercy," he growled. He kicked off his undershorts, then grasped her shoulders and laid her back on the mattress.

He crouched over her, his gaze drinking her in. "Lana. You're driving me wild." Parting her legs with his knees, he swept his hands down her sides, then up the tender insides and covered her mound with his palm. Hot bliss washed through her. Through her satin panties, his thumb traced her seam and circled her clit, his touch feather-light.

Desperate for more contact, she arched her hips.

With a rumbling laugh, he tugged her panties down and slid toward the foot of the bed until his belly rested on the mattress between her parted legs. He stroked both thumbs over her folds. "Such a beautiful pussy. You're so hot and wet for me."

His touch left her speechless, only able to whimper.

He lifted her thighs over his broad shoulders, then lowered his head. Was he going to—oh God, he was! She'd only ever done this once, with a guy who couldn't find her clit. But Jojo had excellent aim. He pressed an open-mouth kiss to her sex, hot and slick and so good she felt the top of her skull lift off.

His broad tongue slipped between her folds and glided over the spot that made her heart stop and stars dance behind her closed lids. Torn between wanting to watch him work this miracle and wanting to shut out every sense but touch, she writhed on the bed. He seemed to slip beneath her very skin, his flesh merging with hers to create a symphony of impossible pleasure.

He slid one long finger inside her channel and worked it slowly in and out, each glide brushing a magic place that made her jolt. Her hips undulated of their own accord. Mindless, breathless, she clutched the sheets as his tongue swirled and flicked. She shrieked his name as her climax crashed through her in a white-hot rush.

Moments later, when the waves subsided, she registered his muffled chuckle between her thighs. "That's one."

"There's more?" she gasped.

Grinning, he rose on his elbow and wiped his glistening mouth. "Baby girl, there's lots more." He nipped her sensitive inner thigh and worked a second finger inside her, stretching her to receive his thick cock.

She shivered in anticipation tinged with fear. Why did she pick such a huge guy for her first time? He was going to split her in two.

"Lana," he murmured into her neck, "I want this to be good for you. The minute it isn't, you tell me and I'll stop."

"Okay," she rasped.

"Promise me," he growled and worked a third finger inside her. The fullness ached and stung, but with an edge of pleasure that deepened with each thrust.

"I promise." Panting, she lifted her hips to ride his rhythm. "I want this. I want you."

"Touch yourself." He placed her hand over her clit. His rapt focus fired her blood. Electric sensations danced between pleasure and pain. She's never felt anything this intense.

Slowly, he withdrew his fingers, rolled away, and pulled a condom packet from his jeans pocket.

Mesmerized, she watched him tear open the foil and roll the thin sheath over his shaft.

Her last few functioning brain cells zapped to life. "Jojo, wait."

He paused, his hand on his cock, fire dancing in his eyes.

"I'm on the pill."

He tilted his head. "But you've never—"

"It helps with my periods. Have you um—"

His smile bloomed wide. "Got tested the minute you agreed to go out with me. You know, just in case. I'm healthy."

She stretched her limbs, as pleasure-soaked and languid as a cat in a sunbeam. "Then let me feel you bare inside me."

Flames flared in his eyes as he quickly peeled off the condom. Reclining beside her, he pulled her thigh over his hips so she straddled him. "You're in control, Lana. Do what feels good."

Bracing her hands on his chest, she lowered her sex to glide back and forth over his cock. As rigid as heated marble, he burned her in the most delicious way. Already, she felt a second climax building, a pulsing glow between her thighs.

She rose on her knees, and he fisted the base of his cock and notched the fat, blunt head at her entrance. Holding his gaze, she lowered herself slowly. The crown slipped inside, and his eyes fluttered half-closed. He pressed his thumb to her clit. "That's it. Slow. Sweet. So tight."

Encouraged, she sucked in a breath and bore down. A sharp sting drew a gasp. He gripped her hips and tried to lift her off his body.

"No. It's okay." Breathing through the burn, she felt it ease. She slid down another inch, then another. Jojo bit his lip and searched her face. She pressed down again, taking him deeper. When she felt the scratch of his hair against her folds, she rocked her hips, letting her inner walls adjust to the strange new feeling of fullness, indescribably satisfying.

She understood now that sex wasn't just physical sensation. She felt at once in control, possessed, and deeply connected to Jojo. Each movement of her body gifted him pleasure, and his reaction built her own excitement. The pain was nearly gone now. She rose on her knees and sank down in one slow glide. Jojo's abs jumped, and he unleashed a feral grunt. She'd known it was there, a wildness behind his careful gentleness. And she craved more.

Up and down she rode him, each stroke more delicious than the last. Pleasure edged away the last of the pain. Leaning back, she felt Jojo's thighs tighten beneath her palms. His thumb ground over her clit—too hard, too sharp.

"Softer," she hissed, "like this." Guiding him, she lightened his touch. His hips bucked in short, sharp digs. His cock hardened impossibly as he watched her through half-closed lids, his jaw tight.

Moving faster now, he moaned her name over and over, gripping her hips while he drove up into her.

Bubbles fizzed in her blood. Panting, she closed her eyes to focus on the electric sensations.

He grasped the back of her neck. "Look at me, baby. Let me see what you feel." He raked his fingers into her hair and fisted them. The tug on her scalp flashed flames down her spine. His cock churned faster. Her nerves crackled.

"Jojo, now." Her climax broke like thunder, stealing her breath. With a roar, he rolled her beneath him, hooked her knee over the crook of his elbow, and pummeled her until his whole body went rigid, his head thrown back, mouth open on a gasp. His cock throbbed inside her, flooding her with warmth, and nothing had ever felt so fiery, so sharp, so sweet.

He collapsed atop her, then rolled onto his back and clutched her to his sweat-slicked, heaving chest. "Ku'u ipo," he murmured again and again, his fingertips tracing whorls over her back.

"What does that mean?"

He smoothed her hair from her damp forehead. "Beloved, angel, my wildest, sweetest dream."

Heat and light spread through her chest and down her limbs until her whole body tingled. She kissed him, soft and wet. Split wide open, defenseless, her beating heart his for the taking. And she wanted him to claim it, wanted him to wrap his arms and smile and love around her and hold her always.

"Ku'u ipo," she repeated against his lips. "I like it."

Grinning, he enfolded her. "It's yours."

# Chapter Eleven

♥

Thursday Seahawks games always filled Bangers to the rafters, so tonight Jojo checked IDs while Spike worked crowd control on the sidewalk. It had been a great game, but the night was still young, and the bar teemed with thirsty, rowdy fans who stuck around for Dawn's post-game event, a college derby with teams of Puget Sound University Lumberjacks, Tacoma Community College Titans, UW Huskies, and WSU Cougars competing in cornhole, cup flipping, and darts. A community college grad himself, Jojo was rooting for the Titans.

"Good to go. Enjoy your evening." He stamped a late arrival's hand, then peeked inside, searching for Lana. There she was, flitting through the crowd like a hummingbird. God, she was beautiful, her spirit bright enough to light the whole bar. Grinning, he turned to his next customer.

"Dude, are you serious?" He held the next customer's fake ID under his flashlight. "I could do better with my grandma's old printer. Come back next year."

"Go pound sand, you dumb-ass jock." The disappointed kid snatched his useless ID and shuffled away.

"Right back atcha, buddy." Even the most obnoxious customers couldn't drag down his mood. His body still tingled from last night. Waking up beside Lana was almost as sweet as watching her come apart in his arms—even if he had to sneak out early to avoid running into her brothers. Of course, he'd slept through his phone alarm, lulled deep into dreamland by the best loving of his life, but Lana's sleepy kisses woke him better than any ringtone ever could. Too bad they didn't have time for another tumble before breakfast, but she'd promised to plan their next night together ASAP. The eagerness in her goodbye kiss this morning filled him with so much warm, fizzy joy, he was still floating.

Truly, this was the start of something magical.

On her way to the servers' station, Lana caught his eye, flashed a sassy grin, and waggled her eyebrows. He slapped a hand to his heart and pantomimed a swoon. She blew a kiss, then pivoted with a flip of her long braids and short skirt.

Happy, fluffy bunnies hopped inside his rib cage.

A manicured hand waved an ID under his nose, snapping him back to the cold, blustery sidewalk.

"Hi, Jojo," the hot blonde cooed. "It's my birthday."

Her gaggle of girlfriends tittered.

He kept his expression bland. "Happy birthday, Janie." A regular and an obnoxious flirt, the only staff guy she didn't hit on was Gus, Dawn's not-so-silent business partner, whose baggy ass was permanently attached to the last barstool. And Spike, of course, but no one dared to flirt with Spike.

Janie rubbed her tits against Jojo's arm. "Know what I want for my birthday present?"

He rolled his eyes. "Move along, birthday girl. Other people are waiting to come inside."

She stuck out her lower lip. "Not until I get a kiss from my favorite bouncer."

How to get her off his back without making a scene? He leaned through the doorway and waved. "Yo, Spike."

Chest to chest with a cocky frat boy, Spike snarled. The kid pulled a face and retreated, his friends following like a line of startled baby ducks. Stroking his bushy beard, Spike ambled to the entrance. "S'up?"

"Janie here's got a birthday wish. She wants a kiss."

Janie's eyes widened. She backed away, palms up.

Jojo smothered a laugh. This was going to be good.

With a grunt, Spike pulled the toothpick from the corner of his mouth, pitched it to the sidewalk, and grabbed Janie's hand. She squeaked as he bent her backward over his massive thigh and planted a noisy smooch on her neck.

Janie's friends gasped.

Spike set the flame-faced flirt back on her feet and snapped a salute, his face placid. "Happy birthday, Miss."

As the women filed inside, Jojo roared with laughter. "Spike's got moves. Who knew?"

"Of course he's got moves." Maci stepped through the door, holding a tray of wings and tots. She handed one paper boat to Jojo and another to Spike, who also got a shaker of hot sauce and Maci's finger planted in his chest. "Now, I'm trusting you with my special sauce. You bring that back, you hear?"

Spike gave her a rare smile. "Yes, ma'am." Tucking the bottle into the pocket of his leather vest, he returned to his post, where he doused his wings in fiery sauce, inhaled the meat, and chucked the bones in the gutter.

Jojo glanced from bouncer to chef. Something cooking between these two?

Eyeing Spike, Maci sucked her teeth, then gave a low, musical laugh.

The new chef was a helluva change from Diego, who hardly ever left the kitchen during his shift. Maci liked to stretch her legs, as she explained it, and get direct feedback from customers. And she was a looker—tall and willowy, her dark skin glowing under the streetlamps. Wearing a colorful head wrap instead of a chef's cap, she looked like she'd taken a wrong turn from some tropical island and stumbled into Tacoma. Jojo still wasn't sure why she took the Bangers job; she evaded questions about her past. All he knew was she'd left some high-end Seattle restaurant after a dispute with management.

Maci stretched her arms high overhead, took a deep breath of cold night air, and heaved a contented sigh.

"You like the scent of car exhaust?"

"It's a pleasant break from the smell of fried food. Last night, I dreamt I was being chased by a giant, sizzling chicken monster with a dozen wings." She gave him an appraising look. "So, you and Lana, eh? Good for you."

Grinning, he hooked a thumb in Spike's direction. "You got a soft spot for Spike?"

Maci perused the fuzzy ogre for a moment, tapping her lips. "He's a grump, but I do like a man who can handle some spice." With a chuckle, she went back inside, where Dawn was taking the stage to begin the evening's competition.

"Cornhole round one," she bellowed into the mic. "Cougars versus Lumberjacks."

While the crowd hooted and clapped, Jojo's thoughts drifted to Saturday's party at his parents' house. His aunties, uncles, and cousins were coming down from Seattle—a big, happy mob. He hoped Lana wouldn't be put off by their nosy questions. Though they meant well, his family's in-your-face approach wasn't everyone's cup of tea.

"Thirsty, big guy?" Lana sashayed through the door and proffered a cranberry-and-soda garnished with every fruit on the bartenders' tray.

"Yeah, all this sitting on my ass is exhausting. Thanks, beauty." He took a sip, then pecked her temple. "How'd you sneak up on me? I didn't see you coming."

"Ninja training." Her playful grin sparkled as she snagged a tot from his paper dish. "Gotta keep my boyfriend hydrated."

"God, I love hearing you say that." He pulled her hand to his lips and kissed it.

"Hydration?" She batted her lashes, flirting for all the world to see.

"Boyfriend." He dipped another tot in spicy cheese sauce and held it to her mouth. Her soft lips closed over the crispy, gooey morsel, brushing his fingers, and his dick surged in his jeans.

Lana's phone sounded in her apron pocket, the opening piano riff from Bob Seger's "Old Time Rock and Roll." She frowned. "That's Kenny's ring tone. He only calls during my shift if it's an emergency." She set her tray on Jojo's stool and called him back. As she listened, the color drained from her face, and her hand clamped onto his arm. "Oh no! When? Which hospital?"

Jojo's heart plummeted to his feet. One of the boys?

"I'll be there as fast as I can." She clicked off the call, tapped her screen, then shook her head. "No, I've gotta tell them in person." A line etched between her brows as she peered into the barroom. "Shit, it's so crowded tonight."

"What happened?"

Her tear-bright eyes pinned him. "It's Kenny. He—" Her chin trembled. "The EMTs think he had a heart attack." She snatched her tray and wobbled back inside.

"Hold on, now." Jojo bolted after her, slung his arm around her shoulders, and scanned the crowd for Dawn. There she was, up by the pool tables, holding a clipboard. Jojo's shrill whistle jerked her attention to him and Lana.

She hustled over, her face twisted with concern. "What's wrong, kiddo? You're pale as a ghost."

Lana clutched her middle and rasped, "It's Kenny, my neighbor."

"The one who watches your brothers?"

"He's hurt, hospital..." Her voice broke on a sob.

Dawn squeezed Jojo's arm. "Take her home."

Eyes scrunched tight, Lana shook her head. "I can drive."

"Bullshit," Dawn snapped. "You're shaking like a leaf. Go on, you two."

"But the bar—" she protested.

"We'll handle it. You go take care of your family."

Leaning on Jojo's strong arm, Lana stumbled to the staff room, collected her things, and dropped her car keys into his palm. Dawn was right—no way could she drive with her heart in her throat and her hands shaking like aspen leaves.

Outside, he beeped the Camry open with her key fob, helped her into her seat, then crouched beside the passenger door. "Just breathe, ku'u ipo. We'll get through this, okay? Whatever you need, I'm here for you."

Lips pinched in a tight line, she nodded. Hot tears streaked her face as her mind raced from one disastrous outcome to the next.

Jojo adjusted the driver's seat all the way back, then cranked the ignition. He kept his hand on her knee, heavy and warm, as they rolled down 6th Avenue. The gathering clouds chose this moment to unleash pelting rain, as if weeping for Kenny, for their adopted grandparents, for yet another agonizing loss.

Pressure pounded inside Lana's skull. Nausea twisted her guts as a vortex of shock and pain threatened to swallow her—but she didn't dare lose control. Her brothers needed her. So did Carol, who had no family in Tacoma. Oh God, what must she be feeling now?

It was raining like this the night Lana got the call that shattered their family. By the time she and the boys arrived at the hospital, Mom and Dad were gone. And now her surrogate grandpa was fighting for his life. Despite not having set foot in a church since her parents' funeral, she crossed herself and prayed fervently for Kenny's survival, her hands clenched beneath her chin. But prayers couldn't hold back an icy flood of memories—the rain, the flashing ambulance lights, the doctor's grim expression. "I'm so sorry, Miss Lopez. We did everything we could."

Her words scraped her tight throat. "This was my mom's car." She patted the dash. "I feel close to her here."

Often, driving the Camry brought back comforting memories of the long talks she and Mom shared while riding through Tacoma. But now, with Jojo behind the wheel and worry consuming her, Mom's voice had gone silent. No sound but the hiss of tires on wet pavement and the thunk of the windshield wipers.

Pain sliced through her. "Oh Mom, what am I gonna do?"

Turning onto her street, Jojo squeezed her knee. "What does she say?"

Her voice broke. "Nothing. She's dead. And now Kenny's dying." With a ragged wail, she folded over.

He pulled into her driveway and shut off the engine. His broad hand rubbed soothing circles on her back. "Lana, you've been through more loss than I can imagine. But you're not alone, okay? We'll figure something out."

"Okay," she rasped, clinging to his promise like a buoy.

He brushed her tears away with his thumbs, and that reassuring touch calmed her enough to face the next hurdle. "I have to tell Leo and Pedro. Will you come with me?"

"Of course." He pressed a soft kiss to her forehead.

Leaning on his arm, she limped up the stairs and unlocked the door. Electronic music pounded from down the hall.

Leo sprawled on the sofa, headphones on, flipping through his tablet. A pang of guilt stabbed her. He looked so peaceful, and it was her job to shatter that peace.

He glanced up, then jolted upright. "Hey, Jojo." He pulled off his headphones. "Wait, it's only ten-thirty. Aren't you guys supposed to be at the bar?"

Lana sat on the coffee table facing him. Jojo stood beside her, his hand on her shoulder.

"Did you hear the ambulance?" she asked.

Leo's brows contracted as he looked from her to Jojo. "No, I, uh..." He gestured to the discarded headphones. "What happened?"

For her brothers' sake, she had to deliver the news calmly. She laid her hand on Leo's knee. "Carol called. Kenny had a heart attack."

Leo gaped, blinking through tears. "What? No! Is he—"

Jojo sat beside him and slung an arm around his shoulders. "We don't know yet." He glanced at her for confirmation.

She nodded.

"What about Carol?" Leo bolted to his feet. "We gotta help her."

"She's on her way to the hospital." An icy tide of memory washed over her—the nonstop phone calls, contorted faces, tight hugs that strangled her, demands for information—all while she was still numb with shock.

"It's best if we give her a little time. Right now, she probably doesn't know anything more than we do." She pushed to her feet and started down the hallway. "I'll tell Pedro."

"No, wait," Leo called, his voice sharp with alarm.

Turning back, she stared.

"I, uh..." He flapped his hands, his startled gaze darting from her to the hallway beyond.

Jojo rubbed his shoulder. "Little man, sometimes it's best to rip off the Band-aid."

What a good brother, trying to protect his little bro from the news. She gripped Pedro's doorknob and felt the base vibrating the metal. What was with these two and loud music? It was a wonder either of them could still hear. She knocked. No answer, so she twisted the knob.

Pedro's quilt covered the bodies on the bed, but their undulating movements left no doubt. Pedro and Haley were going at it like rabbits.

Lana clutched her forehead. "Are you fuckin' kidding me?"

She turned her back as the kids scrambled for their clothes.

"You told me no one would bother us," Haley wailed.

Pedro's voice rose an octave. "Babe, Leo promised to stand watch. And Lana's never home this early."

Clasping her half-fastened top closed, Haley hustled past. She spun in the doorway and faced Lana. "I'm sorry," she croaked, and shot Pedro a look of pure fury. "And I'm sorry I trusted you. It was my first time, Pedro. It was supposed to be special." She stormed out.

Pedro clutched the quilt to his chest. "Thanks a lot, Lana." A vein popped out in his neck. "I'm in love with her. We used protection, just like you said." His chin trembled. "You ruined everything."

Jojo stepped through the doorway. "Can the attitude, little man. Your sister's got some news." He squeezed Lana's shoulder.

She sucked in a shaky breath. "It's Kenny."

Pedro blanched. "Oh God. Is he dead?"

Leo entered the room, red-faced and teary-eyed. "I'm sorry, man. I tried." He dropped onto Pedro's bed and wrapped his gangly arms around his brother. Her heart twisting with sympathy, Lana joined them. They enfolded her, and the three of them wept together.

Jojo's soft voice broke through their teary huddle. "Can I get you something?"

She shook her head. "No, we—"

"Some hot chocolate?" Leo asked with a sniffle.

That was their dad's trick. When the boys were little and in trouble for yet another stupid stunt, Dad delivered a stern talking-to and an appropriate punishment, then signaled the beginning of forgiveness with a round of hot cocoa.

"Coming right up." Jojo cracked a sympathetic half smile and backed out.

Pedro sniffled into Lana's shoulder. "Is Kenny going to die?"

"I'm sure they're doing everything they can for him." She hugged her brothers tight, and their connection helped her breathe through waves of fear and grief and shock, slowly wrestling her emotions back under control. Leo and Pedro needed her now, and their needs had to come first.

She'd done this before, and she could do it again. Keeping her feelings locked down tight allowed her to hold her family together. With so many decisions to be made, there was no time to sink into grief.

Except she'd failed. The one selfish thing she's done, keeping her Bangers job, had backfired. She'd been a fool to think Kenny and Carol could keep a lid on teenage stupidity. Pedro and Haley were only fifteen, for Chrissakes. What if she got pregnant?

If she'd been home instead of at Bangers, this wouldn't have happened.

Despair gutted her.

She squeezed Pedro's arm. "Once we hear from Carol, you and I will be having a talk about responsibility and consequences."

He nodded, his chin trembling.

She pushed to her feet and went to join Jojo in the kitchen. He stood at the stove, stirring a fragrant pot of cocoa.

He turned at her approach. "They okay?"

"They're heartbroken." She clutched the table's edge as tears overtook her.

"Hey now." He wrapped her in his sturdy arms and rocked her. "We'll get through this, ku'u ipo. We'll find a way."

A fresh wave of grief buffeted her, turning her knees to water.

He eased her into a chair, set a steaming mug of cocoa in front of her, and sat facing her, his giant hand cupping her knee.

She choked back a sob. "I can't do this without Carol and Kenny. The tías were right. I should've quit Bangers long ago and found a daytime job."

Jojo's brow rumpled. "Now, let's not rush into anything."

She looked around the familiar kitchen, Mom's funny chicken figurines atop the cabinets that Dad painted turquoise just to please her one gray Tacoma winter. "This is the only home my brothers have ever known. They've been through so much loss. And Carol's been so generous with her time and love. Now she needs my help to take care of Kenny." *If he even makes it.* "How stupid was I to think this arrangement could last?" She swiped her streaming eyes. "Three more years."

"Until?" So much tenderness shone in his dark gaze. His sweetness only magnified the tragedy.

"Till Pedro turns eighteen and finishes high school. Then I can start to rebuild my life." She gripped Jojo's hand. "But giving up Bangers will be so hard."

He pulled her onto his lap and tucked her head under his chin.

"Listen." His voice rumbled through his chest. "Don't decide tonight. We'll figure something out."

"We?"

"You, me, Rosie, Dawn. You've got lots of people on your side. There's got to be a solution."

She shook her aching head. "No, this is my family, my responsibility."

He kissed her temple. "There's more to family than just blood. Now, let's take your brothers their cocoa."

Wiping her tears, she straightened her shoulders. "Thanks, Jojo. You're a good man."

His lips parted as if he were about to say something, then quirked in a crooked smile. "Anything for you, ku'u ipo."

She clung to those sweet words as she trudged down the hall toward her new, grim future.

# Chapter Twelve

♥

Dawn's eyes bulged. "Jojo, are you sure?"

God, he hated this part. He hated the whole damn situation. But a night of churning his bedcovers and chewing on every feasible solution to Lana's dilemma yielded only one clear path: The sacrifice would be his. He hadn't seen her since last night, but they'd spoken on the phone after she returned from the hospital. The weariness and defeat in her voice only solidified his decision.

"I'm sure." He pasted on a smile he didn't feel and let his gaze wander over the photos on Dawn's desk, Christmas parties, Cinco de Mayo celebrations, last year's Anti-Valentine's party and Halloween Bash—each bittersweet memory pierced his heart, but looking at them was easier than facing Dawn's crestfallen expression.

"I've got enough training clients now, and a job offer from that fancy new gym up 6th Ave. I can't be a bar bouncer forever. As much as I'll miss you all, it's time to move on."

Dawn leaned onto her elbows and tented her fingers. "I don't buy it. You've been balancing your training business, your job at the hospital, and this one just fine."

He shifted in the flimsy folding chair. "I'm not a kid anymore. I can't keep burning the candle at both ends. And in the middle too. I need to focus." His parents had been telling him that for years. Of course, they hoped he'd focus on the medical field. Informing the fam about this course change would add another layer of tension to his birthday party.

Dawn chuckled. "I hear ya. My candle's a puddle of wax. I have half a mind to sell this place to River. He wants to open his own bar someday. Might as well be this one."

"Don't say that, Mama Dawn." He'd never forgive himself if his decision was the first falling domino that ended up toppling Bangers.

She leaned back in her office chair and swiveled. "This isn't about you, is it? Tell me the truth, kiddo. Family trouble?"

He crumbled under her piercing gaze. "Not *my* family."

"I see. Lana's?"

"You can't tell her. Not until I get a chance to talk to her." He quickly explained how Kenny's heart attack left her without supervision for her brothers just as the aunties were closing in. "I remember how easy it was to go astray at that age. Only luck and love and my parents' sharp eyes kept me out of serious trouble. Lana's all those boys have. Her blood relatives couldn't care less about what's best for Leo and Pedro. With Kenny fighting for his life, Bangers is all she has left. We're her anchor, her family." He swiped away a brimming tear. "She can't lose us too."

"So you're going to babysit?"

"In time, maybe she can work out another plan, but right now, she needs me. They need me."

She shook her head. "That's a helluva sacrifice, Jojo."

"She's worth it. They're worth it." He felt the truth of his words ringing in his bones. He cared deeply for Lana and her brothers too. Hell, "care" wasn't a strong enough word. He was falling in love with her.

"Well then." Her eyes misty, Dawn clasped his hand. "We'll call this a leave of absence. You can come back anytime. I hope you do."

The quiver in her voice did Jojo in. Tears slid down his cheeks as he grasped Dawn's hand for a long, long time.

Walking through Bangers, he drank it all in—the lingering scent of beer and tots, the grinning skeletons and bats dangling from the ceiling, the beer signs and sports paraphernalia on the walls, the elaborate mahogany back bar topped with a smiling cherub. The little guy's carved eyes seemed to follow Jojo as he walked to the door.

So many wonderful memories, such good friends. And now he'd be just another customer, though taking care of the boys would leave him few opportunities to drop by for a visit.

Before leaving, he took one more sweeping glance, sucked in a deep breath, and patted the bouncer stool. "I'll be back."

Saturday morning, Jojo rapped on Kai's door. "Heading out to pick up Lana. Remember, Ma needs four bags of ice for the party. She'll skin us alive if we forget."

"Aw man, can't you get it?" came his brother's muffled reply.

Jojo's jaw clenched. He should've left an hour ago, but he'd been too busy rehearsing his speech to notice the time.

He pushed the door open to find Kai still in his pajamas, sprawled on his bed, flipping through *Flex* magazine.

Jojo shot him a dark look. "Got a lot on my plate today, remember?"

"Oh, right." Kai tossed his magazine onto the floor. "Sorry, just a reflex. I'll get the ice. You go give your girl the news." He huffed a laugh. "Man, that must be some excellent sex for you to give up your job."

"It's not about the sex, numbnuts." Which was excellent, not that he'd share that detail with Kai, for Chrissakes. "I care about her. And her brothers. She needs me, and I'm not gonna let her down."

"Yeah, yeah," Kai grumbled as he pushed to his feet. "Knight in shining armor. Go slay your lady's dragons."

Worry gnawed Jojo's gut on the drive to Lana's place. The timing couldn't be worse—introducing his new girlfriend to the fam right after dropping a bomb in her lap. How would she take the news? Would she torpedo his plan out of stubborn independence? Think he was trying to manipulate her into a relationship she wasn't ready for? He prayed his good intentions would outshine her doubts.

Sure, he wanted more than a friendly fling with Lana. He wanted her in his life, in his arms, in his bed, from now until... pretty much forever. But it was way too soon to talk about sharing a future. Today's priority had to be finding a replacement for Kenny and Carol, and he stood ready to take on that job for as long as she needed him.

He'd never been a quick decider, preferring to chew on his options for—well, just look how long it took him to finally choose personal training over his Bangers job. If not for Lana's crisis, he might have delayed that step for years.

This would've gone down easier if he could've told her yesterday, but she'd spent the day comforting Carol in the ICU and her brothers at home, and this wasn't the kind of topic you could share in a text or phone call. He needed to tell her in person, and Dawn said Lana had asked to meet tomorrow morning. Better to present his offer as a done deal.

After leaving Dawn's office, he'd called Spike, expecting the bearded ogre to cuss him out, but he just grunted. "You gotta do what you gotta do. Maybe I'll try out your gym when it's open. Ma's worried about my blood pressure."

Whataya know? The gruff dude had a heart after all.

When Jojo raised his fist to knock on Lana's door, he heard yelling inside. She opened, flashed him a weary smile, then hollered over her shoulder, "If you guys disappoint me while you're at Anna and Diego's, I swear to God..."

"Chill, sis," came Leo's voice from down the hall. "We won't embarrass you in front of your friends."

She stood on tiptoe to peck Jojo's lips, then rested her cheek against his chest. "They're so freakin' slow and disorganized. I thought they'd be better by now."

He wrapped his arms around her and kissed the top of her head. "Want me to lean on them?"

"No, just let me lean on you a minute."

"Gladly." He tightened his hold and rocked her, inhaling the sweet citrus scent of her shampoo. She'd woven her hair into one long, loose braid. The golden ribbon running through it matched her cloud-soft sweater.

Without breaking their embrace, she extended her leg. "I hope jeans are okay."

"You look gorgeous, and you smell delicious." Most of the family would be in Hawaiian shirts and dresses despite the cool autumn breeze. If Lana stuck around, they'd gift her a generous supply of bright floral doodads.

"Eew, they're kissing again," Leo teased as he stepped into the foyer toting a backpack and sleeping bag.

Pedro followed with similar gear. "Check it out, Jojo." He pulled a kids' picture book from his duffle. "This was my favorite when I was little."

"Aww," Lana cooed. "*Go Away, Big Green Monster.*" She ruffled his hair. "You do realize Ellie's just two months old."

He stuffed the book into his bag. "Never too early to start reading."

"You guys spending the night with Anna?" Jojo asked. Those sleeping bags boded well. Maybe he'd get some precious alone time with Lana tonight.

Leo rubbed his hands together. "Diego's gonna let us help renovate his new food truck. Power tools, baby!"

She rolled her eyes. "God help Diego." She kissed her brothers goodbye. "Remember, you're only spending the night if I get a good report from Anna."

Pedro hefted his bags and batted his eyelashes. "We'll be perfect angels."

While he and Lana watched from the porch, the boys stuffed their gear into Leo's old beater, then had a whispered discussion with lots of gesticulating. Leo trotted back up the path, his face solemn. "Will you be okay, sis?"

Misty-eyed, she wound her arm around Jojo's waist and gazed up at him. "Sure. I'll be with Jojo."

"Okay." Leo hugged her tight, then clasped Jojo's shoulder. "Thanks for taking care of her."

Jojo welled up a little as he watched the boys drive away. Their trust meant more than they could ever know. And what a gorgeous day. A light breeze wafted scents of sea and freshly mown grass. Brilliant sunshine intensified the colors of autumn leaves, especially on the big maple holding Lana's treehouse. Should he take her up there to deliver his news? No, better not risk losing the magic of the moment.

He sat on the porch steps and tugged her down beside him.

Lana plucked up a ruddy maple leaf and twirled it by its stem. "Leaves are most beautiful when they're dying." She leaned onto his shoulder. "Just what I need—an effin' metaphor." Her voice cracked. "What if Kenny doesn't make it?" She lifted tear-bright eyes to him, and a swell of emotion nearly stole his breath.

He put his arm around her. "Hey, we can scrap the party if you want."

She shook her head, her forehead pressed to his shoulder. "No way. It's your birthday party."

"You could meet the fam another time."

She raised her head and firmed her chin. "You told them I was coming?"

"Yeah, but—"

"Then I'm coming." She patted his knee. "Besides, I need something to distract me today. And Carol made me promise to go."

"How are they doing?"

"In a couple of days, they're shipping Kenny up to Seattle for a cardiac rehabilitation program. They'll stay with his sister."

"For how long?"

"Best-case scenario, a month." With a sigh, she wound her arm through his and stroked his biceps. "I always knew I'd have to quit Bangers someday and get a day job, but I didn't expect it to hurt this much. Feels like I'm leaving home."

*Now or never.* "You're not."

She peered up at him through narrowed eyes. "I'm not what?"

"Leaving Bangers. You can keep your job."

She blinked rapid-fire. "I don't—"

"I'll stay with the boys while you work."

"But you—"

He cupped her soft cheek in his palm. "It's done, ku'u ipo. I told Dawn yesterday. I'm officially on a leave of absence."

Brows furrowed, heat tilted, she gawked as if he were speaking Swahili. Then she straightened and scooted away. "No way. I can't ask you to do that."

Yup, stubborn.

"You didn't ask me. I decided it was time. I've got enough personal training clients now. It makes more sense to focus my efforts there."

Lana's face flushed. Just as he'd feared, she looked royally pissed. "Jojo, that's a step too far. You can't overturn your life for me. Why would you do that?"

He fought a rising flood of panic. "For God's sake, Lana, I like you, okay? A lot. A ton. I like your brothers too. Let me do this for you."

"I can't let my family troubles ruin your life."

He captured her hand and held it tenderly in both of his. "You're not ruining my life, you're making it better. Dawn says I can come back to Bangers anytime. I'm just taking a sabbatical, okay? Besides, my parents will be glad I'm finally giving up Bangers. This situation is the push I needed. The more I think about it, the more I like the idea." He pressed a kiss to the back of her hand. "Sometimes fate gives you a nudge."

She yanked her hand away, folded her arms, and glared at her boots.

He was losing her. How to convince her to at least try? He scooted closer until his hip nudged hers. "If you don't let me help, I'll just hang outside your house and sulk until you let me in."

"You're already in." She gave a low laugh. "Well, on the porch anyway."

Hope fluttered in his belly. He tapped her breastbone with his forefinger. "Let me in, Lana. Let me care for you. You don't have to carry all this on your own."

Worrying her lower lip between her teeth, she searched his eyes. Would she find what she needed?

Her fingertips skimmed his cheekbone, his jaw. "Jojo," she murmured, "You're too good to be true."

His stomach fluttered. "Nah, I'm just a guy who's found the perfect woman."

The corners of her mouth quirked up. "You need glasses, my friend. I'm light years away from perfect."

"Perfect for me." Barely breathing, he waited for her to decide. Would she close the distance or close herself off again?

With a low laugh, she shook her head. "Anyone ever tell you you're stubborn?"

Before he could answer, she clasped his nape and drew him down into a kiss—tentative at first, then hot and demanding. Her tongue teased his lips apart and swept inside, all silken seduction. Desire roared through him, gilded with hope. Winding her braid around his fist, he tugged to angle her head and deepen the kiss.

A loud wolf whistle from the sidewalk jolted them apart.

The noise came from a group of teens slouching down the sidewalk toward 6th Ave. The taller one flashed them a thumbs up and hollered, "Git some!"

Lana ducked her head and laughed.

Flushed and breathless, Jojo pressed his forehead to hers. "If I weren't the guest of honor, I'd skip the party and spend all afternoon wrapped up in you."

"Now, now, can't do that." She pecked his lips. "I'm blown away, Jojo. And grateful." Another kiss, softer and more lingering. "But it's such a big sacrifice. If this goes south, it could ruin us."

Hope strengthened and glowed, filling him with lightness. "Tell you what—let's try it for now. If you change your mind or find a better solution, we'll reassess."

Her gaze slid away on a deep inhalation.

He stroked her arm. "C'mon, Lana. The boys know we're together."

"Yeah, they do. They idolize you." She laid her soft palm on his cheek. "They couldn't have picked a better role model."

Tears prickled his eyes.

"Okay, we'll try it for now." She wound her arms around his neck. "You're pretty amazing, you know that?"

Joy engulfed him, bright and shimmering. Deep down, he'd half-expected her to refuse his offer. Heedless of gawking neighbors, he pulled her onto his lap. She wriggled against him, nestling her soft ass against his aching cock.

Her lips brushed the sensitive skin beneath his jaw. "How long until the party?"

"Dad said the Kalua pork will be ready at two. That gives us an hour."

She tunneled her fingers into the Henley he'd layered under his Hawaiian shirt. "I'm pretty nervous about meeting my boyfriend's family."

He laughed into her hair. "God, I love hearing you say that."

"What, family?" Her fingers eased past his belt, heading for his ass.

"Boyfriend." He claimed another deep, wet kiss.

Her other hand wandered over his chest, trailing delicious sparks. "Well, boyfriend, does your family know about my situation?"

"I've told them the basics."

"I don't know if that makes me feel better or worse." Her smile brimmed with mischief. "You know what would ease my nerves?" She wriggled her hips, and his nerves crackled.

Her chestnut eyes darkened with desire. When he cupped her breast through her soft sweater, she moaned deep in her throat.

For someone who was a virgin until a few days ago, Lana knew damn well what she wanted. Though hungry for more ever since that night, he'd worried about pressuring her. Looked like there was no need to hold back.

He traced the shell of her ear with the tip of his tongue. "Want to go inside? We'll have to be quick."

She arched her neck on a sigh. "I can do quick."

Giggling, they hurried up the stairs. He kicked the front door shut and lifted her against it, gripping her hips. Like a horny spider woman, she wrapped her arms and legs around him and kissed him breathless. Her hot, questing tongue and hungry mewls fired his blood. She tugged his shirt up, bunching it at his armpits.

"That's not gonna work, babe."

"I want your skin against mine." The hunger in her voice was undeniable.

Still holding her aloft, he pivoted toward the sofa, deposited her there, and unbuttoned his Hawaiian shirt, quickly shedding it and the Henley beneath.

Lana stripped off her sweater and shucked her jeans, then rose on her knees and, with a sexy grunt, wrestled his belt open, yanked his zipper down, and drew out his cock. "There you are, gorgeous," she murmured. She brushed her lips over the aching tip, then sucked it deep into her mouth, her sharp nails clutching his bare ass.

Pleasure nearly stopped his heart—the silken slide of her tongue, the urgent pull that tightened his balls. He hissed through clenched teeth and tumbled her back onto the sofa cushions. Dropping to his knees, he stripped her panties off and buried his face between her thighs. She was so wet for him, her folds plump and slick. Holding her squirming body with one hand on her stomach, he lapped and nibbled, then gently scraped his teeth over her swollen clit. She bucked her hips and moaned. God, her sounds, her taste, her velvet pussy and silken skin fired him with pulsing need.

He thrust a finger into her tight channel and crooked it, searching for the magic spot that made her jolt. Her eyes flew open on a gasp.

Grinning, he rubbed his cheek against the satin of her inner thigh. "You still sore, ku'u ipo?"

"No." She was panting now, mouth wide open. "I need you inside me. Please, Jojo."

Masculine pride filled his chest at the sight and sound and taste of his woman begging for his cock. But he knew he wouldn't last long, so he licked her with broad strokes of his tongue until he was sure she lay trembling on the edge, then reared up and notched the swollen head at her entrance. Supporting his weight on one arm, he sank into her tight, wet heat. God, she was glorious, the firm grip of her thighs around his hips, the tight clutch of her hands on his lats, the sweet welcome of her pussy. Being inside Lana felt like heaven—like home.

He pumped in and out in measured strokes, battling the urge to race toward climax. He needed to get her there first, needed her to feel how much he treasured her, how much more than physical their connection was. Holding her gaze, he reached his thumb between them, searching for her clit. With a gasp, Lana squeezed her eyes shut, flung her head back, and shouted his name. Her inner walls fluttered around his cock. At last, he surrendered to cresting pleasure, fucking her fast and hard until his climax burst like a million blazing stars.

Gulping air, he lowered onto his elbows, his sweaty chest pressed to her soft breasts. Skin to skin, gasping in sync, grinning like happy goofs—this was how he wanted to stay forever.

She stroked his scalp. "Thanks. That helped immensely."

"Nerves all gone?"

Her throaty laughter shook her belly. "You melted my nerves, my bones, my muscles..."

"Your heart?"

"Yeah." She kissed him. "You're amazing." Another sweet kiss. "Wonderful." Yet another. "A beautiful beast."

The words "I love you" pounded in his chest and nearly escaped his throat, but he held them back, sensing it would be too much just before meeting his family. He'd wait until the time was right. He had Lana in his arms, and he had her trust. The rest would fall into place.

# Chapter Thirteen

Giggling, Lana clasped Jojo's hand as they trotted down the steep slope of 31st Street toward his parents' house. He'd had to park way uphill, since his relatives had already claimed every parking spot within two blocks.

"Everyone will know why we're late to the party." She'd checked and rechecked her clothes and repaired her braid, unraveled by their frantic quickie, but her giddy grin refused to be tamed.

Sex with Jojo left her buzzing with energy, like someone had turned up the volume on all the good stuff—the salty scent of the Sound, the cool breeze on her cheeks, the shimmering colors of flowerbeds and autumn leaves.

He squeezed her hand. "Down there on the left."

Colorful balloons bobbed from the gateposts on the two-story butter yellow house with white trim. A "Happy Birthday Jojo" banner fluttered above the wide porch—not unlike the nervous flutter in her stomach.

"Gorgeous house." Expensive, too, like all the houses in the Proctor District, especially ones with this kind of view.

He opened the wooden gate and motioned her through. "My parents worked damn hard to afford this place. Still do."

At the top of the stairs, he squeezed her hands and sucked in a deep breath. *Yikes!* He was just as nervous as she was. "You ready to meet the fam?"

*Nope, not really.* She grinned up at him. "Let's do it."

His lips twitched, then he threw back his head and laughed, a deep, sexy rumble that loosened anxiety's claws.

"Ku'u ipo, we just did it." He smooched her lips. "And you were magnificent."

When he opened the door, a cacophony of voices and laughter drifted out, along with a rich, meaty scent that made her stomach growl.

Jojo sniffed and grinned. "Kalua pork, Dad's specialty. Wait till you taste it."

"Your dad's Hawaiian too?"

"No, but he learned to cook Hawaiian food when he and Mom were dating. Said it helped charm her family. Must've worked, because the ohana love him."

He led her to the back of the house where a tall, dark-skinned man with a shaved head bent over the kitchen island. So this is where Jojo got his powerful build—Mr. Williams must have a hard time fitting those broad shoulders through doorways.

The large, sunny room buzzed with activity—people coming and going, chopping and slicing, snatching bites and getting their hands swatted by Mrs. Williams.

Jojo boomed, "Hello, fam."

All conversation stilled as a dozen pairs of eyeballs zeroed in on Jojo and Lana's joined hands. Her scalp prickled under their scrutiny.

Then cries of "Jojo" and "birthday boy" rang out.

Jojo's dad wiped his hands on his apron and flashed a dazzling smile. "Well now, this must be Miss Lana. Aloha, sweetheart. Welcome to our home." He hugged her tight, his embrace warm and welcoming despite his imposing size.

Clearly, excellent hugging skills were another Williams family trait.

"Glad to meet you, Mr. Williams."

"Now, now, none of that formal nonsense." He thumped his chest. "I'm Joe, and I think you've already met my wife, Kalea."

"Yes, at Jojo's garage."

Joe laughed. "My boys and their weights. Have you tried one of Kai's nasty protein shakes?"

Jojo guffawed. "Dad, seriously. You think I want to drive her away?" Father and son exchanged back thumps. Then Jojo led her around the room, introducing her to more aunties, uncles, and cousins than she could possibly remember. A pair of squealing kids tackled Jojo, who lifted one in each arm and smooched their cheeks. It was all so freakin' cozy and cute she wanted to cry.

This was what she'd been missing ever since she lost Mom and Dad, this easy camaraderie that came with shared history and blood. With her grandparents gone, her cousins all in eastern Washington, and her odious tías as gatekeepers, losing her parents meant losing this wonderful feeling of belonging.

She sniffed hard to hold back threatening tears while Jojo filled paper cups from a foil pan of Chex Mix and handed one to her.

She nibbled, then wrinkled her nose. "What's that ocean taste?"

"Furikake. It's a Hawaiian thing. It grows on you."

A tall, sturdy woman about Jojo's age wearing a hot-pink Hawaiian shirt, jeans, and flip-flops strode forward with her arms spread wide and gave Jojo a back-slapping hug. "Good to see you, brah. You takin' good care of my car?"

"Of course, sistah." He wriggled from her embrace. "Lana, meet my cousin Mikala. She sold me the Challenger."

"Good to see my baby cousin so happy." She pulled Lana in for yet another hug. Lana giggled, a little uncomfortable but also charmed. She'd missed this too. Her parents were huggers, but her brothers not so much, unless they were hurting or supremely happy. Come to think of it, they'd been more affectionate lately. Was that a good sign or a bad one?

"Auntie," Mikala hollered. "Come see. Jojo has a girlfriend."

"We've met." Mrs. Williams approached, wiping her hands on a kitchen towel. Today she wore a bright floral dress and jeweled flip flops, her dark hair loose with a white plumeria blossom behind her left ear. She set down her towel and crossed her arms, her expression hard to read.

"Bringing a girlfriend home, eh?" She lifted her chin. "That's a big step."

"Yes, ma'am." Jojo tightened his grip on Lana's shoulder. "It is."

Her stern face relaxed into a smile. "Well, that's good." She enfolded Lana in a hug even squishier than Joe's. Lana inhaled her jasmine perfume and sighed with relief.

Over her shoulder, Mrs. Williams called, "Mikala, get me a flower, eh?"

From a basket on the sideboard, Mikala plucked a floral hairpin. The older woman attached it behind Lana's left ear. "Welcome, sweetheart."

"Thank you, Mrs. Williams. You have a beautiful home."

"Pffsht." She waved her hand. "It's Kalea, if you please. You've made quite an impression on our Jojo. I must say, I'm surprised he's set his heart on a young lady with kids to look after."

Her intense scrutiny made Lana squirm. "Yeah, I come with a lot of baggage."

Jojo fixed his mom with a narrow-eyed glare. "Leo and Pedro are not baggage, Ma. They're good kids."

She raised her palms. "I'm sure they are."

Joe called, "Dearest, come help me shred the pork." Kalea moved to his side, and the couple huddled over the pan of meat, whispering and throwing glances in Jojo and Lana's direction.

Her throat tightened. Kalea's disapproval of her family situation could be a major obstacle to their budding relationship. Not that she blamed her. In the older woman's place, she'd worry too.

Flashing a tense grin, she hooked her arm through Jojo's and whispered, "Can we go outside?"

"Sure." He led her onto the deck, which offered a magnificent view of the Puget Sound. After greeting several cousins sprawled on deck chairs and love seats, two more cousins working the grill, and a half-dozen kids chasing each other around the lawn, he brought her to a bench hidden between overgrown rhododendron bushes.

For a few minutes, they enjoyed the silence and the view. Jojo scooped her legs across his lap and gently massaged her calves.

She leaned onto his shoulder. "Did you already tell them?"

"About quitting Bangers? Not yet."

"Your mom will think I'm trapping you into something you're not ready for."

He pressed a kiss to her temple. "It's not a reflection on you, ku'u ipo. She's just being a mama bear. For all practical purposes, Kai and I haven't really left the nest yet. We're over here all the time."

She leaned into his caress. "That's not a bad thing. I wish I had a family like yours."

He waggled his eyebrows. "Play your cards right, and you will."

Her whole body stiffened.

"Too soon, huh? Okay, I'll tell Mikala not to hide your engagement ring in the birthday cake."

Wide-eyed and slack-jawed, she gawked up at him.

His lips twitched.

"You rat!" She socked his arm. "That's not funny."

"It was, though, just a little." He kissed her nose. "You shoulda seen your face."

How could she be mad it him when he was so damn cute and playful?

He pulled her all the way onto his lap. "Ma will come around. And it's not like we're rushing into anything. I'm just helping my beautiful, amazing girlfriend by hanging out with her brothers in the evenings until she figures out her next step. I can help them with their homework, maybe train a little, kick their asses at Minecraft…"

"Minecraft? More like Mortal Kombat. Those boys will splatter your avatar all over the screen." She snuggled into his chest.

Up on the deck, someone banged a pot. "Time to eat."

Everyone trooped up to the deck, where the feast was laid out on a line of folding tables. Jojo handed her a platter-sized paper plate. "First thing, Dad's kalua pig."

"From a hole in the ground?"

Joe laughed, a deep, booming sound just like his son's. "From the oven." He clapped Jojo's shoulder. "Sorry, son. Your mother vetoed another hole in her lawn." He gestured with his fork. "Lean meat on this platter, fatty meat on that one."

Grinning, Jojo helped himself to fatty meat. "I'll train it off tomorrow."

Lana followed suit and whispered, "We'll train it off tonight."

Jojo groaned. "You're killing me."

One of the grill chef cousins stepped between them. "Try the huli huli chicken. It's so good, you'll want to leave Jojo and come home with me."

Jojo snorted. "Nice try, Noa."

Lana eyed the platter of glossy, burnished chicken thighs. "I don't know, Jojo. This is mighty tempting."

He pressed a hand to his forehead and struck a comical wounded pose.

"Just kidding." She smooched his cheek, then filled the rest of her plate with macaroni salad, rice, and green salad.

Jojo bypassed the salad.

His mom closed in, hands on her hips. "See? They move out, and they stop eating their veggies."

In line behind them, Kai protested, "I put veggies in my smoothies."

Kalea smacked his arm. "You need to *chew* your veggies. Take some salad." She elbowed Lana. "Boys. Am I right?"

She wasn't wrong. Leo and Pedro had to be prodded to eat anything green. But they'd love this grilled pineapple.

One of Jojo's aunties handed her a plastic cup of punch. "Hawaiian rum," she said with a saucy grin. "Drink enough of this and you won't need hula lessons. Keu a ka' ono."

"Means bon appétit." Jojo pointed to a picnic table where several cousins his age beckoned. For the next hour, they shared easy laughter, delicious food, and probably a little too much rum punch, which turned down the volume on her jitters. As guest of honor, Jojo fielded a steady stream of greetings, hugs, and good wishes, along with raids on his plate by an adorable toddler who "snuck" to their table on tiptoe and stole potato chips. When he finally seized the giggling child with a roar, held her upside-down, and blew raspberries on her plump tummy, Lana's heart melted into a puddle of goo.

After dinner, Kai called dibs on Lana for a rowdy game of volleyball.

"No fair," Jojo protested when her team trounced his. "You're a ringer."

She smirked and poked his ribs. "Star libero on my high school team."

Kai hooted. "Jojo's too distracted by luuurrrve!"

"Jealous, much?" After blotting his glistening brow with paper towels, Jojo slung his arm around her and strolled to the back fence, which was the perfect height to lean on and drink in the view. The setting sun burnished the Sound to rose gold and darkened the wooded islands and headlands. In the surrounding trees, paper lanterns and strings of party lights flickered on, echoing the sky's soft glow. Out on the Sound, a sturdy little tugboat nudged a huge container ship toward the port. Pleasure craft dotted the water, their white sails blushing pink as this amazing day drew to a close.

Jojo hugged her tight and rested his cheek against the top of her head. "Autumn goes out in a blaze of glory, eh?"

Cozy and content, she patted his chest. "Big muscles, big heart, and a poet too. You've got it all, Jojo."

He gave her a sweet, boyish grin. "If I've got you, then I've got it all." He winced and dragged a hand over his mouth. "Sorry, that was pretty cheesy."

She nuzzled beneath his chin. "Good thing I love cheese."

"Thank God." He kissed her forehead. "And see? The fam loves you."

"Your family is great. I hope they don't change their minds about me once you drop the bomb." Was it just the cool evening breeze, or did a tickle of warning prick her skin? Moments like this were too good to last.

Over the wooded hills on the other side of the bay, the sun's rays flared, then dimmed.

Jojo's mom called from the porch "Come on, lovebirds. Time for cake."

Jojo felt Lana stiffen in his arms. "Are you going to tell them now?"

Damn it, she was still spooked. He'd miscalculated badly. He figured she deserved to hear his offer before anyone else, but waiting to see how his parents would take the news—well, that was a lot to ask of someone who'd just lost her safety net. And Mama's frosty reception didn't help. Eventually, Lana would come to understand how similar she and his mother were—both worriers, both fiercely protective of family.

He pressed a kiss to the top of Lana's head. "I'll tell them after the cake."

Mama and Auntie Kanani, her older sister, came onto the deck with a blazing cake and platter of haupia, his favorite Hawaiian dessert. His cousin Noa strummed his ukulele, Auntie Maile shook her ulu'ulis, the little kids clacked pū'ili sticks, and everyone sang *Hau'oli Lā Hānau*, a Hawaiian birthday song

"Aww, guys, you're the best." He made a wish involving Lana, a large bed, and privacy, then blew out the candles.

"Birthday boy eats first." Dad served him and Lana piña colada cake and haupia.

"What's this?" She whispered, pointing to the wiggly white square on her plate.

"Kind of a cross between coconut pudding and Jello. Try it."

She took a bite and moaned her approval.

"Speech, speech!" Kai called.

"Have you set a date?" one of the girl cousins added.

Her mouth full of cake, Lana made a choking sound.

Jojo raised his palms. "Woah now, pump the brakes, sistah."

Everyone laughed—even Lana.

He snarfed up the last of his dessert and set down his plate. Hopefully, the birthday cake's good juju would carry him through this part. He sucked in a deep breath and faced his family.

"Mahalo nui loa, everyone. I couldn't ask for a better ohana." He swiped a hand over his damp forehead. "Thirty, wow. Feels like an important milestone."

Kai hooted. "Time to sign up for AARP."

Jojo pointed at his chucklehead brother. "You're right behind me, brah. But seriously, turning thirty is a good time to reflect on where my life is going."

Cousin Mikala yelled, "He's totally gonna propose."

Lana's fork clattered to the ground.

He steadied her with one arm and forced an affable grin. "In front of all of you? Think again."

"You okay?" he whispered.

Her nostrils flared, but she gave a tight nod.

He cleared his throat. "Anyway, I've decided it's time to—how did you put it, Dad? Pick a horse instead of trying to ride the whole damn stable."

To Lana, he murmured, "Dad loves cowboy movies."

"Yippee kay yay!" yelled one of the cousins. Everyone laughed.

Jojo laced his fingers through Lana's. "So I'm quitting my job at Bangers."

The reaction was mixed—applause from older relatives and moans of disappointment from younger ones. Mama and Dad exchanged whispers.

"From now on, I'll concentrate on building my personal training business." He fished a stack of business cards from his shirt pocket. "Got a website and everything. So tell your friends, eh?"

He answered Lana's questioning glance. "Charlie set it up for me." He handed her a card and gave the rest to one of the tween cousins. "Pass those out for me, bud."

Auntie Kanani took one with a shrug, tucked it into her bra, and clapped her hands. "Let's go, girls. Time for your dance."

*Okay then, not such a big deal.* Relief dropped Jojo's shoulders back to their normal position—until he turned and bonked right into Mama, who'd planted herself in his path.

She scowled at his business card, a deep worry line etched between her eyebrows. "Are you quitting your hospital job too?"

He hurried to reassure her. "Not until I build up my client roster. That'll take some time."

Mama's frown deepened. Lana worried her lower lip with her teeth. This was heading south fast.

He clasped his mother's shoulders. "Don't worry, I'll always have my phlebotomy job as a backup."

"Why now?" Dad asked.

His heart hammered his ribs. *Keep cool. Smile. You got this.*

"Like I said, I'm thirty. Time to pick a lane, and"—he laced his fingers through Lana's—"Lana needs my help."

Talk about deer in the headlights. She froze under his parents' scrutiny, wide-eyed and pale.

Mama folded her arms. "That's an enormous responsibility, son. You sure you're ready for that?"

Jojo recognized the steel glinting behind her soft tone. He was tiptoeing through a minefield now. Not that he needed his parents' permission to do the right thing, but alienating them would make this harder on everyone, especially Lana.

"Yes, ma'am. I'm ready." He squeezed Lana's shoulder, and she gazed up at him with a wavery smile.

Dad huffed. "You two are serious, then."

*I sure as hell am.* He smiled down at Lana and lifted an eyebrow.

His brave little warrior raised her chin. "Jojo is a wonderful man. I can't believe he's willing to do this for me, but I'm grateful."

Dad clapped Jojo's shoulder. "Ohana is the most important thing." He gave Lana a fond smile. "That means family."

Mama harrumphed. "More like hānai."

Jojo explained, "That means adopted family." He faced parents. "And that's just as important."

Mama dropped her gaze and took a big breath. "Yes, it is." She kissed Jojo's cheek, then Lana's. "You're a grown man, Jojo, and it's your decision. But we're always here if things don't work out." Arm in arm, she and Dad moved away to chat with the aunties and uncles.

Jojo drew Lana toward the tall hedges, away from the others. "Well, that was ninety percent not awful."

She gave his arm a playful punch. "I'd say fifteen percent terrifying."

Noa stepped up, because, of course, someone had to interrupt. The Kama-Williams clan had no concept of privacy. "What was that about?" He shot a sideways glance toward Mama and Dad.

"I'm quitting my Bangers job to help Lana take care of her brothers. It's just the three of them, and their hānai grandparents can't help anymore."

"Huh." Noa tilted his head. "So you guys are moving in together?"

His cousin's nosy question ignited a glow in Jojo's chest. How sweet would that be—waking up each morning with Lana's soft body nestled against him, her silky hair spread over the pillow.

He squeezed her hand. Oops—she'd gone bug-eyed again.

"No, nothing like that. I'm just hanging with the boys while Lana works."

"Cool." Noa turned to Lana. "He's good with kids. The little cousins are always climbing him like a jungle gym. Hey, show's starting." He ambled toward seats set up facing the deck.

Alone again, Jojo hugged Lana and massaged her stiff back muscles until he felt her relax a little. "See? That went fine."

"I'm not so sure," she muttered into his chest. "Everyone's looking at me funny."

"Nah, that's just their nosy normal. They're not used to seeing me with a girlfriend."

"Come on. I've seen you leaving Bangers with women."

There she went, tensing up again. If he wasn't the guest of honor, he'd sneak off somewhere and give her some real stress relief.

"Sure, I've had lady friends, but I never brought one home." He bent down and pressed a kiss to her tight lips. "Because none of them were special to my heart." He kissed her again, light, teasing brushes that loosened her scowl. "But you are, Lana."

She nestled into his hold, but her voice still wavered. "This is moving so fast."

"What do you mean, fast?" He'd given up his job, introduced her to his family, and she still wasn't convinced? He threw up his hands. "Since the day you came to Bangers, I've been dropping hints like the Easter Bunny drops eggs. When you lost your parents—well, I couldn't approach you after that."

Her liquid gaze met his, gleaming with emotion. "But you wanted to?

He brushed a stray tendril of hair behind her ear. "Every. Single. Day."

The corners of her lips quirked up. "I wish you'd told me."

"Have you met you?" He waved his hand in front of her chest. "You've got this force field. Major defensive vibes. For a while, I even thought..." He spluttered to a standstill.

She arced an eyebrow. "You thought what?"

His cheeks flushed hot. "That maybe you weren't into guys? But Rosie set me straight."

Her eyebrow crept even higher. "You've been talking to Rosie about me?"

"She knows you better than anyone, right? We both love you, and we want you to be happy, and..."

Lana clutched his shirt. "Wait, you love me?"

Groaning, Jojo pinched the bridge of his nose. "Shit. That wasn't supposed to happen tonight."

"Excuse me?" Now she sounded pissed.

Frustration tightened his throat. Why couldn't he explain in a way that made sense? "I wanted a romantic setting," he spluttered. "Somewhere private with atmosphere, a table for two, fancy food, music."

The sound of a ukulele floated from the porch.

He shook his head. "Well, there you go."

She released his shirt and flattened her palm over his heart.

There was nothing for it but to finish what he'd started. He cupped her face in both hands. Her gaze met his, wide-open and unwavering.

"I'm in love with you, Lana Pilar Lopez. Truly, deeply, all the way to my bones. Have been ever since the day you spilled your tray on me and scolded me for being in the way."

Lana's lips formed a perfect O. Her cheeks reddened.

"You remember, eh?"

"I was such a bitch about it." She rubbed slow circles on his chest and bit her lower lip in that sexy way of hers, sharp white teeth and plump pink flesh.

He skimmed his hands down her sides to rest loosely on her hips. "Traditionally, this is the place where you'd say something like, 'I love you too'. Or maybe, 'Don't worry, you haven't made an absolute ass of yourself, you stupid lunk.'"

Lana laid her cheek on his chest. "I was a total snot to you that day. I'm sorry."

He huffed and rested his chin atop her head. "She's avoiding the topic. Not a good sign."

After a long silence, she whispered, "I'm scared."

"Of me?" He slid his fingertips beneath her sweater, skimming the satin skin of her lower back.

"Of believing this could be real."

"Lana, I'm laying my heart wide open in front of my whole family."

She stiffened. "Yikes. They're all watching, aren't they?"

"Most of them. Cousin Kaleo is too busy murdering that ukulele to notice us."

She shivered in his arms. "I've lost so much, Jojo. What if I lose you too?"

"I'm not going anywhere, ku'u ipo. You can count on me." He nuzzled her hair. "Throw me a lifeline. Tell me what you're feeling."

Her voice cracked. "I can't. Not in front of all these people." She raised her glistening eyes to his. "I need that private moment."

Hope flickered, a tiny flame, but enough to warm his body and soul. "I understand."

"Jojo," Kai yelled, "get your ass over here. We're all waiting on you."

He pressed a kiss to her forehead. "We okay, Lana?"

She kissed him back, sweet and lingering. When she broke the kiss, her eyes sparkled. "We're more than okay. We're freakin' magnificent. Let's go watch the show."

Lana followed Jojo to seats reserved for them in the front row of the makeshift backyard theater while a dozen girl cousins and aunties trooped onto the deck. Dressed in tank tops and colorful skirts and draped in leis of flowers and leaves, they giggled and jostled as they took their places. Cousin Noa, the flirty grill chef, strummed his ukulele while the oldest auntie sang in a rich alto voice. The dancers launched into a graceful hula, their hands floating and fluttering like birds as they stepped and swayed in perfect unison. The littlest dancers were so cute they brought tears to Lana's eyes. All this could be hers—the food, the fun, the effortless sense of belonging—if she was brave enough to grasp what Jojo offered her.

Everyone applauded wildly as the performers filed off the "stage," but the tiniest, no more than five, lingered to bow and throw kisses until her dad scooped her under his arm and carried her off. "Unkah Jojo," she squealed as they passed, her little hands starfishing.

"C'mere, punkin'." He gathered her into his arms as two more cousins took the stage, both with guitars, and launched into song. Jojo patiently allowed his tiny cousin to climb onto his shoulders and pat his bald head in time to the music.

Lana's eyes welled up. Every detail of this day was so damn perfect. Would she make it out the door without dissolving into a puddle of tears? Her chances were small and shrinking fast. Who could spend time with this sweet, funny, gentle man and not fall for him?

Another Auntie took the stage to sing a haunting song, illustrating her words with graceful hand and arm movements. Even though Lana couldn't understand the Hawaiian lyrics, the singer's mellow voice painted a picture of longing for someone or someplace deeply loved.

Jojo whispered, "It's about a woman who lost her lover to the sea, so she walks the beach singing to him."

The singer finished her song to loud applause and not a few sniffles. She pressed her palms together over her heart. "Happy birthday, dear Jojo. You're my favorite nephew, you know."

Several men protested.

"Oh, shut up. It's his birthday." She fixed her twinkling gaze on Lana. "Your turn, honey."

She pointed to her chest. "Sorry?"

"We shared our traditions with you. Now you share something with us." She took the nearest guitar and proffered it. Her smile held a teasing edge—and a definite challenge.

"Hey, now," Jojo protested, "don't put her on the spot. You don't have to sing, Lana."

She nibbled her lip. Jojo had just dropped a bomb on his family out of love for her. He gave up a job he loved for her. This woman was giving her a chance to prove herself worthy of his sacrifice. Their approval was worth a moment of embarrassment.

She rose from her seat. "It's okay. I've got this."

"You play?"

"A little." She wiped her sweaty palms on her leggings and climbed the stairs.

"I'm pretty rusty," she admitted as she looped the guitar strap over her shoulders. Actually, she'd barely touched her guitar since her parents died. Too many memories of singing with them.

Her knees wobbled, so she sat on an empty chair and strummed three simple chords, thankful the muscle memory was still there. "This is a song my mother used to sing to us when we were small."

Arrorró, mi niño

Arrorró, mi Sol

Arrorró pedazo

De mi corazón

Her voice wavered at first, but strengthened as she sang the sweet lullaby. So what if she got the verses out of order and missed a few chord changes? The feelings rang true. When she finished to aww's and loud applause, she had the oddest feeling her parents were clapping too.

"What does it mean?" someone asked.

"Let's see. Something like hush-a-bye my baby, hush-a-bye my sun, hush-a-bye oh piece of my heart." Her voice broke, and hot tears spilled down her cheeks. Being here with Jojo's family pried open the tight lid she kept on memories of Mom and Dad. It hurt, but the pain was bittersweet.

Jojo's auntie laid her soft hand on Lana's shoulder. "That's so beautiful."

Misty-eyed, Kalea clasped her hands over her heart. "And you'll sing it to your children one day."

Jojo raised his palms. "Easy, Ma. Don't start shopping for baby clothes just yet."

Everyone laughed, thank goodness.

Jojo stood. "Thanks, everyone, for a truly special day. But I need to get Lana back home."

"You haven't opened your presents!" someone protested.

He dropped back into his chair with a groan.

Lana sat beside him and nudged his shoulder. "Open your presents, ku'u ipo. Did I say it right?"

"Perfectly." He gave her a grateful smile.

Lana reflected as she watched the gift-wrap carnage. Sharing this day with Jojo drove home how much she'd missed family. She felt the loss like a physical ache, a phantom limb. Sure, the Bangers crew was family, but this was different, deeper, the kind of love that persists even if you're mad at each other. The kind you can count on. The kind that, when you lose it, rips your heart to shreds.

A half-hour later, she helped Jojo pack up T-shirts with teasing slogans about getting older, plus miscellaneous musclehead gear, and a new speaker system for his garage gym—a group gift from his cousins. When they loaded the birthday loot into his car, she spotted an overnight bag in the trunk.

He flashed a sheepish grin. "We could go to my place, but Kai and the cousins would descend on us when the older folks get tired of their noise."

Lana desperately needed that private moment he spoke of. In fact, if she didn't get it soon, all this suppressed emotion would burst forth in a hot, seething mess. But guilt poked her. It wasn't right to foist Leo and Pedro on her friends overnight. With their squabbling and noise, the boys could be a handful and a half. And they were her responsibility.

"Let me call Anna real quick."

Anna answered, masculine laughter ringing out behind her. "Don't worry about it," she told Lana. "The boys are great with Ellie. They even helped me clean up after she blew out her diaper. What did they call it?"

"A shit-pocalypse," Pedro yelled.

Lana nibbled her lip. "Are you a hundred percent sure?"

"Of course. The food truck is closed tomorrow. Diego's making breakfast empanadas." Anna lowered her voice. "Now go enjoy your man. Everyone in this house thinks it's about time you two got together. That includes your brothers. They're all, 'Jojo this, Jojo that.' I think they're as gaga for him as you are."

Lana's pulse sped. Whether or not she proclaimed her feelings out loud, she'd already crossed that line. No more protecting Leo and Pedro from the fallout. She glanced over her shoulder at Jojo, waiting patiently for her to decide. More than her body and her time, he craved those three little words. He deserved the truth.

She tucked her phone away and faced him with a nervous smile. "Let's go home."

# Chapter Fourteen

♥

Lana knotted her hands in her lap as Jojo pulled into her driveway. Weird to see her home so quiet and dark. When the boys were home, they left lights blazing and a sonic trail of music and shouts. Tonight, the house was holding its breath—just like her.

No more light and easy. No more telling herself this was just a friendly fling without real consequences. Her confession pulsed in her chest. She had to tell him soon, or she'd burst.

She wove her fingers through Jojo's and gave a weak laugh. "Strange to have the house to ourselves."

His lips pinched in a straight line, Jojo searched her face.

The gravity of this moment tightened her chest. She had the power to hurt him deeply by withholding what he needed to hear, but the words stuck in her throat. Why did this have to be so damn difficult? She should be braver than this, and stronger.

She blew out a breath, then reached for the door handle. "Get your bag, Jojo. This is our private moment. We may not have another one for a long time."

He gave a solemn nod.

As they approached the porch steps, he put his arm around her, and despite his enormous strength, she had the odd feeling he was leaning on her. As she slid her key into the lock, the glow-in-the-dark skeleton leered down at them, its plastic grin mocking her cowardice.

*Mind your business, you undead creep.*

Jojo's hand covered hers, and that warm, comforting touch calmed her jitters a bit. "You want me out before the boys get back?"

She inhaled deeply, letting the cool night air soothe her jangling nerves. "No. I want you here, Jojo."

His lips twitched. "Even if your brothers know we're doing it?"

She huffed a laugh. "They're teen boys. Doing it occupies 95% of their brains at all times, right?"

"Yeah, but not where their sister is concerned." He cupped her cheek, his expression solemn. "Finding me here in the morning means no more pretending we're just friends. Are you ready for that?"

She pressed her hand to his broad chest. "Are you ready for teenage attitude and stupid jokes? And stinky socks on the living room floor? And gobbling all the good snacks before you even get a bite?"

His smile widened, as luminous as the moon. "I'm ready for all of it, Lana. And not just because I want you." His hands skimmed down to her hips and snugged her close. "I care about you and the boys. I want to be there for you."

Grinning, she propped her chin on his chest. "I want the same for you, Jojo. And I don't like the idea of kicking you out of bed at the butt crack of dawn. Besides,"—she skated her fingertips over his pecs—"you're damn hard to wake up."

He chuckled. "Ma used to dump ice water on me to get me up in time for school."

That intriguing tickle at the back of her brain flared to life. She hadn't planned on asking him this—in fact, until this moment, she'd dismissed the idea as too outrageous to consider. But he'd offered her the perfect opening, and for once, she switched off her doom-spinning mind and listened to her gut.

"If you're going to spend every night with the boys, maybe you could, you know, just stay here?"

He drew his head back and blinked rapidly. "You mean, like, move in?"

Her heart thundered. Clearly, Jojo wasn't ready for this level of intimacy. Had she lost her freakin' mind?

"I mean, if you want to," she spluttered. "You could go back to your place whenever you get tired of our noise. But we've got room in the garage for your weights and equipment, and—"

Eyes bright and sharp, he gripped her shoulders. "Lana, does this mean you love me?"

Why was she so tongue-tied around him? What happened to unflinching Lana who said what needed to be said?

"For Chrissakes, why else would I trust you with my brothers? I even let you into my treehouse." Her voice wobbled. "This is hard for me to say, because saying it means I stand to lose everything. Again. Do you get how terrifying that is?"

He gave a slow nod and whisked a tear from her cheek with his thumb.

Beneath her palm, his heart hammered, just like hers.

Waves of heat and cold raced over her skin, but she filled her lungs and pushed out the truth. "I love you, Jojo Makoa Williams. Being with you makes me happy. You're so kind, and funny, and gentle, and beautiful, and sexy, and—" She knew she was rambling but couldn't stop the cascade of words. "And the boys adore you, and your family is great, and I think if we try, we really could—"

Her feet left the ground as Jojo lifted her in a bear hug and kissed her breathless. Shifting her weight onto his massive thigh, he fumbled for the doorknob and murmured against her lips, "If you don't want to shock your neighbors, you better open this door."

She turned the key and they tumbled over the threshold.

Off balance, he lurched across the room and collided with the bookshelves. Her volleyball trophy clattered to the floor.

"Don't worry about it." She kissed the broad column of his throat, then tongued his earlobe.

"I'm not worried about anything but you." Still holding her aloft, he tried to peel off her sweater but only succeeded in bunching it at her armpits. With a frustrated growl, he set her on her feet and pressed her to the wall, his erection hard against her belly.

A thrill shot through her at seeing this powerful man rendered clumsy by lust. She wanted to tease him and pleasure him and make him feel as wild and reckless as she felt in his arms. She pulled back and, holding his fevered gaze, tugged her sweater over her head and tossed it toward the couch.

Jojo unfastened her bra, then crouched to lick and suckle her breasts. His hungry grunts and moans sent sparks sizzling across her skin. Kneeling at her feet, he peeled off her leggings and panties, then caressed and kissed his way up her legs. Her core pulsed with need and anticipation. Grasping her calf, he draped her thigh over his shoulder and dove in, his strong fingers digging into the flesh of her ass while his tongue drove her mad with licks and swirls and flicks, stoking her pleasure until climax slammed her in a vortex of bliss and heat and love for this amazing man.

When she came to, she found herself clutching the bookcase with one hand and stroking his soft scalp with the other. His cheek rested against her thigh as he murmured sweet nothings into her pussy. The sight was so cute and comical she couldn't help laughing. "You're so good at this. My coochie thanks you."

Chuckling, he stripped off his shirt, used it to wipe his glistening mouth, then tossed it away to land on a lamp across the room. He unfastened his jeans, then rose to his feet and kicked them off too. The brush of his bare chest and belly against her sensitized skin set off aftershocks of bliss.

He clasped her face between his giant paws and kissed her deeply. She tasted her arousal on his tongue.

When he broke the kiss, desire simmered in his eyes. "I'm in love. Your pleasure means everything to me, Lana."

Her sex throbbed, aching to be filled. With a feral growl, she clutched his back and swirled her tongue over his dark, flat nipples.

Chuckling, he stripped the elastic from her braid and teased the strands loose. "Hungry, ku'u ipo?"

"Ravenous." She rubbed her breasts over the broad expanse of his chest. "I love your skin, your strength, your beautiful body, your soulful eyes, your goofy jokes, your neon car, your noisy family, your big, big heart..." She peppered him with praise and greedy kisses.

His strong fingers dug into the flesh of her ass as he lifted her again and pressed her to the wall. His weight and heat intoxicated her.

"I've waited so long to hear you say that." He kissed her, sweeping his tongue into her mouth on a hungry moan. The fat head of his cock prodded her entrance. "My Lana." He slid in a few inches, his girth stretching her deliciously. "My angel." A few inches more. His eyes drifted half-closed.

She drank in every detail as pleasure loosened his features, wishing she could slide beneath his skin to feel what he felt.

With a deep, slow push, he filled her completely. His head lolled back on a groan as his cock plunged in and out in measured thrusts, drawing out the experience to keep them both on the edge.

"You feel so good, ku'u ipo. I want to stay like this always."

"I want that too. God, I love to feel you moving inside me." She clutched him, arms tight around his neck, thighs gripping his hips. He thrust in to the hilt, and she rotated her hips, pulling a moan from his corded throat.

"My beautiful man, my love."

He groaned and sped his movements.

"That's right, love. Fuck me deep and hard." It felt so freeing, so exhilarating to relinquish control and give voice to every filthy thought. Pleasure and power tangoed through her body, spinning her higher and higher.

Jojo's grip on her hips tightened. Deep inside her, his cock grew even thicker, harder. "Angel, I can't...oh sweet Jesus. Touch yourself."

The savage rasp in his voice shot like lightning straight to her core. Obeying his command, she slid two fingers between them and ground her clit in tight circles. Pleasure coiled low in her belly, ready to burst. "I'm so close. Let yourself go."

With a groan, he captured her mouth, devouring her with teeth and tongue while his cock pistoned in and out. Climax blazed through her, wracking her in spasms of bliss. Eyes shut tight, mouth gasping, she keened her joy. Jojo stiffened, then shuddered as wet heat flooded her.

Primal delight glowed in her breast. She did this. She rode her man until he lost control. He was hers, and she was his.

Lana was a mermaid, her ebony hair floating on sapphire currents, her sinuous lower half encased in sparkling scales that scratched his thighs deliciously as she slid down, down, down until her lips closed on his aching cock, sucking him into wet heat. Jojo gasped, clutching at ropes of kelp, struggling to stay rooted in this sweet, sensual dream. But wakefulness tugged, stronger than a riptide, pulling him back to the surface.

His eyes flew open on a gasp. His hands clutched sheets, not seaweed, and Lana's dark head bobbed between his outstretched thighs.

She lay curled up on the edge of the mattress, one hand stroking his thigh, the other cupping his balls. The scratch of her nails and velvet caress of her tongue nearly levitated him off the bed.

"God, Lana," he croaked.

She released his cock with a champagne-cork pop and grinned up at him. "Good morning. Found a way to wake you up without ice water."

He fisted a handful of her hair. "Please don't stop."

"I won't." Giggling, she swirled her tongue around the head of his cock. "No mercy for you, big boy."

Pleasure built fast, a glowing pulse at the base of his spine. His balls tightened. His belly and leg muscles jolted. "Wait." Rising on one elbow, he tugged on her hair. "I want to make you feel good too."

Sexy devilry danced in her dark eyes. "Tonight." She gave his cock a languid lick. "Right now, I'm a little sore."

Too far gone to protest, he dropped back onto the pillow and let her work her magic as she licked and sucked him to a swift climax.

When the delicious shudders subsided, he lay panting, spent and glowing and so filled with love for her he feared his skin would burst, too fragile to contain this enormous, intoxicating feeling. He pulled her into his arms and kissed her deep and hard, then released her with an apologetic laugh. "Sorry, morning breath."

Her giggle was so damn cute. "Wow, I guess I really am in love." She kissed him again, then wrinkled her nose. "Yeah, gotta get some mints for the nightstand."

He rained kisses over her face and throat and beautiful naked breasts.

"Jojo, we can't spend all day in bed." She wriggled from his grasp. "The boys are on their way with breakfast empanadas, and if we don't get out of bed, they'll eat them all." She smooched his nose. "I mean, I love you, but empanadas..." She vaulted from the mattress and trotted toward the bathroom, her ass cheeks jiggling enticingly.

Jojo propped himself up on his elbow. "Are you a hundred percent sure you're ready for them to see me here?"

She popped her head through the door, a toothbrush in her hand. "Well, you should put some clothes on first, but yeah." She blew him a kiss. "Let's make it official."

With a whoop of delight, he rolled out of bed, ran to the bathroom, and wrapped his arms around her from behind, lifting her off the floor. "I adore you, Queen Lana, bringer of light and love and beauty and blowjobs. I am your humble servant. I kowtow before you." He set her down and fell to one knee because there wasn't enough space in the tiny room for a proper prostration.

Laughing merrily, she flicked him with her towel. "Where did this flowery language come from?"

"That medieval game Pedro likes. I was Sir Stabsalot." He kissed his way up her legs, then stood, scratching his bare belly. "Do I have time to shower before they get here?"

She smacked his ass. "Go wash off the sex funk. I'll set the table."

Fifteen minutes later, the front door slammed open, and the boys tumbled into the kitchen where he and Lana were already at the breakfast table drinking coffee and nibbling cantaloupe. Jojo's stomach tightened. He forced his shoulders down and his jaw to relax. Despite Lana's reassurances, he worried they would resent him as an interloper in their tight-knit little family.

Pedro's eyes widened, then he grinned and poked Leo's ribs. "Told ya."

"Nah, man. I told you. Morning, lovebirds." Leo set down a foil pan and peeled back the lid. A cloud of savory steam escaped.

Pedro grabbed a slice of melon. "You staying here now, Jojo?"

He glanced at Lana for guidance, but she just smiled and bit into an empanada.

He cleared his throat. "Would it be okay with you if I do? At least until we figure out a plan going forward."

A long silence fell in the little kitchen. He was sure they all heard the hammering of his heart. Leo and Pedro conducted a silent conversation of squints and bugged-out eyes, raised eyebrows and splayed fingers—communicating in that almost telepathic connection siblings shared, just like him and Kai.

Jojo's gut twisted. What had he and Lana been thinking? He couldn't move in here and upset their family's rhythm. Of course, the boys would resent him.

Finally, Pedro sucked in a deep breath. "Will you guys be moving into Mom and Dad's room?"

"That's a big step." She rubbed Jojo's knee. "We'll decide together when it's time. All of us."

Pedro exhaled and visibly relaxed. "Cool. Hey, Jojo, wanna play Death's Dungeon?"

He dropped his head back and laughed, feeling the tension melt away. No way had he expected such a nonchalant reaction. "After breakfast, I'm moving some stuff over here. Want to help?"

Leo grumbled under his breath, but Pedro smacked his brother's arm and grinned. "Sure. We're glad to help."

The boys grabbed empanadas and left, and soon the sound of clanging swords and blood-curdling screams drifted from the living room.

Jojo collapsed back in his chair. "For a minute there, I thought they were gonna tell me to pack sand."

Lana massaged his shoulder. "My brothers are crazy about you. They're too teenage cool to jump up and down about it." Her smile flattened. "Oh, but what about Kai? Will he be okay with this?"

Jojo rubbed his chin. "Yeah, this leaves him without a room-mate to share the rent. I'll cover my half until he finds some-one. Hey, can I help with the rent here?"

"What rent? Mom and Dad's insurance paid off the mort-gage." She squeezed his biceps. "But there are a lot of little jobs you could help with around the house. The back gate sticks, the porch paint is peeling—"

He laughed again, awash in relief and gratitude. "Mr. Fix-it at your service."

"What happened to Sir Stabsalot?"

"I'm a man of many skills." With a growl, he yanked her chair closer and kissed her neck.

"I've noticed." Giggling, she pushed him off. "Now, eat your breakfast. You're going to need your strength." She waggled her eyebrows, a lusty promise sparkling in her eyes.

"Am I, now?" He helped himself to one of Diego's excellent empanadas, stuffed with fluffy eggs, melty cheese, and spicy chorizo. Simply heaven, sharing breakfast with his playful, saucy women in her—now their—sunny kitchen, so much nicer than the grubby one he shared with Kai. This was more than he'd hoped for, and he would do whatever it took to make Lana glad she gambled on him.

After breakfast, Lana showered, and Jojo joined the boys in the living room just in time to see Leo gut Pedro's dragon in an explosion of CGI gore.

"Hey," he asked. "Do you guys have a pocketknife?"

"What for?"

His cheeks flushed. "I want to carve our initials into the tree out front. It's Lana's special place, and I thought..." Okay, so it was a corny idea, but his dad had carved his and Mom's initials into the big locust tree in their backyard, and Mom still got misty-eyed when she rubbed that memento.

The brothers stared at him, then at each other. They burst into laughter.

His cheeks heated. "Kinda lame, huh?"

"Nah, man, it's romantic," Pedro said, "but don't you know that's bad for the tree? C'mere." He led Jojo down the hall to his bedroom, where a desk was covered with art supplies and half-finished comic book panels.

Jojo's eyebrows shot up. "Impressive artwork." Clearly, he had a lot to learn about these two.

Pedro dug his toe into the carpet, but his proud grin belied the humble gesture. "I like to draw. Go ahead, take some Sharpies. Draw something in the treehouse. It's our family tradition."

Jojo blinked hard, touched to his core by the kid's welcome gift. "I'm not much of an artist."

"Doesn't matter, man." He thumped his skinny chest. "Draw what's in your heart."

Well then. Looks like Lana wasn't the only member of the Lopez family who had something to teach him. Dad always said things happen for a reason, even if we mere mortals can't see it. Maybe God brought Lana and these boys into his life to teach him about love and family.

Armed with a pocketful of Sharpies, he climbed the ladder and drew his initials and Lana's on the treehouse wall, then surrounded them with a multi-colored heart. Simple but pretty, an appropriate gesture to mark the start of their new life together.

He folded his arms on the half wall and gazed out at the street below, lined with mature maples, elms, and chestnut trees in full autumn glory. A trio of kids rode by on skateboards, followed by a galumphing shaggy dog. Would their own kids play in this treehouse one day? Would they trick or treat down there? Grinning, he sank into rosy dreams of a future with Lana.

# Chapter Fifteen

♥

"If Lana says no, it's no." Jojo toed off his Crocs and propped his aching feet on the coffee table. After a long, rough day at the clinic plus two new training clients, the last thing he needed was a fight. But no sooner had he opened the front door than the boys cornered him, bearing offerings of over-cooked frozen pizza and Dr. Pepper. Clearly, Leo had been appointed spokesperson. Pedro watched the debate, chewing on a cuticle and bouncing nervously on his toes.

Leo screwed up his face into a childish pout. "But if it were up to you—"

Jojo felt for the kid, but he remembered well the stupid shit he and his jock friends perpetrated down on Ruston Way, a stretch of waterfront road that attracted cruisers, potheads, and muscle car enthusiasts. Those parties featured promi-nently in his personal high school greatest hits reel, but if he let the kids go and Lana found out—

Of course she'd find out. Her eagle eyes didn't miss a trick, and he'd never risk losing her trust, especially now when they were just settling into their new shared life.

"C'mon Jojo, be cool," Leo pleaded. "You were our age not long ago. All my teammates will be there."

He raised his palms. "I remember what those kegger parties were like. Almost got busted more than once. When I think about my parents having to come bail me out..." He shook his head. "No way am I putting Lana in that position."

Leo's pitch rose to nails-on-a-chalkboard level. "She doesn't have to know."

He gave the kid his best stern bouncer glare. "I'm not betraying your sister's trust. You know what's at stake. One screw-up, and you two end up a hundred miles apart in eastern Washington."

Pedro broke his silence. "But Haley will—Argh!" He knotted his fingers in his hair. "You're not our dad, Jojo. You can't just move in here and start giving orders."

He winced. So much hung on this crucial conflict. He leaned forward, elbows on knees, hands clasped, and carefully wiped all signs of irritation from his face. "Look, I get it. You're almost grown men, both of you, and it sucks not being able to do what you want when you want. But know this—I'm not trying to replace your dad. No one can ever do that."

Pedro glared through tear-bright eyes. "That's right, you can't. So don't try."

Leo grasped his brother's arm, his sharp-eyed expression clashing with his soothing tone. "Easy, bro. There will be other parties. Let's watch *Fear Street*."

"But we—"

"I'll make the popcorn. Come help me." He tugged his little brother into the kitchen.

Jojo blew out a breath and pressed his palms to his eyes. He knew damn well this fight wasn't over, but at least they'd got through the first skirmish without bloodshed.

Returning a few minutes later with a brimming bowl of popcorn, the boys settled into their beanbag chairs to watch their gory pick of the night. They even passed Jojo the popcorn. With a grin of relief, he stuffed a handful into his face. Maybe this parenting gig wasn't really that hard after all.

A cozy glow filled his chest as he watched the brothers mock the characters on the screen and toss kernels at each other's heads. What would his and Lana's kids look like? They'd be lucky to have these two as uncles.

During a slow point in the movie, Pedro pivoted and propped his folded arms on the coffee table. "Jojo, how do you get a girl to like you?"

"That depends on the girl. Are we talking about your girlfriend from the football game?"

Pedro's brows drew together. "She's not my girlfriend anymore, since you guys caught us, you know, doing the deed. She blames me for ruining her first time. I told her Kenny's heart attack wasn't my fault, but—"

"But sneaking her into the house behind Kenny's back was."

Pedro dropped his chin onto his arms. "We figured since Kenny missed his ten o'clock check in, he'd fallen asleep." The inner corners of his brows drew up. "I love her, man. How do I convince her to give me a second chance?"

Jojo leaned over and rubbed the kid's shoulder. "I don't know Haley, so I can't answer that. But patience is a good start. Why don't you write to her? Tell her how sorry you are, how much she means to you. Let her read it in private and think it over."

Pedro brightened. "Yeah, a love letter. And maybe a ring?"

Jojo laughed. "Slow your roll, little man. One step at a time."

He pulled out his phone and started typing.

Jojo hoped the girl would give him another chance. He was a sweet kid, less of a hothead than Leo, and seemed to be genuinely in love. Love could make a man do reckless things, like moving in with his new girlfriend and her hormone-driven brothers, but sometimes it all worked out for the best.

On the screen, the killer's axe landed with a splat.

Huddled with Dawn during a late-night lull in drink orders, Lana flipped through her phone. "Okay, I've got pics from last year's Halloween bash scheduled to post all weekend. See?" She swiped through dozens of photos. "Shots of the costume contest winners, the competitions, and the staff." A delicious shiver slid down her spine when she came to a photo of Jojo in green body paint, a leather vest open over his bare chest. He and Spike dressed as zombies, and damn! Undead looked good on him.

Dawn clapped her shoulder. "Looks great, kiddo. Don't forget to mention the food and drink specials and door prizes."

"On it, boss." She loved crafting the social media messaging for Bangers' big events, and the Halloween party was the biggest of the year. Thanks to Dawn's connections, she also had contracts to handle social media marketing for the dumpling place up the street, plus a vintage clothing boutique, and a record shop pushing vinyl records as holiday gifts. You'd think they'd wait until after Halloween, but Christmas seemed to start earlier every year.

An alert flashed on Lana's phone, a direct message from Karina Lee, a friend from high school and older sister of Davonté, one of Leo's teammates. Weird—she hadn't thought of Karina in years. It would be nice to catch up later. She started to tuck her phone into her apron pocket, but it shrilled in her hand.

"Go ahead," Dawn told her. "Might be your brothers."

She didn't recognize the number. "Hello?"

The caller sounded out of breath. "Lana, it's Karina. Check the post I sent you. The cops are on their way. My parents are going to skin Davonté alive."

Cops? She flipped back to the message and tapped the link. Her stomach plummeted.

Wobbly and bleary-eyed, Pedro perched on a boulder, the glassy waters of the Sound behind him. He was making a dramatic speech punctuated by sweeping arm gestures. "I love you, Haley-boo," he slurred. "You're my life, my everything. Please—" He sank to one knee, then toppled over and disappeared from the screen. Someone yelled, "Oh, shit!" The camera went wonky, swinging from pavement to running feet.

Beneath the post, comments were piling up rapidly.

**So romantic!**

**Swoon!**

**Get it, P!**

**If that b*tch won't take him back, I will!!**

In the comment thread, she found another video snippet of Leo supporting his bloody brother. In the background, Haley's voice was unmistakable and tight with fury. "You stupid ass. Someone call 911."

Blood pounded in her ears. How the hell did the boys end up drunk on the waterfront? Where the fuck was Jojo? She called his number, but it rang and then switched to voicemail. How could he flake out on her like this?

Lana jolted when Dawn's hand fell on her shoulder. Shocked by the sight of her brother's literal downfall, she'd forgotten the boss was standing right there. Great. Another scoop of disaster on this shit sundae.

"Go on, kiddo. Family business trumps tater tots. Take care of your brothers."

She bit her lip hard, hoping to hold back angry tears. No such luck.

"C'mere" Dawn pulled her into a tight hug. "Don't be too rough on them. Kids will be kids."

"Yeah, but these kids had to post their stupid stunts on social media. If my tías find out, we're toast."

She bolted for the parking lot, unlocked her car with trembling hands, and steered toward the waterfront.

·♥·♥·♥·♥·♥·

A loud bang jolted Jojo awake. "Wha-?" He rubbed his sleep-crusted eyes, trying to make sense of the scene before him.

Lana stood in the doorway, fists clenched, nostrils flared, eyes blazing. The boys huddled behind her.

Adrenalin shot through him, kicking his heart into overdrive. He bolted to his feet. What the hell happened? He was watching a movie with Leo and Pedro, and then...

Leo's face held a sickly green tint, and a large bandage covered Pedro's forehead.

"What happened?" he croaked.

"Tell him," Lana snarled through tight jaws and pushed both brothers toward him.

Pedro stared at his blood-spattered shoes. "We waited until you fell asleep, then snuck out."

Leo hugged his arms over his chest as if expecting a blow—which his sister looked ready to deliver. "All my teammates were there. I couldn't look like a wuss," he whined.

"You lied to me?" Jojo shook his head slowly, hoping for some morsel of explanation that would make all this less awful. Disastrous. Deadly.

An icy wave washed through him. Lana would never trust him again.

Pedro flapped his scraped hands. "I just had a couple of drinks. You know, for courage." He wobbled, then righted himself. "Haley was there with some senior asshole."

Leo whirled on him. "Hey. Manny's not an asshole."

"That bastard had his hands on my girl," he roared, then turned his teary gaze to Jojo. "You understand, right? I love her. I've gotta win her back. I had that whole speech you told me to write."

Jojo's stomach lurched. He couldn't let Lana think this idiocy was his idea. "I told you to send her a message, Pedro, not go make a speech." He spread his hands in a desperate plea. "Lana, I told them they couldn't go to the party, I swear."

She threw her car keys on the table so hard she knocked the popcorn bowl onto the floor, spraying kernels across the carpet. "Let's review." She stabbed a finger toward the boys. "You both disobeyed my specific instructions. Leo drove drunk. Pedro could've had a concussion or worse." Advancing, she poked Leo's chest. "And guess who posted the whole thing to TikTok? This dumbass. Did it never occur to you the tías could see?"

The brothers exchanged a baffled look.

Oh no. Could they really be that stupid? Then Jojo remembered some of his own idiotic teenage near misses. Of course they could.

Pedro snorted. "Old people aren't on social media."

Lana's phone sang out an unfamiliar ringtone: the Darth Vader theme from *Star Wars*.

The boys' eyes widened. Leo gulped and whispered, "Tía Valeria."

Lana hit *Speaker* and held up her phone for all to hear. A shrill voice made Jojo wince. "This has gone too far, Lana. You've proved you can't keep those boys out of trouble. We're coming tomorrow. I expect them packed and ready to go." Without giving Lana a chance to respond, the sharp-tongued tyrant disconnected.

Despair slammed him, squeezing the air from his lungs. The boys had betrayed him. Even worse, they betrayed Lana, who'd sacrificed so much to keep them together. And he'd let them all down. His hopes toppled like dominos—one screw-up after another, bam, crash, boom. He had to stop that last domino from falling, but he couldn't move, couldn't speak. Rooted where he stood, he watched Lana crumple, all her fiery emotion snuffed out.

She shook her head slowly, her expression dull and slack. "I tried. I thought I could handle this."

He reached for her. "This is my fault. If I hadn't fallen asleep..."

"For fuck's sake, Jojo, you're working two jobs. You're not superhuman." She sank onto the sofa and folded over, clutching the back of her skull. "I don't know what I'm going to do."

Panic sped his words. "I'll talk to your aunties, explain it was my fault. I'll—"

"No." Her voice rang hollow. "This happened because I let you take over my responsibility." Eyes closed, she shook her head. "I'll handle it. This is my family, not yours."

"But it was my screw up. I fell asleep, and—"

She didn't even look up. "I should never have put all this on you, Jojo. That was unfair of me, and fuckin' irresponsible. If I'd been here, I would've known they were up to something. I can read their tells."

Finally, she raised her glossy, reddened eyes to his. "You're too kind-hearted, and they played you like a game console."

"No," Leo shouted, his voice tight and squeaky. "This isn't Jojo's fault. Don't you dare blame him."

Lana glared icicles at her brothers. "You. Go. To. Bed."

The boys gave him a final mournful glance, then trudged down the hall.

Lana clutched a sofa pillow to her middle and rested her cheek there, the way she used to rest it on his shoulder.

Before he broke her heart.

A tear rolled down her pale cheek. "It's time I did what I should've done the moment Kenny got sick. I'm quitting Bangers."

"Lana, no." He sank down beside her and drew her into his arms, but she resisted, stiff as the dead and just as cold.

From the hallway bathroom, he heard the unmistakable sound of puking.

She pushed to her feet and walked away without a backward glance.

# Chapter Sixteen

"Fifty-two, fifty-three, fifty-four." Jojo's muscles burned like hellfire as he cranked out one-armed pushups. Stinging sweat blurred the garage floor beneath him. Good. He deserved the pain. He needed it to numb the ache of loss.

It wasn't working, though. He didn't sleep last night, too busy berating himself over losing Lana and the boys. Three years of yearning, one month of bliss, and then—splat, everything destroyed by his inattention. She would never trust him again, never let him near.

His phone's ping drove him to his feet. He tapped the screen, hoping against hope it was Lana. But no, only Pedro again, pleading with him not to give up on them. All morning he and Leo had sent groveling texts, apologizing and taking responsibility. Poor kids. Almost as agonizing as losing Lana's love was knowing he couldn't keep their evil aunties from separating them.

**Too late, little man,** he texted. **Nothing I can do.**

"Yo, dungeon master," River yelled as he jogged into the garage, followed by Eddie. He pulled up short when he spotted Jojo's expression.

"That bad, huh?"

Jojo huffed a mirthless laugh.

River immediately dropped his teasing and clasped Jojo's arm. "What's wrong?"

"Everything, my friend. Every fuckin' thing." He quickly recounted the whole debacle—falling asleep while on kid watch duty, the boys' flaming screw-up, Lana's defeat, his banishment. "I have literally never had a worse day in my life."

Eddie whistled. "Man, that's rough. But we all screwed up at that age. I was as strait-laced as they come, and even I got busted for stupid shit."

River snorted. "You still are strait-laced."

He waggled his eyebrows. "Not anymore. Rosie brings out my kinky side."

River threw a wadded-up hoodie at him. "Eew. I don't wanna picture that."

Eddie tossed it back. "Says the dude who's always grabbing Charlie's ass at work. Exhibitionist, much?"

Jojo pinched the bridge of his nose. ""Shut up, will you?"

The guys muttered apologies.

He sank onto a weight bench. "Of course, we all screwed up when we were young. But none of us lost our families. We all had that support. Now Lana's wicked-witch aunties are taking the boys away from her. And from each other."

Eddie's eyes narrowed as he drew himself up to his full height. "They can't do that. Not if she has legal custody."

"They can't?"

"We went through something like this with my cousin. His wife took off with a guy from work, and he spiraled. When he went into rehab, his ex's parents tried to grab custody of their kid." He pulled his phone from his shorts. "My uncle Pete is a family lawyer. I'm calling him now."

"Hold up." Lana wouldn't appreciate more interference, especially from him.

River grasped Jojo's arm. "Family helps family. Big as you are, you're not gonna stop us from protecting our own."

Misgivings nibbled Jojo's gut with sharp, ratty teeth, but his phone lit up with another message from Pedro. He couldn't imagine what it was like for the poor kid, losing his parents, then being ripped away from his siblings and girlfriend, his school and home, everything he'd ever known.

He clapped Eddie's shoulder. "Call your uncle."

Even if he never regained Lana's trust, he wasn't ready to give up on the boys.

Lana huddled in her treehouse and watched the neighborhood wake up. A delivery truck rumbled up the street. Across the way, a young dad loaded his minivan with kids' soccer gear. Traces of morning mist clung to treetops and lent a spooky air to Halloween decorations on porches and in front yards. A shiny crow landed on a branch just outside. It ruffled its feathers, cocked its head, and regarded her with sharp, beady eyes.

"Hi, Humphrey. Sorry, I didn't bring snacks."

The bird grumbled a corvid curse and flapped away.

"Letting people down seems to be my specialty these days." Not that crows counted as people, but still...

Propping her folded arms on the half wall, Lana breathed in the cool, peaceful air. Soon she'd lose this precious morning solitude. She'd be on her way to some soul-numbing day job, a bullet she should've bitten long ago. Better to live on beans and ramen than face another custody battle. So what if the Bangers crew felt like family? Leo and Pedro were her real family, and now she'd have to fight to keep them together. Drained by disaster, she yearned to sink into her sorrow and just surrender. What would it be like to be responsible only for herself? But selfishness was out of the question.

An icy blade of regret slid between her ribs. *If I'd been home last night, this never would've happened.*

She huddled on her cushion, buffeted by images of pleasures she'd never taste again: sexy snuggles beneath the stadium blanket she gave Jojo, exploring Tacoma together, spending time with his wonderful family, waking up wrapped in his arms, flirting at Bangers—lost possibilities drifting away like the morning fog.

A tear slid down her cheek. If only she could turn back time and skip falling for him. If only she could prevent her parents from leaving for the date night that ended with their deaths. She scanned the treehouse walls, searching for some magic portal to a time before all this pain. Her eye fell on a new image: JW + LL encircled by a rainbow heart.

She curled into herself in a protective gesture, but it was too late. Long-held grief crashed through her, bone-chilling and brutal, stealing her breath. Sobs quaked her aching chest.

"Mama," she keened. "Why did you leave me? It's too much. I can't do this alone. Daddy, I need you." On and on, she wept and lamented, finally giving voice to heartbreak and loss.

When the storm passed, her head was pounding, but a fraction clearer. The slamming of a car door below snapped her back to ugly reality. With Jojo gone, she had to find a way to block the tías' custody grab.

She checked her phone. No call-back from the Ed Lockwood, the lawyer who Kenny and Carol prevailed on to help her win custody last year. Contacting him was a long shot, since he'd retired and moved to Phoenix. She'd need a new lawyer, and to afford that, she'd have to take out a mortgage on their home.

"Lana," a deep voice boomed.

*Oh God, no. Not now.*

Sure enough, Jojo stood below, peering up at her. Dressed in faded gym clothes, with deep shadows around his eyes, he looked as ragged and gutted as she felt, and just as gorgeous as ever. Her heart squeezed.

He grasped the first rung. "I know you don't want to see me, but please, hear me out."

"No," she snarled in a voice she barely recognized as her own. "I'm losing my family, Jojo. I can't take care of your feelings too."

And because the universe was merciless, an upstairs window flew open, and Leo leaned out.

"You gotta help us, Jojo. She's just giving up."

"Damn it, I'm not giving up," Lana yelled. "I'm thinking. Something you should learn to do."

Jojo climbed another rung, one hand extended in a plea. "Listen, Lana, I found someone who can help."

"I don't need your help, Jojo. I've got this."

Relying on him had brought them all enough grief. Her first instinct had been right, but she'd ignored it, too caught up in her selfish desires to face the ugly truth. Until her brothers were eighteen and safe from the tías' grasp, she had no time for love. Better to cut things off now. Jojo's heart would heal. He'd move on, find someone with less baggage. He deserved an easy, uncomplicated life—not the tangled web she'd snarled him in.

Pedro shouted from his window, "Jojo! Lana took my phone. Can you get a message to Haley?"

Across the street, the neighbors' windows scraped open.

Great. Now the whole frickin' neighborhood was watching. Even though Jojo's proximity would scramble her brain, she had to leave her sanctuary and shut down this shit show.

Just as her feet touched the ground, a sleek Lexus pulled into the driveway and disgorged both stiff, scowling tías. They must've hit the road as soon as they hung up.

Both boys ducked back into their rooms and slammed the windows. Barely breathing, Lana clenched her hands at her sides.

Jojo glanced from her frozen face to the car. "Your aunties?" She nodded.

He draped his arm around her shoulders and faced the interlopers. She tensed under his touch but didn't shrug him off. Right now, she needed all the support she could get—even Jojo's.

Tía Valeria lifted her nose. "Well, well. The boyfriend who fell asleep. Nice choice, Lana."

"I told you, Tía," Pedro called from the porch, "it's not his fault. It's ours."

Tía Camila sniffed and addressed her older sister. "Those boys are always egging each other on. Remember when we visited ten years ago, and Leo dared Pedro to throw water balloons at us?"

"Really?" Lana growled through gritted teeth. "You want to break up our family over water balloons?" Her mama bear hackles bristled. Family or no, she'd like to tear these invaders limb from limb.

Tía V slid into a saccharine tone. "It'll be easier on you, dear. You can sell this sad little house and get on with your life."

Leo charged forward, with Pedro on his heels. "This is our home. We grew up here." He put one arm around his brother and the other around Lana. "We're a family. You're not separating us." He looked at Lana, his eyes bright in a silent plea for reassurance.

The lines around Tía V's mouth deepened. "Don't be so selfish, young man. Can't you see what this stress is doing to your sister? You want her to keep working as a barmaid forever?"

*Barmaid? Listen, you snooty dinosaur—* Lana lifted her chin. "I'm fine, Valeria. I can handle my family without your help."

"Nonsense." The older woman pursed her lips and raked her narrow gaze over Lana from head to toe. "You look exhausted."

Jojo gave Lana's shoulder a gentle squeeze. "She looks beautiful. And strong—strong enough to stand up to you two."

Tía C clucked her tongue. "Come off your high horse, young man. Lana's only in this for the money. We've heard about all the benefits you get—Social Security, state assistance, food stamps."

Lana felt the top of her head lift off. "Are you effin' kidding me? That's why you want custody? So you can get the money that barely keeps these two in clothes and school supplies? You want to rob their college funds?" Fists itching to connect with their smug, smarmy faces, she strained toward them. The boys and Jojo held her back.

Lana's phone rang.

Jojo nudged her. "You'll want to take that call, ku'u ipo."

"Not now," she hissed.

"Yes, now. Please." The sharpness in his tone gave her pause.

Let the tías wait. She clicked the green phone icon. "Hello?"

"Hello, is this Lana Lopez?" She didn't recognize the caller's voice.

"Speaking."

"My name's Pete Volkov. Eddie's my nephew. I'm a family law specialist. Eddie says you're in a pickle."

# Chapter Seventeen

♥

Lana's Halloween started off with a shitty bang—a frantic text from Pedro, who forgot to have her sign a permission slip for a class trip. Of course, today was the deadline.

Already dressed in heels and a skirt for her job interview later this morning, her fourth in a week, she strode into the lobby of Stadium High School.

Halloween decorations every-freakin'-where—painted ghoulish faces leered on the windows, paper skeletons and ghosts fluttered from the ceiling, and posters announced tonight's Monster Mash Ball. Clutching a hall pass, a zombie bride hurried past, her ragged train fluttering after her. In the office, behind a counter laden with pumpkins and candy, the receptionist adjusted her sparkly witch hat. "Can I help you, miss?"

"I'm here to sign a permission slip for Pedro Lopez."

"Can I see some ID?"

Lana slid her driver's license across the counter.

"Hang on." The woman searched a stack of wooden cubbies. "Here you go, hon."

Lana scribbled her signature. "Where are they going again?"

"Wright Park Conservatory. There's an exhibit of carnivorous plants. Perfect for Halloween, right?"

"Sounds like fun." Lucky Pedro, he got to feed bugs to creepy plants while she continued her—so far— fruitless search for a job to replace Bangers, though nothing could replace the friends she was leaving behind.

*Quit being so dramatic*, she reminded herself. It's not like she'd never see them again, but tonight would be her last shift at the beloved bar, and she teared up every time she thought about it. At least Jojo wouldn't be there. No way could she hold her shit together if she had to confront his sad-puppy face. She hadn't seen him since he helped her banish the Wicked Tías of the East. He'd respected her wish for distance, and she was grateful.

But God, she missed him. She had to keep her guard up 24/7, or else sweet memories crept through, tempting her to call. What could she say, though? The damage was done, their infant love squashed by cold, hard reality.

When she gave notice last week, Dawn bribed her with a bonus to stay through Halloween. "No one does our social media like you, kiddo."

Reluctant to let her work family down, Lana accepted, but that meant checking on her brothers every hour. She'd downloaded a tracking app for their phones, just in case—probably an unnecessary precaution now that Leo and Pedro understood the impact of their stupid stunt and how much they stood to lose if they screwed up again.

Rosie and Charlie helped find nighttime care for the boys, but that was only a temporary stopgap. And Carol called yesterday with more bad news—Kenny had a second minor heart attack, resulting in bypass surgery.

Completing the trifecta of disaster, this morning Lana received a fat packet of legal papers from the tías' lawyer. Just as expected, they were petitioning for custody—Leo with Tía V, and Pedro with Tía C. Eddie's uncle Pete said she stood a good chance of keeping the boys together so long as they didn't get into any serious trouble. Knowing how close they came the night of their team party, she wasn't holding her breath.

Lana thanked the secretary, accepted a baby Snickers, then froze as a familiar figure entered the office—Jojo's mom, dressed in a crisp suit and pulling a large, wheeled case. They locked eyes, and the older woman gave her a warm, sad smile.

Lana forced her jaw to unclench. "Hi, Kalea. What brings you here?"

"I provide audiology support for the school district—hearing screenings and equipment for students with hearing impairment." She tapped her pursed lips, then beckoned. "I'm setting up in the conference room. Give me a hand?"

"Oh, I have an appointment."

"It'll just take a minute. I could really use your help."

Reluctantly, Lana followed her down the hallway to a room dominated by a large oval table.

Kalea motioned her inside and began unpacking electronic equipment from her case. "Look, I don't usually butt into my boys' personal lives. They're grown men." She lifted an eyebrow. "That's a phrase to remember when your brothers are a little older and still acting like fools. No matter how much you want to interfere, they're grown men."

Lana winced. How much had Jojo told his family about their split?

Untangling a knot of cables, Kalea continued. "But it hurts my heart to see my boy in such pain." She gave a knowing smile. "And you too, dear. You both seemed so happy just a few weeks ago."

"He told you?"

"Not much. Whatever trouble your brothers got into, he blames himself. Even after I reminded him of all the stupid things he and Kai did in their teen years." She clipped a lavalier microphone onto Lana's lapel and slid headphones over her own head. "Say something in a normal tone, please."

"I don't know what to say."

Kalea laid a soft hand atop hers. "Of course you don't. This is your first time dealing with teen knuckleheads. I'm afraid it won't be your last." She adjusted a dial on a small control panel. "A little advice from a veteran mama who got through it?"

Lana nodded.

Kalea squeezed her hand, her gaze kind but insistent. "Forgive them. Then forgive yourself. If I beat myself up every time my boys did something dangerous, I'd never have survived. And look at them now—" Her smile brimmed with fondness. "Still knuckleheads, but they've grown into good men. So will your brothers. You'll survive this."

She unclipped the microphone. "And if you should want to talk to Jojo, you'll find him in his garage, punishing himself with heavy lifting and Kai's disgusting protein shakes." She chuckled. "I don't pretend to understand it, but he says it helps."

As she left the school, Lana considered the wisdom of Kalea's words. Her brothers were still young, but they were old enough to know right from wrong, and they'd deliberately deceived Jojo. He deserved better than ungrateful kids who took advantage of his kindness and a girlfriend who blamed him and pushed him away.

She'd never reproached him aloud, but her stony silence spoke volumes. Of course, he'd think she held him responsible. Regret snaked through her. This mess wasn't Jojo's fault. He was just a well-intentioned victim of Leo and Pedro's scheming.

But she still couldn't face him, not until she untangled the snarl her family life had become. Her own broken heart didn't matter. She had to focus on fixing this.

Shoulders slumped after yet another depressing, pointless job interview, Lana descended the stairs to the basement apartment Rosie and Eddie rented in Dawn's house—one more painful reminder of what she was giving up. So far, only Dawn and Rosie knew tonight would be her last shift at Bangers, because she couldn't bear the pain of a protracted goodbye. But of course, everyone had heard about her breakup with Jojo. News traveled fast in a tight-knit circle like theirs—a circle she'd soon be outside of.

Even though Dawn would be at the bar well into All Saints' Day, her house dripped with Halloween decorations from corny to creepy, including a huge grinning spider on the front door. Lana drank it in with a wistful smile. Mama Dawn loved to decorate for every occasion—the bar, her outfits, and her home.

*God, I'll miss her.*

Eddie answered Lana's knock, looking cute as a bug's ear in pumpkin printed socks, gym shorts, and a jack-o'-lantern T-shirt that showed off tight little muscles—thanks to Jojo's training.

*Ouch.*

"Hey, Lana. Come in." Taking her hand, he pecked her cheek and pulled her inside their cozy apartment. A ski-chalet style gas fireplace crackled merrily, driving away the drizzly damp outside. Rosie waved from her drawing table, set in the corner beneath twinkle lights and star-shaped paper lanterns. The dining table was covered with Eddie's notebooks—neatly organized plans for his future bar.

Lana smiled at the contrast—the bodacious, blue-haired tattoo artist and the strait-laced, skinny businessman were an odd couple for sure, but they'd meshed their very different styles in this cozy home that radiated color, warmth, and good vibes.

What kind of home would she and Jojo have built together?

For the hundredth time that week, a stab of regret pierced her.

Eddie gathered up his notebooks, then gave Lana a narrow-eyed look and shook his head. "I'll make you guys some tea."

Rosie enfolded her in a hug, then released her and gave her a similar head-to-toe inspection. "You okay, sis?"

Lana sniffed hard. "Nope. But life goes on, right? What do they say? When a window closes, a door opens?"

"Something like that." Rosie pulled out a dining chair and pushed Lana into it. "Eddie, bring cookies, too, would you?" She patted Lana's shoulder. "Are the boys all set for Halloween?

"Yeah, they're staying with Anna and Diego to hand out candy. They wanted to take Ellie trick-or-treating, but Anna says she's too little. Never thought I'd see my brothers so gooey over a baby."

"Maybe next year."

She slumped in her chair. "Next year, my life will be so different."

Eddie returned with a teapot, mugs, and a plate of oatmeal cookies. Rosie pulled him down for a smooch. "Babe, could you give us an hour?"

"Sure." He shot Lana a look of concern. "Just let me get dressed. Mom and Dad need help with the new steam press."

A moment later, he headed out for his parents' dry cleaner shop. "Enjoy your girl talk."

"What a prince." Lana blew on her steaming mug. "I feel bad, kicking him out of his own home."

Rosie flapped a hand. "He was going to help his parents today, anyway. And he's a smart one. He knows when it's best not to ask too many questions." She crunched into a cookie. "How was your interview?"

"Total dud. They're looking for experienced bank tellers."

"Any other leads?"

Lana leaned onto her elbow with a sigh. "There's an educational aide position at the boys' school."

"Cool. You could keep an eye on them."

"They'd hate that. And the position pays way less than what I earn at Bangers."

Rosie tapped her pursed lips. "Eddie's parents probably have an opening at the dry cleaner's, but they don't have the best track record at hanging onto employees who aren't Eddie." She opened her tablet. "Let's see who else is hiring. Maybe cleaning at the hospital?"

Lana shuddered. "Pee and barf? No thanks. Besides, Jojo's there."

"Right. Sorry." Rosie patted her hand. "You could finally start your own social media marketing firm. Go freelance, like Charlie?"

"Charlie's got a degree in computer science. I never even finished my associate's. Who's gonna hire me?"

"Daycare?"

"Long hours, crappy pay."

"Grocery clerk?"

"New hires work nights and weekends. I need a day job."

"Restaurant server? Barista?"

"Ditto."

"Ugh." Rosie snarled her fingers in her blue curls. "Are you sure you want to quit Bangers? We'll miss you so damn much." She pulled a sad puppy face. "Especially me and Jojo."

Lana's jaw dropped.

"Sorry, I know you don't want to talk about him."

"Jojo's coming back to Bangers?"

"Didn't you hear? Sorry, I thought everyone knew. Dawn needs him for the Halloween party."

Fabulous. She'd hoped the Bangers party would be a fun distraction from her shit can of a life, but now her last shift would be a minefield of dodging Jojo's wounded gaze and her own raw emotions. And no way could she break her promise to Dawn.

She straightened with a grim smile. "You know what? I need a break from thinking about Jojo and jobs. Show me your tattoo designs."

Rosie grinned and wiped crumbs from her hands. "Cool!" She fetched her sketchpad and flipped through the pages. "Let's see—I'm working on a new dragon."

"No, go back. That one's cute. A little vampire?"

Rosie squirmed in her seat. "Just a project for a friend."

*Thunk.* "Jojo?"

"Yeah. Sorry."

She squeezed Rosie's arm. "Don't be. He's your friend. You don't have to give him up." Her voice broke. "Only I do."

"Oh, hon." Rosie gathered her into a soft, squishy hug. "Take a few days. Catch your breath. You don't have to solve everything all at once."

*But I do! If I don't get a handle on this, my whole world will unravel.*

Summoning her last iota of self-control, Lana pushed her chair back. "Thanks for listening, Ro. I'd better get ready for work. I need all the tips I can get."

# Chapter Eighteen

♥

"Looking good, Jojo!" Janie cooed as she presented her hand to be stamped. Of freakin' course she was dressed as a sexy black cat with acres of sparkly cleavage on display. And of course she rubbed said cleavage against his arm just as Lana passed with a tray of Halloween cocktails. Her eyes caught his for a nanosecond before she pasted on a tense smile and turned her back.

He backed out of Janie's reach. "Enjoy your evening. Next. Let's move it along, people. Costume contest starts at ten." It was going to be a good one this year, judging by the long line of partiers stretched down the sidewalk. He spotted scores of sexy witches, angels, devils, cats, nurses, nuns, plus superheroes, a cheeseburger, a taco, and enough zombies to take over 6th Ave—and that was just the women. Not that any of them came close to Lana's heart-stopping beauty.

He dragged the back of his hand across his mouth. Why did he let Dawn talk him into working tonight?

Of course, it was damn hard to say no to Mama Dawn.

"Mean as he is," she told him, "Spike can't handle the Halloween crowd on his own, and I don't have time to train a new guy."

Rationalizing like mad, he reminded himself he'd hardly see Lana tonight, but knowing she was inside made it impossible not to check on her. He turned it into a game—stamp twelve hands, then look for Lana. Stamp twenty more, then peek through the door.

There she was, flitting through the crowd. She glanced his way as she set down a pitcher of beer and a brimming platter of tots. She looked dismal. Dressed as a sassy witch, she might as well be a zombie with those dark shadows beneath her eyes, her black-painted lips pressed in a tight line. Was she not sleeping, just like him?

The urge to go to her was nearly unbearable. He wanted to reach out, hold her, ease her burdens and kiss that tense scowl off her beautiful face. But he'd blown his chance. The only way he could help her now was to honor her wishes and stay away.

Spike ambled over, tugging at his tight t-shirt printed with Rosie's design—a grinning Jack-o'-lantern above a plate of tots. The rising steam looked like little ghosties. Dawn ordered size 2XL for both bouncers, but Spike's was snug over his round belly.

He grunted. "How long's it gonna take until this thing fits?"

"Keep it up with the planks and weights, and it'll fit by New Year's." He'd been astonished when Spike showed up to their morning workout session a few days ago, but he welcomed the challenge of training his fried-food loving, grumpy-ass coworker. If he could whip Spike's grumpy ass into shape, he could train anyone.

A pirate wench showed her ID. "Looking good, Spike."

Spike's bearded jaw dropped.

"See?" Jojo smacked his arm. "It's working already."

Spike took a slug of his soda. "Thanks for comin' back, man. You gonna stick around?"

He shrugged. As far as he knew, Lana was still determined to quit, so it wasn't like he'd keep bumping into her. Why was she here tonight? Probably doing Dawn a favor, just like he was.

Rosie popped out with soda refills for him and Spike. She patted his arm. "Aww, no green skin this year?"

"Looks like you beat me to it." In her silver-lame space girl dress and lime-green body paint, she was a shoo-in for best staff costume. She'd swapped her blue hair color for neon green—or was that a wig? You never knew with Rosie.

"Hey." He drew her aside. "Did Lana know I'd be here tonight?"

"Yeah, I told her." She narrowed her eyes. "Will you be cool? She's really fragile right now."

"Or course. No worries." It was way too late to win her back anyway, and trying would only hurt her more than he already had.

He peered through the door, wishing he could join the fun inside. Behind the bar, River, Kiara, and Eddie slung specialty cocktails at lightning speed. Maybe River's "Beetlejuice" rum punch would lessen the pain of avoiding Lana. God, she was so cute in that pointy hat and short black dress that flipped with her sharp turns.

Remembering Rosie's warning, he jerked his focus back to the line outside. "Next, C'mon, c'mon, have your IDs ready, people."

A half hour later, Maci brought them each a to-go box of tonight's special: bloody "bat wings" drenched in fiery red sauce, and tots drizzled with black and orange. A sparkly spider pinned to her skull-print head wrap jiggled its googly eyes. "Go on, try it. Don't be scared." She elbowed Spike. "I went extra-light on the poison."

The bearded grump dug in, closed his eyes, and grunted.

Maci patted his shoulder. "I like a man with a healthy appetite." She lifted her chin. "What's the matter, Mr. Jojo? Don't like my cookin'?"

He dutifully took a bite. The rich, complex spice of Maci's sauces complimented Shelby's crispy tots perfectly. "What's in the sauce?"

"The orange one is pumpkin habanero, and the other is black beans with garlic." With a teasing smile, she poked his shoulder. "You know, to keep away the vampires."

He forced a smile. "Thanks, chef. Incredible as always." No need to take out his gloomy mood on Maci or anyone else.

She gave a crisp nod. "You need your strength tonight, so eat up, or I'll send Miss Lana out to twist your arm."

She sashayed back inside with Spike's gaze glued to her swaying hips.

Spike stroked his beard. "Guess she didn't get the memo about you and Lana. Sorry, man."

Apparently, the chef was the only staff member who hadn't heard. It sucked, having everyone tiptoe around him like he was about to burst into tears.

A few minutes later, Dawn poked her head through the doorway. "How you two holding up?"

"Great, boss." Spike snapped a salute. "Just keep the wings coming."

She gave Jojo a sympathetic smile and mouthed, "You okay?"

He nodded, not meaning it.

She hooked a thumb over her shoulder. "You're wanted at the photo booth."

"Ugh. It's not Janie, is it?"

Spike guffawed.

"Just a bunch of middle-aged ladies. One of 'em's a friend of mine, recently got divorced and needs cheering up. Do it for me?"

"Sure." With an aggrieved sigh, he entered the fray. No sign of Lana. She must be in the kitchen fetching a food order. He elbowed through the rowdy, bouncing crowd toward the photo booth set up in the back corner. On the way, he passed Kai and his buddies, huddled at a high top over a pile of wings and a pitcher of Pumpkin Porter.

"You okay, bro?" Kai asked, for once without an ounce of sarcasm.

"I'll survive." He thumped his brother's shoulder.

Dawn had outdone herself with the decorations this year. Cobwebs, spiders, bats and skeletons dangled overhead. Glittery pumpkins on the tables held flickering battery-operated candles. Charlie passed with a tray of cocktails dripping with corn syrup died scarlet to look like blood.

"You okay, Jojo?" she asked, her brow rumpled in concern.

"Never better," he lied.

As he brushed past a table, a folded cardstock sign tumbled to the floor. He picked it up and read the instructions: "To enter tonight's mega-prize drawing, post your Halloween party pics on social media with #BangersHalloweenBash." Lana's work. She should be doing more of this instead of hunting for some grubby day job. If only he could make her see—

"Yoo hoo, muscle dude." A wobbly woman waved her black-tipped fingers from the photo booth. "We're ready for you."

Jojo bit the inside of his cheek, hoped his grimace passed for a smile, and let the tipsy ladies deck him out in a vampire cape, devil ears, and a purple feather boa. While they posed him like a Ken doll, he spotted Lana approaching the stage. She said something to the DJ, a lanky dude wrapped up mummy-style in toilet paper, and pointed to the clock above the bar—the clock that ticked down the hours until this ordeal would end. As much as he hated letting Dawn down, coming here tonight was stupid.

Michael Jackson's "Thriller" rang out, and tipsy partiers stampeded toward the miniscule dance floor, waving their arms like zombies and nearly knocking Lana off her feet. Jojo lurched forward instinctively, but the DJ had already pulled her up onto the low stage and out of harm's way. Her gaze skimmed the crowd until it zeroed in on him. The sadness in her eyes stabbed him like a stiletto.

"All done, ladies?" Jojo peeled off his goofy accessories and tried to slide between dancers toward the door, but flying elbows and waving hands poked and pummeled him at every turn. Surrendering to fate, he flattened himself against the window and waited. Again, as if magnetized, his gaze found Lana's. Aside from the night of their breakup—and of course, that awful period when she lost her parents—he'd never seen her look more miserable. And there wasn't a damn thing he could do about it.

Rosie sidled up, her tray propped on her hip. "It's her last shift. Wish I could convince her to stay, but you know how hard-headed she can be." She hip-bumped him. "Maybe you'd have better luck?"

He heaved a sigh. "I'm the last person she'll listen to."

The dance ended, and Dawn mounted the stage, dressed in her goofiest costume yet, a rainbow unicorn, complete with a sparkly rainbow T-shirt, glittery rainbow tail, furry pink boots, and a hat with a unicorn horn. Her stubby dreadlocks were tipped in pink glitter, too. She grabbed the mic and pumped her fist in the air. "All right, spooky people. Are you ready for tonight's scary story contest?"

This again? Dawn loved a storytelling contest. On Valentine's Day, it was a worst first date competition; for Saint Patrick's Day, dirty limericks; and last Christmas, it was the "best Christmas miracle ever," a sappy sob fest.

"We've got a great prize for the best tale of terror—a water-view room at the Golden Cloud Inn, dinner for two at Anthony's, and a gift certificate from Magic Leaf Dispensary." She waggled her eyebrows. "If you can't have fun with all of that, you're probably dead. I'll start the ball rolling." She rubbed her hands together. "So, when I was a kid, there was this old, abandoned house on 22nd Street." Off she went, blah, blah, blah, while most of the crowd drifted to their tables.

Lana hopped down and got back to work, her usual sassy strut just a weary trudge. Seeing her so deflated hollowed his chest. And then, an idea tickled. A stupid idea probably, but maybe it would help. He had to do something, or else he'd burst from pent-up sorrow and frustration. And she couldn't hate him any more than she already did.

Dawn finished her tale to a smattering of applause. "All right, who's next?" She scanned the crowd with an expectant grin.

His hand shot up. "I'll go."

"Jojo!" his divorce-party fan club crowed. Other patrons hooted. Lana's brow rumpled as she flashed a "What the hell are you up to?" glare.

He jumped onto the stage and took the mic. "So, y'all know I'm a phlebotomist. Kinda like a vampire, right?" Giggles rang out from the crowd. "This is a story about blood—more blood that you've ever seen. So if you're squeamish, maybe plug your ears."

His tipsy ladies leaned in, their gaze rapt. At least someone was listening. Hard to tell if Lana could hear him through the rumble of conversation, so he raised his voice. "Teen boys do stupid shit. It's a known fact. Just ask my numbnuts brother over there."

Kai grinned and waved. Someone hollered, "Jojo has a brother? Swoon!"

Across the room, Lana turned away to gather empty glasses.

"You know that new science building at PSU? The one with the pointy tower? When they were building it, there was a ton of lumber lying around. We'd sneak out there at night with our bikes, build ramps and shi—Sorry, Dawn. Ramps and stuff."

The boss tossed her head and laughed.

"One night, we built this ramp taller than me."

Someone whistled. At the bar, Kiara poked Lana, who shook her head.

"Stupid, right? And rickety. I dared Kai to make the jump. He landed wrong and broke his humerus. Really nasty fracture, bone poking through the skin. Nicked the brachial artery." He pointed to a spot near his armpit. "Blood spurting out, splashing on the ground, on me when I tried to stop the bleeding. I was terrified."

Everyone, even Lana, pivoted to stare at Kai, who flexed his arm. "Twelve screws."

Jojo continued. "He forgave me. Only God knows why."

"Wasn't your fault, man. I was trying to impress you." His brother's grin held a sheepish note.

Jojo's eyes grew misty. "And look at him now—stronger than me, even. I'm proud of you, bro."

Kai pounded his chest and pointed at Jojo.

"But his recovery took a long time, and the medical bills were huge. The whole neighborhood came together to raise funds. That's when I learned that family is so much more than blood." He swiped his eyes with the back of his hand, drawing a chorus of awws.

Lana's gaze dropped to her feet.

"And now I've got a friend in a similar situation. No one's bleeding on the outside, but her family's under attack by a couple of really evil witches."

She finally met his eye, her expression steely, her hand knotted in her apron.

*I'm sorry, ku'u ipo, but you need to hear this.*

"She's the strongest person I know, but even she can't handle this alone."

Lana's icy stare softened. Her lips parted.

"And she won't let me help her because I screwed up big time and lost her trust. Maybe I can never get it back, but I want her to understand it's okay to let people in." He put his whole heart into his words and his pleading gaze. "She got family right here who'll help her through it."

Another chorus of "Aww." Someone yelled, "We love you, Jojo."

He grinned and waved. "I love you guys too. But I love my friend more. I hope she believes me." He shrugged. "We'll see.

That's my scary story—'cause losing someone you love is the scariest thing of all."

*The scariest thing of all.*

Jojo's eyes burned into hers, across the crowd, through the thick, beer-and-tater tot-scented air, through her fear and despair and stubborn independence.

When he climbed onto the stage, her stomach clenched, bracing for a clichéd grand gesture, a public plea for her love. But no. He didn't beg for another chance, didn't rhapsodize about his feelings. He simply reminded her she wasn't alone.

His gaze brimmed with yearning, but his words were self-less.

As he stepped down from the stage, people glanced around, searching the crowd for the object of his affection.

Breathless, she ducked behind a cobweb-draped pillar and clutched her fists over her fluttering chest.

At a moment when every day took another big bite out of her time, her attention, her strength, her heart—Jojo didn't take, didn't demand. He gave.

He'd arranged for Eddie's lawyer uncle to defend her custody of the boys. When the tías stormed her defenses, he stood by her side, steady and comforting, even after she'd told him she had no room for his feelings.

He sacrificed his job at a bar they both loved.

He gave her hope.

He didn't just declare his love: he proved it.

Even if she never took him back, he was still trying to help—not just her, but her brothers too.

And that's the very definition of love, selfless and pure.

A sweet ache pressed inside her ribs, a swelling tide that buoyed her above the sticky bar floor.

She loved him. She was stronger with him. There had to be a way to make this work.

That shrill voice at the base of her skull, the one insisting she could, should, must handle everything on her own? It was a liar, a self-defeating fiction sculpted by grief and pain. Clutching life's steering wheel gave her a false sense of comfort, but this latest disaster proved there would always be things she couldn't control.

If she welcomed Jojo in, she might get hurt. And the boys might too. He could change his mind or reveal a side of himself he'd kept hidden. Hell, he could even die, like her parents did.

But the truth of his declaration reverberated in her bones. He loved her, and she loved him. Maybe—terrifying as it was to admit—she needed him.

With a deafening crack, the dam inside her crumbled, inundating her with swirling, fizzing emotion, pushing her from her hiding place. There Jojo stood, a few tables away, watching for her to emerge. His anxious gaze pierced her. What an act of courage, laying his heart bare in front of all their friends.

Not just friends. *Family.*

She closed the distance and gently clasped his forearm, stroking the tightly corded muscle. "That was quite a story."

"I meant every word." He took her hand and pressed it to his heart. His gentle touch brought a sense of balance and calm, steadiness in the storm of misfortune spinning around them.

"I was wrong to push you away. I'm sorry."

"I'm sorry I fell asleep."

"And the boys are sorry they snuck out."

His laugh rumbled beneath her palm. "I know. They've told me a thousand times." His hand settled at the small of her back. "Think they've learned their lesson?"

"Time will tell." She nestled closer. "But if they screw up again, I want you by my side to help me handle it."

His dark eyes glowed with hope and promise. "Yeah?"

"Absolutely." She rose on tiptoe and laced her fingers behind his nape. "Did you really mean what you said about wanting to focus on fitness training instead of this?"

"Yeah, actually. It's going pretty well."

She pressed her lips to his. "I miss you. The boys miss you. I don't want to live one more day without you. Move back in with us? To stay?"

His smile bloomed so wide and bright she felt its warmth all the way to her toes. "Yes, ku'u ipo. I love you. I'm yours—now and always." With a flick of his wrist, he sent her flimsy witch hat sailing across the barroom. Then he dipped her backward, safe and supported in his arms, and kissed her breathless.

Dawn's husky voice rang out over the mic. "Well, it's about damn time."

Washed in applause, warmed by Jojo's strong, tender embrace, Lana grinned into his kiss, at long last one hundred, million, gazillion percent sure. In Jojo's arms was exactly where she was supposed to be.

# Chapter Nineteen

Jojo slid the last bin of his belongings into place on the shelves in Lana's garage.

*Our garage,* he reminded himself with a wide grin.

With the boys' help, he'd found space for most of his stuff, but not his gym equipment. Kai had asked to keep all that in place to ensure he would see Jojo on the regular. "You know," the big goof said, digging his toe into the floor, "in case you get all tangled up in love and forget about me."

"Not gonna happen," Jojo assured him with a tight hug. "I'm not leaving one family for another, I'm knitting two families together. Besides, you'll find a new roommate soon—probably that cute nurse you've been sharing tots with at Bangers."

Kai's blush confirmed Jojo's suspicions. Good for him. About time little bro put himself out there.

When Jojo opened the kitchen door, a wall of delicious smells hit him. Tonight Lana was cooking the boys' favorite meal to ease their first "family meeting." Though they'd rehearsed this discussion for the past few days, worry still twisted Jojo's stomach. Would her brothers resent his intrusion into their cozy home? If it were up to him, he'd ease in slowly, leaving any talk of ground rules until later. But Lana insisted it was crucial to hash out everyone's expectations and feelings up front.

Judging by the hours she'd spent banging pots and pans, she was nervous too. God, she looked cute with that fluffy apron tied over the jeans shorts she wore to Bangers. Autumn leaf tights tonight, and gold-spangled sneakers—his sassy, sexy, soup-slinging sweetheart.

He snuck up behind her, pulled her long braid to one side, and planted a smooch on the back of her neck. "Smells delish."

She patted his hip. "Me or the soup?"

"Yes." He wrapped his arm around her middle and pressed her soft curves tight against him.

"Hey." She wriggled free. "No frisky business before dinner. We need to focus on the boys."

He slid his hands up to cup her breasts. "What about the girls?"

She rapped his knuckles with her wooden spoon. "They'll be waiting for you when I get back from work."

"Eew. Quit molesting our sister." Pedro groused as he shambled into the kitchen and dropped into his seat. Leo followed right behind, no doubt drawn by the tempting scent of dinner.

"Ready?" Lana whispered.

"You bet." He smooched the top of her head.

"Liar." Flashing a teasing grin, she patted his cheek. "Carry this to the table, pretty please?"

While she dished up salad, along with stern looks when the boys protested, he filled their bowls with hearty cheeseburger soup, then passed the cheesy garlic bread. Apparently, cheese was the key to their hearts—he filed that away for future use.

Everyone dug in, filling the spaces between bites with chitchat about their day—his at the clinic, the boys' at school, and Lana's at her computer—she was taking on more social media clients who wanted a boost for the holiday season. On the surface, they seemed at ease, but Pedro and Leo kept darting nervous glances at each other and at him. They were as on edge as he was.

Finally, Lana pushed away her barely touched bowl and cleared her throat. "Okay, so Jojo and I want to talk to you two about this new arrangement. You know, expectations, boundaries, feelings."

*All the difficult, embarrassing, important stuff.*

Jojo gulped. A helluva lot was riding on this conversation.

She took his hand and gave him an encouraging nod.

He swigged his lemonade, then launched. "I want you guys to understand that I'm in no way trying to step into your parents' shoes. Neither is Lana. Because no one could ever do that."

"Absolutely," Lana added. "But Jojo and I are the adults in this house—for now, at least. We want your input, and we will respect your feelings, but sometimes we'll make choices you don't like. When that happens, you can't sneak behind our backs. You've gotta talk to us, okay?"

Pedro shot Leo a sharp look. Leo lowered his gaze and chewed his lip.

Lana squeezed Jojo's hand and lifted an eyebrow.

*My turn.* "And I promise you guys to always be honest and take responsibility for my own screw-ups."

"Same goes for me," she added. "How about you two?"

Pedro raised his chin. "I promise."

Leo continued to stare at his lap, glum and silent.

This had to be hard for the kid. At almost eighteen, he probably thought of himself as the man of the house.

"Leo?" Lana fixed him with a stern glance.

He finally raised his head and narrowed his eyes at Jojo. "You're not leaving us again, are you? 'Cause that was rough. We were just getting used to you, and then—bam!"

"Lana was hurting too," Pedro added. "You may be big, Jojo, but there are two of us, and if you hurt her again, we will kick your ass. Hand to God."

Looks like the brothers'd had a rehearsal of their own. Good for them. Feeling protective of Lana was something all three of them shared.

Lana interjected, "Now hold on. I'm the one who sent Jojo away."

"And you're not doing that again, right?" Pedro's brows drew together. "If you guys get mad at each other, you're gonna talk it out like grown-ups." He puffed out his skinny chest. "Like me and Haley. We had a problem, but we talked through it, and now we're tighter than ever."

*Lectured on adult behavior by a fifteen-year-old.* He chuckled under his breath, then glanced at Lana. She was trying to keep a straight face, but her shoulders quivered with suppressed laughter.

Jojo slid his chair closer to Lana's and squeezed her knee. "I'm not going anywhere. I love Lana, and I'm committed to building a life with her."

The soft kiss she pressed to his cheek kindled thoughts inappropriate for a family dinner—but they had to get through this before Lana left for her shift at Bangers.

He faced the boys. "Folding me into your lives won't be easy, and I'm sure there'll be times when you resent me for taking up space in your home. When that happens, just be honest with me. And fair. And I promise to do the same with you." He crooked his pinkie finger and extended it to Leo.

Leo gawked at Jojo's hand for a moment, then cracked up. "Dude, do you know how weird you look right now?"

"That's a sacrifice I'm willing to make for you, little man. Pinkie swear?"

"Fine. Okay. Pinkie swear." Leo hooked his little finger with Jojo's. Pedro did the same. Then both brothers hooked pinkies with Lana, giggling as they accidentally upended the breadbasket.

Jojo filled his lungs. *Whew! Got through that with no blood spilled.*

Lana poured another round of lemonade. "Speaking of Haley, let's talk about protection and consent."

Both boys groaned.

He and Lana exchanged a look. She'd asked for his help on this part, and he'd spent every free moment over the past few days looking up how to talk to teens about sex.

She folded her hands on the table. Her whitened knuckles belied her calm tone. "First of all, we hope you'll save your first time for a partner you're in love with and committed to."

Jojo placed his hand over hers, rubbing her knuckles softly. "Trust me, guys, sex is a gazillion percent better with someone you love."

Lana gave him a fond smile, then leveled a finger at the boys. "And you absolutely must use a condom correctly, every single time."

Leo and Pedro squirmed in their seats.

"I mean it. Every. Single. Time. Because if you don't, the consequences could be huge."

Pedro chewed his lip for a moment, then asked, "Do you?"

Jojo tightened his grip on Lana's hand. Holy cats, kids asked the darndest questions. How did she want him to handle this?

The corners of her mouth ticked up. "No," she answered with impressive poise, "but we're in a committed relationship, and I'm on birth control."

Pedro jutted his chin. "You told me no form of birth control is a hundred percent."

Leo's next question nearly knocked Jojo out of his chair. "Are you and Lana gonna have kids?"

For God's sake, they'd only just moved in together. Still, the possibility of kids one day was one of the many topics they'd covered during their sleepy, post-sex cuddles.

Lana answered calmly, "That's a definite possibility. But for now, we're being careful and responsible. We need time to get to know each other as partners first. Because believe me, having kids changes everything. You guys know that, right?"

The boys nodded.

How did she stay so calm faced with these personal, probing questions? Lana's strength of heart was truly amazing.

Jojo wove his fingers through hers. "And if Lana does end up pregnant, we'll face that decision together."

The look she gave him filled his chest with sunshine and his love-soaked brain with giddy dreams of forever and always. Her trust was the most precious gift he could ask for, and he would devote the rest of his life to proving himself worthy—starting with this.

Tearing his gaze from Lana's beautiful face, he straightened his shoulders and faced the boys. "Speaking of birds and bees and such, you also know that what you see in porn is complete bullshit, right?"

Judging by their reddened cheeks, the boys had already sampled online porn. How could they not? It was freakin' everywhere. And they needed to hear this.

"Here's what porn gets wrong. Sex is supposed to be good for both partners, not just the man. Now, I'm not poking my nose into that subject, but if you ever want to talk about that—"

Leo curled his lip. "With the guy who's boffing our sister? Eew."

*Fair enough.* "I was thinking of River and Eddie. Or Diego."

"Or Kenny," Lana added. Though he was still rehabbing from surgery up in Seattle, he video chatted often with the boys.

Pedro goggled at his older brother. "You think they still do it?"

Jojo chuckled. "You've seen them together. Very affectionate. I bet Kenny could teach me a thing or two."

Clearly, he'd just blown the kids' minds. Good. Never hurt to expand your thinking.

Lana smacked the table with her palm. "And this is important—you've gotta treat your partner with respect. I know guys feel a lot of pressure to hook up, like it's some kind of merit badge, but if you want to do something sexual and your partner isn't sure, backing off is the only right choice." She gave Pedro a hard look.

He answered with a sheepish grin. "Understood. Haley and I—well, I apologized for making our first time such a disaster. We won't try again until she's ready, and she says that'll take time." He shrugged. "I'm a patient man."

Chuckling, Lana leaned onto Jojo's shoulder. "Now, where have I heard that before?"

Well, what do you know? The conversation he'd been dreading turned out to be not so terrible after all. No angry words, no recriminations, just honest communication.

Beneath the table, Lana kneaded his thigh. He felt his cheeks heat just as a scrap of bread landed with a plop in his soup bowl, splashing his shirt with cheesy goo.

"House rule number twenty-seven," Leo said with a snarky grin. "No making out at the table."

Lana snatched up the now-soggy bread and tossed it back, hitting her brother in the forehead. "House rule forty-two: food is for eating, not throwing."

"You guys got a list of all these house rules?" Jojo asked, blotting his shirt.

Pedro snorted. "We mostly make them up as we go."

Jojo pushed back from the table. "Okay, guys. Lana has to get to work. What say we do these dishes, then veg out to a slasher movie?"

Leo curled his lip. "I've got a history essay due tomorrow."

"And I've got a geometry test," Pedro grumbled.

Jojo stood and gathered plates. "No guarantees, but I'm pretty sure I passed both those classes. And studying goes better with Lana's apple pie, right, ku'u ipo?"

The look of sheer gratitude she gave him was almost as delicious as the sweet kiss she pressed to his lips. Standing on tiptoe, she whispered, "You're the best, Jojo. When I get back, I'll show you just how much I appreciate you."

"With apple pie?"

She giggled and gave his ass a smack. "Is that what we're calling it now?"

# Epilogue

Lana raised her glass high. "To Leo!"

"To Leo!" friends and family chorused.

Perched on the back stoop, surrounded by clusters of balloons, Leo beamed. Two hours after the ceremony, he still hadn't removed his graduation robe. As far as she was concerned, he could sleep in it. Seeing him cross that stage was such a sweet relief. Almost as sweet as when the family court judge banged his gavel and dismissed Camila and Valeria's custody suit as "a contemptible waste of this court's time." She'd never forget the way their smug faces crumpled beneath his withering glare.

Jojo slung his arm around her shoulders, pressed a kiss to her temple, and whispered, "You did it."

"We did it." She leaned into his embrace and let it all wash through her—the delicious lightness in her chest, the happy, celebratory energy, the incredulous glow on her brother's face. Despite all they'd been through, tragedy and teenage screw-ups and emotional tempests and marauding tías, this sweet spring day found them celebrating Leo's transition to adulthood—with honors, no less, and an award for the most improved student athlete.

With the help of Kenny and Carol, who'd returned home in January, and the Bangers guys, who'd become surrogate big brothers to Leo and Pedro, and the Williams clan, who welcomed both boys with open arms, here they stood, celebrating this glorious victory.

Pride and love lifted her spirits higher than the magnolia tree towering over their little backyard. Guests packed the small space—Kenny and Carol, the Bangers crew, Jojo's family, plus Haley and her parents, probably there to keep an eye on the lovebirds. Dad's brother Alonzo had driven up from California with his new wife and step kids, and a few cousins from eastern Washington even made the trek west to celebrate. Lana almost wished the tías had come so she could rub their noses in Leo's success.

She wiped a tear and wound her arm around Jojo's waist. "He's really going to be okay, isn't he?"

"He really is. Look at all these people he's got on his side."

Another tear dribbled down her cheek. Damn it, she'd promised herself to focus on joy, putting grief on the shelf just for this one special day. But milestones like this would always be bittersweet.

"I wish Mom and Dad could see this. They'd be so proud."

He hugged her tight and kissed the top of her head. "They're watching, ku'u ipo. And I'm sure they're very proud—of Leo and you both. You've done an amazing job."

His tender words pulled a sob from her throat. Overwhelmed, she clung to him as he rubbed soothing circles on her back. Curse these tears—the last thing she wanted was to dampen Leo's celebration with her runaway feelings. He deserved one perfect, happy day.

A second set of arms closed around her from behind. Leo snuffled into her hair, his voice cracking with emotion. "Thanks so much, sis. This is the best graduation party in the history of graduation parties."

Her laughter burbled through tears. "Even without the keg you wanted?"

"No bigs. There's a kegger tonight on Ruston Way."

Eyes wide, she spun, big-sister finger armed to stab his chest.

Leo raised his palms and flashed a teasing grin. "Just kidding. Besides, you think I'd admit to underage drinking in front of Tacoma's most bad-ass bouncer?"

Now that Kenny and Carol were home again, Jojo had returned to Bangers, mostly on the weekends, "To keep in touch with my crew." Lana had cut back her Bangers shifts as well. Between her marketing classes and her growing roster of social media clients, she had less time for slinging beers and tots, but she squeezed in shifts to rest her brain and bask in the love of her chosen family.

A metallic clang pulled their attention to the long buffet table set up by the back door. Maci gave a serving pan another whack with her spoon. "Food's ready. Come get it while it's hot."

"Awesome." Leo bolted for the chow line. After four years of noshing on the leftover bar food Lana brought home, he'd requested Bangers' goodies for his grad party. Maci had prepared three kinds of wings and her pineapple-pepper slaw. Diego brought empanadas from his food truck. Shelby bought huge foil pans of smothered tots, and Jojo's parents supplied grilled huli-huli chicken and macaroni salad.

Lana detached herself from Jojo's clasp. "I better go help serve."

"Oh no you don't." Looking like a garden-fairy queen in her fluttering floral dress, Carol hooked her arm through Lana's and towed her toward the serving line. "You've earned the chance to relax and celebrate."

Kenny pecked Lana's forehead. "That's our Lana—always thinks she's got to do everything by herself."

"Okay, okay." She laughed. "I just want Leo's party to be nice."

"Then let your friends do their thing." Kenny accepted a glass of Kiara's rum punch. "Thank you kindly, my dear."

"You too, Mama Bear." Kiara filled Lana's glass, then smooched her cheek. "Enjoy my special chill-the-eff-out recipe."

"Look out now," Jojo said with a chuckle. "Shelby will get jealous."

"Nah, she knows I'm not the cheating type." Kiara flashed a saucy grin.

Carol scooped slaw onto Lana's plate. "How's it going with your client roster, hon?"

"Really well. I've got three new clients this week—a bridal resale store, a paint and sip business, and that Hawaiian shop on 6th Ave. Pretty sure someone had a hand in sending them my way." She goosed Jojo, who raised his hands.

"That was Mama, not me." He turned to Kenny, "We good for Saturday night? Dawn's got a limbo tournament at Bangers. She needs us both."

Kenny grinned. "Bring us some wings, and it's a deal."

Carol bristled. "Kenneth Everett Dalca, you are not eating fried chicken! Do you want another heart attack?"

Behind the buffet table, Maci threw back her head and laughed. "I'll bake a batch for you, Mr. Kenny. Now, where did that man go?" She twisted to peer over her shoulder and hollered, "Silvio!"

"Hold your horses," Spike grumbled as he backed through the kitchen door carrying a tray of wings.

Lana goggled at Jojo and fought back a giggle. Of course the big meanie's given name wasn't Spike, but Silvio?

Jojo's lips quivered, but he kept mum as Spike reached around Maci and snagged a wing. "Use the tongs, you brute." She slapped his hand away, but her fond smile belied her sharp tone.

"Just washed my hands, I swear." Was that an actual grin on Spike's fuzzy face?

As they moved up the line, collecting wings, empanadas, and tots, Lana whispered, "Maci goes for dad bods?"

He chuckled. "Seems every time I turn around at Bangers, Spike's in the kitchen."

The carved cupid atop the back bar had struck again.

With their glasses and plates full, she and Jojo made their way to a table beneath the big magnolia tree. Everything was delicious, of course, especially Diego's shrimp and chorizo empanadas. Before cutting the sheet cake Rosie had topped with Leo's portrait painted in icing—a damn good likeness, down to his smug grin—the graduate rose to make a speech.

Tears prickled Lana's eyes before her brother uttered a word. "Oh crap, here we go again," she muttered as she dug in her dress pocket for a tissue.

Jojo's arm came around her shoulders and snugged her close. "Everyone cries at graduations. Don't worry about it." He smooched her temple. "Just means you have a big heart."

Standing beside the cake table, Leo swiped at his eyes and gave a sheepish smile. "Hope I can get through this. First of all, thanks to everyone for coming. It really means a lot." His watery gaze skimmed the crowd. "Losing Mom and Dad, well—it was rough, you know?" His voice broke, and Lana fought the urge to throw her arms around him and comfort him, just like when he was a squirmy little kid.

"Next, I want to thank Kenny and Carol, our neighbors who sorta adopted us. You guys are the best, and I love you." Leo's voice wobbled again. "And my little bro, Pedro. For a smart-ass kid, you can be pretty wise. Thanks for kicking my butt when I needed it. I'm counting on you to watch out for Lana." He cracked a crooked grin. "If Jojo will let you."

Pedro swiped his eyes with his napkin, and Lana's heart squeezed again.

Leo's watery gaze met hers. "Lana, what can I say? You were right about pretty much everything. So today, in front of everyone, I want to apologize for all the grief I gave you. You remember—" He adopted a whiny tone. "You're not my mom, you can't make me—all that crap." He sniffled hard. "You're the strongest person I know, and you always kept me pointed in the right direction, even when I was a royal pain in your butt. You're the best role model I could ask for."

Hot tears rolled unchecked down Lana's cheeks. This sweet moment made it all worthwhile—the fights over homework and housework and curfew and taking responsibility. Even the college years she missed out on faded to mere trifles in the face of her brother's gratitude.

"I love you, little bro," she choked out.

All around them, people sniffled and honked into tissues and napkins.

"And Jojo," Leo continued, "You came into our lives because you were crushing on my sister, but your love was big enough for me and Pedro too. Thanks for never giving up on us. You've got a heart bigger than—" He spread his arms wide. "I'm so glad you're part of our family."

A chorus of "Aww," rumbled from the guests.

Lana beamed up at Jojo, her gentle giant who never gave up on her either, even when she blamed him and pushed him away. Gratitude surged through her in a steady pulse that connected her to this amazing man—her partner, her friend, her love.

After Leo finished his thank-yous and cut the cake, she kicked off her shoes, propped up her aching feet, and nestled into the curve of Jojo's arm. Between getting the boys out the door in time, perching on hard stadium bleachers through the two-hour graduation ceremony, and last-minute party prep, it had been a helluva day.

"It was a long, hard road, but we made it." She kissed Jojo's jaw. "One down, one to go. You think Pedro will make it?"

"I have no doubt." He lifted her hand to his lips. "With your eagle eyes on him, he'll do fine."

Speak of the devil, Pedro and Haley trotted around the side yard, hand in hand and giggling.

Pedro beckoned to Jojo, who jerked upright in his seat.

"Now?"

He beckoned more urgently. Haley giggled and blushed.

"Give us a minute," Jojo told him.

Stepping up behind his little brother, Leo tucked his hands in his armpits and flapped his elbows. "Bok bok buh-gawk."

Lana straightened in her chair. Should've known their good behavior wouldn't last through the evening. "Why are you guys being so rude to Jojo?

With a huff, Jojo stood and held out his hand. "Lana, would you do me the honor of a stroll?"

She blinked in confusion. "Stroll? The party's still going. I can't just leave."

"We won't go far. I promise."

Beside Pedro, Haley jiggled from foot to foot. At the next table, Rosie whispered to Charlie, who shushed her and quickly turned her back.

*They're up to something, all of them.*

Jojo's smile held a nervous edge as he wiggled the fingers of his extended hand.

"Okay. But just for a minute." With a weary sigh, she let him pull her to her feet.

Jojo tucked her arm into the crook of his elbow and led her to the treehouse in the front yard. "Up you go."

She gawked. "Really? You want me to climb the ladder in this dress?" She squinted at her brothers, huddled in the side yard, then up at her childhood refuge. "Do I hear music up there?"

Jojo lifted one eyebrow. "Climb up and find out."

"But it's getting dark."

He dug in his pocket, and lights flickered on in the tree-house. "Now, if you please."

How could she resist that sweet puppy face? With a resigned shrug, she started to climb. The twilight breeze whipped her skirt around her legs.

"Nice view," Jojo muttered as he followed.

"If you wanted to look up my dress, all you had to do was ask."

His fingers slipped beneath her skirt and stroked the sensitive inside of her thigh, just above her knee.

"Jojo, honestly. We have a very comfortable bedroom, and—"

What she saw inside the treehouse stole her breath.

Moving carefully, she hauled herself upright into the little space, transformed tonight into a magical treetop fairy palace. Paper hearts in shades of pink, red, and purple fluttered from the ceiling between crisscrossed strings of twinkle lights. Rose petals lay scattered around velvet floor cushions she recognized as Rosie's. Pink and silver balloons bobbed in the corners.

Mouth gaping, she pivoted slowly, taking it all in. "What's this?"

Where Jojo's face should be, only air.

"Lana." His warm, broad hand closed over hers.

"Oh God," she squeaked and clenched her free hand over her heart.

He knelt at her feet, his eyes enormous and glistening in the dim light, his lips softly parted, a velvet box cupped in his trembling hand. A diamond winked up at her, a tiny star lighting the way to their shared future.

Her heart fluttered like hummingbird's wings. Her knees liquified. Only his steady grip kept her from crumpling to the floor.

"Ku'u ipo, four years ago you caught my eye, and then you caught my heart. It's yours now. I'll never get it back." His voice trembled, but he sucked in a breath and continued, never dropping his gaze from hers. "I want to spend the rest of my days with you. And your brothers. And their partners, their kids, whoever comes along. I want to walk through this life by your side forever." His chest rose and fell. "Will you marry me?"

Joy, pure and brilliant, lifted her in a hot swell that danced through her veins and sang in her bones. Jojo knew she'd want privacy at this moment, so he chose her special refuge, the site of their first kiss. He understood her, saw her deepest, most guarded self and embraced it all—her mess, her pain, her family, her complicated history. With gentle determination, he slid beneath her armor and folded himself around her heart.

She opened her mouth, but happy tears choked her words. That wouldn't do, not for a moment they'd share with their grandchildren.

She cleared her throat and tried again. "Yes, Jojo. I'll marry you."

A luminous smile wreathed his features. "Really?"

"Really, truly, absolutely." She sank to her knees and threw her arms around his neck. "My ku'u ipo. My sweet, beautiful man. My love." Pressing her lips to his in a tender kiss, she drank in this moment, a precious memory she'd cherish forever.

With a joyful whoop, he dipped her in a backbend that toppled them onto the cushions. Laughing into their kiss, they clutched each other tight, hearts beating in tandem, limbs tangled, indescribably happy.

Below, on the lawn, someone yelled, "Well?"

"Oh, right." Chuckling and fumbling in the near darkness, he slipped the ring onto her finger. After another lingering kiss, he pulled a narrow cardboard box from beneath a cushion. "Your brothers' idea." He extracted a pair of birthday sparklers. "Actually, they suggested bottle rockets."

Giggling, they lit their glittering wands and waved them through the open doorway.

Cheers and whistles rang out below.

Laughing until her eyes streamed, Lana leaned onto Jojo's firm shoulder. "So much for our private moment."

"Hey, marriage is about family, right?" He kissed the tip of her nose. "Shall we go down?"

"In a minute." She pulled him down for another kiss. "You went to all this trouble. Let's enjoy it a little longer."

He smiled against her lips. "Well, I had help. Rosie, Charlie, Leo, Pedro, Haley—I'm afraid this will be on her Instagram. Then there's my mom, Carol..."

She nuzzled his neck, relishing the scrape of his beard shadow against her skin. "Family. Can't escape them."

"Do you want to?"

"Maybe for a few days." She nipped his earlobe.

"How about a Hawaiian honeymoon?"

"Mmmm." She pressed her forehead to his. "Sun and sand and my favorite Hawaiian. Sounds like heaven."

Thanks for reading Jojo and Lana's story! Want a little more? Go to https://dl.bookfunnel.com/yguu5ds0ro for a bonus epilogue. You won't want to miss the shenanigans Jojo and Spike pull when a troupe of male strippers come to Bangers! You'll also get *Cupid's Silver Spark: A Bangers Tavern Romance Novella*, yours free for joining my monthly reader newsletter.

If you enjoyed *Sweet, Slow Sizzle*, please consider leaving a review on your favorite bookseller's site, Goodreads, or Bookbub. Or all three!

Read on for cocktail recipes from *Delicious Heat*. But first...

# Books by Sadira Stone

♥

**Christmas Rekindled: Bangers Tavern Romance 1**
**Charlie & River's story**

*When two Scrooges unite to save a bar in trouble, a kiss under the mistletoe sparks the sexiest Christmas miracle ever.*

Bartender River Lundqvist has a damn good reason for hating Christmas. Bangers Tavern is the perfect place to lay low over the holidays—until Charlie walks in. His first encounter with the saucy server nine years ago was utter humiliation. Her reappearance stirs up powerful desires and hopes for a new start. But the timing is all wrong.

Back in Tacoma to care for her estranged dad over the holidays, freelance web designer Charlie Khoury braces herself for the suckiest Christmas ever. A temporary job at Bangers Tavern gives her a chance to escape Dad's criticism and blow off some steam. But why does the hunky bartender seem to hate her?

A pretend girlfriend is just what River needs to keep his family off his back—until a kiss under the mistletoe flares hot enough to melt the North Pole. When greedy developers threaten Bangers Tavern, River and Charlie must team up to save it. Their sizzling chemistry feels like the real thing—but everyone knows rebound relationships don't last.

Come to Bangers Tavern for an enemies-to-lovers tale of reconciliation, found family, holiday cocktails, and the steamiest Christmas miracle ever.

### Opposites Ignite: Bangers Tavern Romance 2
### Eddie & Rosie's story

*A mismatch sparks the hottest flames.*

Blue-haired, buxom, and bodacious, server Rosie needs her job at Bangers Tavern, where her work family adores her weirdness and supports her hunt for a tattoo apprenticeship. When too much New Year's bubbly tumbles her into a sweet, shy coworker's bed, she craves more. But guys like Eddie never stick with girls like her.

Strait-laced, soft-spoken, and skinny, barback Eddie has a huge crush on his curvy, tattooed coworker. Their New Year's surprise is a dream come true—until his grandma walks in on them.  Eddie begs Rosie to fake-date him to appease his old-fashioned family. He's already keeping secrets, so what's the harm in one more? But the longer he pretends with Rosie, the deeper he falls.

Their boss lays down the law: No relationship drama at work, or you're fired. Rosie's everything Eddie ever wanted—but to keep her, he'll have to drop a terrifying truth bomb on his loving but stifling family. And Rosie must trust her bruised heart with the guy who nearly crushed it.

Come back to Bangers Tavern for a steamy, laugh-out-loud, opposites-attract romance that ignites in all the worst ways—and the best!

### Delicious Heat: Bangers Tavern Romance 3

**Anna & Diego's story**

*Cupid has lousy timing.*

After kicking her cheating husband to the curb, nurse Anna Khoury discovers she's pregnant. When Bangers Tavern's hunky chef makes heart eyes at her, she dismisses that delicious thrill as the last thing she needs. Single motherhood will take all her strength and focus. Anna's battered heart can't take another blow.

Chef Diego Vargas is aiming higher than burgers and tater tots. His dream—his own food truck, the Empanada Angel, but he'll need his family's support to pull it off. Meeting Anna leaves him thunderstruck, even though his attraction to her threatens all his plans. Call it fate, call him crazy, but he's determined to prove he's in it for keeps.

With a belligerent ex-husband and two overprotective families set on breaking them up, Anna and Diego will need more than red-hot passion to pull them through. His career and her baby's future are on the line.

Come back to Bangers Tavern for a spicy tale of forbidden love that will warm your heart...and other parts...and make you hungry for empanadas!

## Cupid's Silver Spark: A Bangers Tavern Novella
## Carla & Jeremy's story

*Will Cupid's misfire cost her everything?*

Still stinging from a breakup, Carla Portofino wants nothing to do with Valentine's Day. When her bestie drags her to Bangers Tavern's Anti-Valentine's Bash, Cupid gifts her a swoonworthy silver fox. Maybe a no-strings fling is the remedy for her tattered heart? He seems perfect, until a greedy real estate development scheme tangles them in more string than either can handle.

All Jeremy Franklin wants on Valentine's Day is to escape the lovey-dovey hype. But his pushy friend insists on cheering him up with a trip to Bangers Tavern, where Jeremy meets Carla, a woman so enticing he simply must pursue her. Trouble is, his real estate firm has the hots for her building, and he's not sure he can save her shop from their greedy grasp.

To keep her business, Carla must dare the hardest hurdle of all—trust the enemy. Will her silver fox prove a predator, or will Cupid's arrow strike true?

·❤·❤·❤·❤·❤·

*Hungry for more? Try the Book Nirvana series, steamy contemporary romance set in a quirky bookshop in Eugene, Oregon—because bookshops are sexy!*

### Through the Red Door: Book Nirvana 1

*Letting him inside could be her salvation...or her undoing.*

Clara Martelli clings to Book Nirvana, the Oregon bookshop she and her late husband Jared built together. When rising rents and corporate competition threaten its survival, her best hope is their extensive erotica collection, locked behind a red door. In dreams and signs, her dead husband tells her it's time to open that door and move on. When a dark and handsome stranger's powerful magnetism jolts her back to life and he wants a look at the treasures of that secret room, she can't help but want to show him more.

Professor Nick Papadopoulos is looking for historical erotica. Book Nirvana's collection surpasses his wildest dreams, and so does its lovely owner. A widower, he understands Clara's battle with guilt, but their searing chemistry is too strong to resist. Besides, he will only be in town for two weeks, not long enough for her to see beyond the scandal that haunts his past.

**Runaway Love Story: Book Nirvana 2**
*Fierce passion or long-cherished dreams...she can't hang onto both.*

High school history teacher Doug Garvey is trying to enjoy his last few weeks of summer vacation, but receiving his final divorce decree hits him harder than expected. After a brief fling fizzles, he fears love just isn't in the cards for him. If only he could find someone who's real, someone interested in something beyond herself...maybe a new running partner who can keep up with his more carnal appetite. When sexy, straight-talking Laurel runs across his path, he dares to hope again.

Fired from an art gallery, Laurel Jepsen shelves her pursuit of an art career in San Francisco to help her beloved great aunt Maxie move into assisted living. While out on a morning run, she's harassed by a group of teens until a tall, broad-shouldered hottie steps in, pretending to be her boyfriend with a kiss that makes her wish it were true. But she's only passing through, not looking for a relationship.

Their fierce chemistry burns up the sheets—and the couch, the shower, the forest—but falling in love would ruin everything. Laurel can't stay in Eugene, and he can't leave. Doug's only hope is to convince her the glittery life she's after could blind her to the opportunities already in her path.

**Love, Art, and Other Obstacles: Book Nirvana 3**
*She's a free spirit. He's a one-woman man.*

Rejected by her family for her bisexuality, graphic artist Margot DuPont yearns for a life with no fences, no limits, and no family ties. Between college, work at Book Nirvana, and an art competition, she barely has time for her part-time girlfriend, much less a flirtation with her competitor.

Dumped into the foster system at a young age, ceramics artist Elmer Byrne craves a big, loving family of the heart. His artist family almost fills that need, but something is mi ssing...until Margot. But when he offers his heart, her thorny defenses shatter him.

Thrown together in an art competition that could jump-start one artist's career, but not both, their irresistible attraction forces them to reconsider the meaning of success.

### Gelato Surprise
**A standalone older woman/younger man beach romance novella**

*She came to the beach to find herself—and found him.*

Forty-two-year-old divorcée Danielle Peters ends up alone on her family's annual beach vacation. Maybe time to herself is exactly what she needs. That and gelato from her favorite ice cream shop. But when the owner's intoxicating young nephew offers more than sweet treats, she's tempted to indulge in a hot summer fling before returning home.

Thirty-one-year-old Matteo Verducci craved a fresh start to mend his broken heart, and he's found almost perfection in Ocean View, where he scoops gelato by day and crafts furniture by night. But when a sexy older woman stops to sample his wares—Mamma mia! He only has two weeks to convince her their passion is more than a delicious surprise.

# Author's Note and Acknowledgments

♥

One of the many things I love about writing fiction is the chance to try out on page the many careers I never pursued in real life. In my books, I've run a bookshop (*Through the Red Door*), an ice cream shop (*Gelato Surprise*), a vintage clothing shop (*Cupid's Silver Spark)*, a food truck (*Delicious Heat*), and now a bar! I've also been a photographer (*Runaway Love Story*), a graphic artist, and a potter (*Love, Art, and Other Obstacles*). But I couldn't do it without the generous people who help me get my facts and terminology straight.

Huge thanks to Val Stiglicz, my fellow DoDDS alum and Zumba diva, for educating me on Hawaiian family celebrations.

Though Bangers Tavern is fictional, the 6th Avenue District is very real, and if you find yourself in Tacoma, you should definitely check out this funky neighborhood. And if you've seen a certain iconic 1999 movie rom-com, you're already familiar with Tacoma's Stadium High School. Go, Tigers!

Thanks to King's Books, Destiny City Comics, and Shake Shake Shake, Tacoma landmarks who granted permission to mention their businesses by name. I hope you'll visit all three!

Thanks to my beta readers Laurie Ryan, Marie Tuhart, and Michelle McCraw, my editor Saya of Red Quill Editing, and Dar Albert of Wicked Smart Designs for yet another awesome Bangers Tavern book cover.

And most of all, thanks to my husband for supporting me on my writing journey. You're the BHE!

# Cocktails from
# Sweet Slow Sizzle

♥

### Tequila Touchdown

In a highball glass or tumbler, mix one shot of Añejo Tequila, a tablespoon of lemon juice, a tablespoon of lime juice, half a tablespoon of green chartreuse or fernet branca, and a tablespoon of simple syrup. Add ice and stir. Rub a strip of lemon peel around the rim, then drop it into the glass. Go home team!

### Bloody Vampire

First, decorate at tall, stemmed cocktail glass, such as a hurricane glass. Dip the rim in clear corn syrup, then in red or black sprinkles—or purple? Go wild! Drizzle some red gel icing "blood" down the outside of the glass, or use clear corn syrup tinted with red food coloring. Set glass aside.

In a cocktail shaker, mix a pony shot (1 ounce) of vodka, a pony shot of cherry vodka, and a pony shot of gin. Adjust the amount of booze up or down, depending on how bloodcurdling you want your cocktail. Add a good squirt of grenadine for color, club soda, and ice. Shake well, then pour though a strainer into your prepared bloody glass over plenty of ice.

Garnish with Maraschino cherries and lime wedges. Spookily delicious!

### Kiara's Midnight Martini

In a cocktail shaker, mix a jigger (1.5 ounces) of vodka, 10 drops each of red and green food coloring, and a half ounce (one tablespoon) of Chambord or other berry-flavored liqueur. Stir with a spoon until mixed and black as your ex's heart. Pour the mixture into a martini glass and top with lemon-lime soda. Garnish with blackberries.

Feeling adventurous? Drop a few small pieces of dry ice into the glass to create "smoke." CAREFUL! Sip your drink from the top. The dry ice will evaporate harmlessly in about five minutes. Don't swallow it or touch it with your skin or tongue!

# About the Author

Award-winning contemporary romance author Sadira Stone spins steamy, smoochy tales set in small businesses—a quirky bookstore, a neighborhood bar, a vintage boutique... Her stories highlight found family, friendship, and the sizzling chemistry that pulls unlikely partners together. When she emerges from her writing cave in Las Vegas, Nevada (which she seldom does), she can be found in dance class, strumming her ukulele, exploring the Western U.S. with her charming husband, cooking up a storm, and gobbling all the romance books. For a guaranteed HEA (and no cliffhangers!) visit Sadira at sadiras tone.com.

**Visit Sadira on All the Socials! @SadiraStone**